W9-CHV-726

USA TODAY Bestselling Author

KASEY MICHAELS

SARAH MAYBERRY
TERESA SOUTHWICK

A Summer Reunion

™ **Harlequin**®

TORONTO NEW YORK LONDON
AMSTERDAM PARIS SYDNEY HAMBURG
STOCKHOLM ATHENS TOKYO MILAN MADRID
PRAGUE WARSAW BUDAPEST AUCKLAND

ISBN-13: 978-0-373-83760-1

A SUMMER REUNION
Copyright © 2011 by Harlequin Books S.A.

The publisher acknowledges the
copyright holders of the individual works
as follows:

Recycling programs
for this product may
not exist in your area.

ALL OUR YESTERDAYS
Copyright © 2011 by Kathryn Seidick

ALL OUR TODAYS
Copyright © 2011 by Small Cow Productions Pty Ltd.

ALL OUR TOMORROWS
Copyright © 2011 by Teresa Southwick

CONTENTS

To Karen Reid, with many thanks.

ALL OUR YESTERDAYS

Kasey Michaels

PROLOGUE

THE LITTLE BOY ON THE television screen was busily getting into trouble with his next-door neighbor, something he seemed to do during every show, and Margaret Mary Haswick held a flowered pillow to her face so that her giggles did not wake her baby sister, Victoria, who had fallen asleep beside her on the couch.

Ruthie Baxter, their own next-door neighbor and some-times babysitter, had been having trouble getting baby Stephen to sleep, which was why three-year-old Victoria had been allowed to remain downstairs past the magic hour of eight o'clock, much to Margaret Mary's disdain.

After all, *she* was eight whole years old, and even she had a strict bedtime of eight-thirty. It wasn't fair that Victoria got to break the rules, just because stupid Stephen had colic, or whatever it was called. He sure did cry a lot—that much Margaret Mary knew. She hadn't asked for a brother, and she still wasn't so sure that her mother was right, that one day she'd be glad to have a big strong brother to watch over her and protect her.

But Victoria wasn't so bad, even if sometimes she got into Margaret Mary's bedroom and messed up her dollhouse and stuff. And she was kind of funny, always following her around and climbing on her lap and calling her Mar-Mar because she couldn't say Margaret Mary.

Her mother said she should be proud that her little sister so clearly loved her and looked up to her, and that she, Margaret

Mary, should always set a good example. Whatever that was. She did kind of like it when her mother teased her and called her Little Mother, just because she helped Victoria with her buttons and things.

Thoughts of her mother reminded Margaret Mary that her parents had told her just before they left for dinner that they would bring home a special dessert she and Victoria could share tomorrow. She hoped it would be strawberry shortcake. Strawberry shortcake was her very favorite dessert in the whole world.

The television show ended, but still Ruthie hadn't come back downstairs, so Margaret Mary got up and turned off the set, because now the grown-up shows would come on, and she and Victoria weren't allowed to watch the grown-up shows.

"Come on, Victoria," she said, giving her sister's shoulder a little shake. "Time to go upstairs to bed." Her sister didn't respond except for the slight frown that came and went on her sleep-flushed face, and Margaret Mary sighed, knowing that her sister could sleep through both thunderstorms *and* Stephen's crying, so it would be pointless to try to wake her with a simple shake on the shoulder.

"Wake *up*, Victoria! Time for *bed!* Get up and come upstairs with me, and I'll read you a story, okay? You know you like—"

Margaret Mary looked toward the door, as if she could see who was on the other side of it this late at night. The door was locked, because Mommy and Daddy always reminded Ruthie to lock the door after they left, and to never open it for *anybody,* but just to call her mother if anyone did come to the door, and her parents, Mr. and Mrs. Baxter, would be right over to see who had knocked.

But Stephen was still crying, and Margaret Mary didn't think Ruthie could have heard the knock. Margaret Mary twisted her hands together nervously, wondering what to do.

The knocking came again. This time it was louder.

Margaret Mary ran into the kitchen and pulled over a chair so that she could climb onto it and reach the phone that hung on the wall, and on her second try, managed to push all the correct numbers so that she could tell Mr. Baxter to please come over right away. And maybe call the police, or something.

Her heart was pounding so hard after she hung up the phone. It was dark outside, and it was snowing, and nobody should be knocking on the door. Eight-thirty at night was too late for visitors, so it had to be somebody bad, trying to get in. Mommy wouldn't have said to lock the door and not let anyone in if it was all right for someone to knock so late.

She ran back into the living room and gathered the sleeping Victoria tightly into her arms as she heard voices outside on the porch.

And then Mrs. Baxter's voice got very loud and shrill, and Margaret Mary could hear every word she said. "Oh, no, officer! Those poor sweet babies! What will happen to them now?"

THE WOMAN IN THE WHEELCHAIR, a bright pink cast reaching from her left foot to her knee, wasn't a stranger; she couldn't be, as they seemed to have the same face, the one Tory Fuller had seen in her mirror every day for the past fifty-five years.

Right down to the distinctive salt-and-pepper hair Tory would have, if she hadn't begun taking refuge in hair coloring at least two decades previously.

Realizing she'd been standing still in the foyer of the fantastic beach house, like some human statue or some such silliness, Tory thanked the severe-looking woman who had opened the door for her, and began slowly walking across the expansive marble floor, moving toward the seated Peggy Longwood.

Margaret Mary Longwood.

A smile bright as a thousand suns lit the older woman's face as she held out her hands in welcome. "Victoria," she said quietly. "It's you. After all these years…"

Tory nodded, not trusting her voice. Tears were running down her face now, but she didn't bother to wipe them away. She went to her knees beside the wheelchair and took one of her sister's hands in both of hers. "Mar-Mar," she managed at last. "I called you that, didn't I? I've forgotten so much, but somehow I've always remembered that. Mar-Mar."

And then the sisters were embracing, and the long years they'd been apart from each other fell away as if they'd never happened….

CHAPTER ONE

"GOOD MORNING, DOCTOR, MAY I help you with something?" Theresa, the young unit clerk at the nurses' station, chirped hopefully as she got to her feet, only to be ignored by Dr. Gorgeous, which is what most of the female hospital staff called the cardiac surgeon when he wasn't within earshot.

And with pretty good reason, too. Sam McCormack might be in his fifties, but he was one of those men who, instead of getting older, just seemed to get better. Like George Clooney, Theresa had told her agreeing friends in the lunchroom. Except that Dr. McCormack had light brown hair and he wore it sort of longish and shaggy, so that it often fell down over his drop-dead-sexy green eyes. He was tall, but not too tall, and his face was sort of lean and chiseled, and he sported a great tan, probably because he liked to run for exercise. The day Theresa had seen him jogging out of the hospital parking lot in his shorts and one of those sleeveless running shirts, she'd nearly run her compact car into a light post.

Sam McCormack reached past the clerk to grab a patient chart, only belatedly realizing that someone had spoken to him. "Oh, good morning—Theresa, isn't it?"

"You remembered. Yes, that's me." The young woman breathed, all but melting back into her chair. "Theresa…"

Sam shot the young woman a quick, curious look, and then dismissed her from his mind as he turned and headed down the corridor to the room of his patient and good friend, Bill Helms. Bill was six days post-op on an emergency multiple bypass surgery. Sam was here to spring him, and send him home to his wife and grown kids.

He only needed to see the results of Bill's latest tests and confirm that he was no longer running a low-grade fever. Nope, he was good to go.

Sam was still paging through the chart when he turned into Room 4-34B, where his college buddy was pushing some hospital-issue oatmeal around his plate.

"Wow, would you look at the puss on you," Bill said as Sam pulled up a straight-back chair and straddled it. "Let me guess. You're about to tell me you sewed up my heart inside out, and you have to open me up again."

Sam grinned, sensing that his friend's joke was only half-way jovial; Bill had been an apprehensive patient. Then again, it could be a little unnerving to anyone to wake at two in the morning feeling as if somebody had just parked their truck on your chest. "Yup, you nailed it. Not the inside-out part, but I haven't been able to find my Penn State ring since your surgery, so…"

"Very funny. I'll give you mine and keep yours. No, seriously, I can really go home today?"

"Unless you're addicted to hospital food and beg me to stay, yes," Sam informed him. "Patients recover better at home, I'm ashamed to say, and I know Janie will take good care of you."

Bill pulled a comical face. "She told me she spent yesterday cleaning out the pantry and fridge, tossing all my favorite foods in the garbage. No more potato chips, no more eggs and scrapple for breakfast, no more ice cream, no more beer. That was cruel, Sam. Did you really tell her no more beer?"

"I might have suggested you cut back," Sam admitted. "Everything in moderation, Bill, that's the key. That, and exercise. Janie told me she bought you a treadmill."

Bill snorted. "Yeah, she told me. I think it's payback for

me having bought her that rug shampooer last year for Christmas." He went quiet for a few moments, and then said softly, "Thanks, Sam. You saved my life. I've got a second chance now, and I promise you, I'm not going to blow it." Bill paused for a second. "Sam? You sort of winced there for a sec. What did I say?"

Sam ran a hand through his hair, pushing it away from his forehead; he needed a haircut, he thought randomly. Sometimes it seemed like he always needed a haircut. But he was so busy, on his own perpetual treadmill.

"Nothing," he said, sighing, and then shook his head. "No, not nothing. You said second chance, and I guess it struck a nerve. You have a minute, Bill?"

"Until you sign those release papers, my time is your time," his old friend said. "Come on, you're obviously upset about something. Maybe I can help. And if I can't, at least I can listen. I may not be a whiz in the operating room, but as a psychologist, I don't think I'm too shabby."

Sam grinned. "A child psychologist," he reminded Bill.

"You say potato, I say—come on, Sam. Spill your guts."

"Great bedside manner you've got going there," Sam said, and got to his feet to walk over to the window. He'd do better with his back turned to his friend, and no, he didn't want to know what Bill the psychologist would read into that particular body language. "You remember Tory?"

"Tory," Bill said ruminatively. "I don't know that I—wait. Tory? Victoria Fuller? Oh, wow, flashback city. Our senior year at State. You'd moved out of the frat house and in with Tory. Lucky devil, she was really something else. I thought you guys were going to make a go of it. And then you two broke up, right? She left Happy Valley, never graduated? That was kind of weird, seeing as how we were less than a semester away. So…Tory Fuller. What about her?"

This was going to be difficult. Sam's life, so ordered and

serene, had been busy, yes, but not difficult. He had his work, a small circle of good friends, a new condo not far from the hospital and his office. Everything neat, orderly. If something was missing in his life, he hadn't known it. Or at least he'd never been able to put a name to the feeling that sometimes came over him, a feeling that there should be more to life than professional success.

"Her…uh…her daughter called me a couple of weeks ago," he said at last, his gaze still on the air conditioner units lined up on the flat roof two stories below Bill's window.

"Okay," Bill said slowly. "And?"

Sam turned around to face his friend. "And she said she was pretty sure she's my daughter, too."

Bill leaned back against his raised hospital bed, holding a heart-shaped pillow to his chest as he rubbed at the stubble on his chin. "She said that, did she? And how do you feel about that, Sam?"

"Oh, come on, Bill, don't hand me that shrink talk. How the hell do you think I feel?"

"Well, it could go a number of ways. Surprised. Shocked. Skeptical. Betrayed. Angry—no, scratch angry. Incensed. Cheated. Excited. And there's always the ever-popular scared out of your gourd."

"How about all of the above?" Sam sat down on the side of the bed. "Allie—that's Tory's daughter—asked if I'd take a DNA test, and I agreed. She mailed me her sample and I took care of the rest here at the hospital lab. I got the results yesterday."

"And?"

"And let's say we can eliminate *skeptical* from your list of my possible reactions. She's my daughter. I have a daughter. A thirty-two-year-old daughter, Bill. *Me*. More than that, I'm a grandfather. Three times over."

"Oh, the nurses out there aren't going to be happy to hear that one, Dr. Gorgeous. A grandfather?"

Sam got to his feet once more. "I'm so glad I could count on my friend to be sensitive about this."

"Ah, come on, somebody has to step back a little, see the whole picture. You probably aren't, at least not yet. And what about Tory? Is that why she took off? You didn't want her to have the baby?"

"I didn't *know* there was going to be a baby," Sam said, once again nearly overcome by an avalanche of emotions he couldn't name. He just knew they were painful—a mixture of shock and anger and inexplicable joy that had had him going in circles for weeks, not just since the results of the DNA testing was in. "She just took off, Bill. One day she was there, and the next day I came home from class and she was gone. Her books, her clothes—just gone. Why? I mean, I didn't deserve that. Why didn't she tell me? It was my baby, too."

"All good questions, Sam. Unfortunately, I don't have the answers. But we both know who does. Did this Allie—your daughter—tell you anything?"

Sam shook his head. "No, not really. She just told me that she was fooling around on the internet one day and read something that caught her eye, and that one thing led to another, and another, until she managed to locate Tory's family." He looked at his friend. "Tory was adopted. I didn't know that, either. I lived with the woman for nearly a year, and I didn't know that. I'm not proud of that, by the way. Clearly I wasn't paying as much attention as I should have been."

Bill shrugged, and then winced as the movement clearly wasn't yet comfortable. "We were young, all of us. Carrying heavy course loads, working part-time to help with expenses. If we weren't in class we were studying, working or sleeping. Or, in your and Tory's case, making babies. Sorry, poor attempt at humor. How did Allie go from finding Tory's family to finding you?"

"She admitted to some guesswork there. She knew her mother had attended Penn State, but since Tory didn't graduate, it was a little tricky pinning down the years. Did you know there are old real estate and rental records on the internet? Honest to God, Bill, it's like the world has nothing else to do but upload a bunch of useless information. Anyway, Tory and I had both signed the lease to that apartment over the pizza shop. After that, it was plugging my name into a search engine, and some simple math. And the DNA test. I guess I should be proud of her ingenuity."

"Do you know where she is?"

"Allie? Yes, she and her husband live in South Carolina. With my grandchildren."

"That last part really gets to you, doesn't it, Grandpa? Janie and I are still pushing our boys to get married, so we can have grandkids. But, no, I meant Tory. Do you know where she is?"

Sam nodded. "Allie also found Tory's sister, and Tory's visiting her now in Cape May, although Tory lives in San Francisco. I've got the address of the beach house. I want to see Allie, of course. And her children. But I don't know about Tory. I don't know what to say to her. I'm curious, but I'm also so damn angry…"

"I remember how you were when Tory took off. You really loved her, Sam. You even married a woman who physically reminded me of Tory, not that the marriage stuck. You've been alone for a long time."

"Are you speaking now as my friend or my shrink?"

"Both," Bill said solemnly. "One, my patient needs closure. He's been waiting for it, consciously or subconsciously, for over thirty years. And two, I'd like to see my friend happy. If there's a chance of that, why not take it?"

"Go see her, you mean. I don't know, Bill. I've got every right to be madder than hell at her, except that I keep wondering if it was something I did, or said, or didn't do, didn't say, that made her believe it would be better I didn't know she was pregnant. Maybe I was selfish and shallow, and she didn't think I'd make a good father. And maybe she was right. Maybe I don't want to know what happened to us all those years ago."

"Okay, tough love here, buddy. Maybe you shouldn't be so worried about *your* feelings, and start thinking about Tory. She's the one who gave up college months before graduation and raised a kid on her own. None of that could have been easy for her. You loved her once, right? Or was she just convenient?"

"I loved her," Sam said quietly. And then he added, "I think I loved her. I hope I loved her..."

"All right, that's a start. Be honest with your feelings. You two were young, probably confused. God knows when I thought back to what I was like during my college years it was all I could do to let my boys go off on their own when their time came. Look, you said she's in Cape May. We're here, in Philly. So she's just a quick drive down the Atlantic City Expressway. You have the address, and you probably need a vacation anyway. You own the practice and have plenty of backup—good surgeons, all of them. I've pretty much met them all since I got here. The world won't end if you take a couple of days off. Go. See. Talk. Don't judge her, or start kicking yourself, until you know her side."

"And then report back to you?" Sam asked, summoning a weak smile.

"Oh, you'd better believe it, bucko. This is better than a made-for-TV movie." Bill reached out and squeezed Sam's shoulder. "All kidding aside, and you know I was only trying to lighten the mood a little here, but we usually only go around once, Sam. Sounds to me like both of us may have just been handed a second chance. I know I can't speak for you, but I really don't think either of us can afford to blow it."

TORY CLOSED HER CELL PHONE and slipped it back in her skirt pocket as she made her way to the lounge chair on the balcony just outside her bedroom, sitting down with a near thump. Quickly, before her legs collapsed from under her.

He knows. Sam knows.

"Oh, Allie…" Tory said, burying her head in her hands.

She could get a flight to South Carolina, mend fences with her daughter, if that was possible. Allie had been remarkably mature for someone who'd just found out her natural father was alive, and not just some nameless college boy her mother couldn't remember. She'd said she didn't hate Tory for the lies. But the hurt had been in her voice, coloring her joy at having spoken with her father.

Or she could fly back to San Francisco, tonight, and try to forget anything had happened at all. Tory knew she was good at that. Running away. She'd done it enough.

Too much.

And what about Peggy? How could she leave the sister she was only getting to know? Wasn't it terrible enough that they'd learned their brother, Stephen, was dead, that they'd never be reunited with the baby Tory hadn't even remembered existed? She'd had vague memories of her sister, but none of her brother.

They didn't even have a photograph of Stephen, although the man Peggy had contacted in Australia—Stephen's business partner and friend—had promised he'd send them a few…when he got around to it. She and Peggy wondered if those photos would show the same sort of startling physical resemblance so evident between the two of them. The thick salt-and-pepper hair, the unusually shaded blue eyes, the high cheekbones…the small cleft in both their chins. The only difference between Peggy and Tory, in fact, was that Peggy was a good six inches taller than her younger sister. Not that Tory had yet seen her sister anywhere but in her wheelchair.

It would be interesting when Allie finally met her father, for she resembled him so much more than she did her mother. She had the same green eyes, the same smile, the same sharp mind and even his same dry sense of humor. Sometimes just looking at Allie broke Tory's heart all over again.

She should pack her bags and go to Allie. But she couldn't, no more than she could run back to San Francisco.

Dr. Freeman was coming by later today to tell her the results of the tissue-typing tests he'd run without Peggy's knowledge. Tory would soon know if she could be the one to give her sister another chance at life. It would be like a miracle, overcoming years of not knowing if she had any family still alive, and then being reunited with her Mar-Mar just in time to give her sister a kidney.

Tory sighed, lying back against the chaise, her mind whirling with all that had happened since Allie had phoned her a few months ago, nearly delirious with excitement, to tell her that she'd been able to trace her family from the time of their adoptions.

But Allie hadn't told Tory the full extent of her digging. She hadn't told her she'd found Sam, as well. *Damn internet….*

"Ah, here you are. It's almost time for lunch."

Tory sat up, smiling as her sister wheeled herself out onto the sunny balcony.

"How did the session go?" she asked as Peggy turned the wheelchair to face her and set the brakes. "You look a little pale."

"I always look a little pale. It comes with the territory. But I'm fine, and the session was uneventful. Meaning I didn't screw up and break sterile procedure. I have a horror of that, let me tell you. Luckily, I read *Home Dialysis for Dummies* cover to cover when I first started down this road three years ago."

"You're very brave, you know. I'd be constantly terrified if I knew I needed a kidney transplant."

Peggy gave a small wave of her hand. "You get used to it. No, that's a lie. You learn to live with it. What's driving me crazy is this stupid foot. I don't like being slowed down."

Tory smiled. She and Peggy had only been together for a few weeks, and Peggy had been in that wheelchair for all of them, but if Peggy considered herself to be slowed down, Tory sure hadn't seen any evidence of it. Not by her broken foot, not by her kidney failure. The woman was amazing.

"Kinsey told me she caught you hopping yesterday," Tory said, wagging a finger at her sister. "You could have fallen."

"Kinsey worries too much, and so do you and Eugenia. The doorway to the downstairs powder room isn't wide enough for this stupid chair and I wanted to see what kind of job the painters had done in there. I was holding on to the wall the whole time," Peggy responded almost mulishly. "I only almost lost my balance when Eugenia saw me and started screeching."

"I wish I'd heard that," Tory said, smiling at the thought of Eugenia Babcock, Peggy's long-time housekeeper and cook. Eugenia might be close to Tory's own age, but it was difficult to tell (and Eugenia certainly wasn't telling). Tall, slim, her straight dark hair always pulled back in a tight bun and not showing even a hint of gray (Eugenia said it was natural, but Tory had her suspicions). No matter that Eugenia insisted upon always wearing black, plain dresses that looked very much like uniforms, and no matter her starchy outside, Tory had already figured out that the housekeeper was solid marshmallow on the inside, and would slay dragons for Peggy. For that, Tory could forgive the woman anything.

"You might not have, but Kinsey did, so I ended up being

scolded twice." Peggy grinned, all the way to her sparkling blue eyes, and suddenly didn't look pale, or tired, even with the unable-to-be-disguised dark circles below her eyes. "I believe they think they're in charge of me. It's rather cute when it isn't frustrating."

"Kinsey *is* your physical therapist," Tory reminded her, thinking of the sweet young woman who was currently staying with Peggy, and whom Eugenia privately said should have always lived here, to help Peggy with more than just her current problem.

"In theory she's my physical therapist," Peggy said, winking at her sister. "Let's have a sisterly secret. This ugly cast comes off soon and I'll finally be able to put weight on my foot again and kiss this damned contraption goodbye. After a few therapy sessions I should be fully back on my feet and Kinsey could be out of here and on her way to her next patient before Davy comes home. That would be a shame, because I really do like her. In fact, I'm thinking about doing very poorly when it comes to my rehab."

Tory looked at her sister in shock, and with some admiration. She knew Peggy worried about her son, whom Tory had yet to meet. She said he was too serious, even bordering on dull, not at all the adventuresome young boy Peggy had made famous in her books, where David Longwood was perpetually eight-years-old and known as Davy Daring. Tory had read those books to Allie when she was young, and to find out that her own sister wrote them had been a lovely surprise. "You're matchmaking Kinsey with your son?"

Peggy pressed her hands to her chest, her eyes wide and innocent. "Me? Don't be silly. I'd never do anything as crass and manipulative as that. Let's just say I encourage opportunities. And now, if we're done talking about everything except the look on your face when I came wheeling out here, maybe you'll tell me what's wrong."

Suddenly Tory was back at the very bottom of the "Stygian Well of Despair," as she would have called it in her comic books. That was another thing that had surprised and even shocked the sisters once they'd been reunited. Peggy was a writer of children's books, and Tory had her own successful comic book series. Time and distance couldn't change the fact that genes were genes, and they'd both been born with similar inherited talents. If only they knew if those talents had come from their mother or their father—but that they'd probably never learn.

"Tory? There is something wrong, isn't there?"

She nodded. "I'm that transparent?"

"Pretty much, yes. According to my mother, you'd be a cardsharp's dream. You know, sometimes I think she's fibbing to me when she says she only plays the penny slots. I think maybe she's hitting the poker tables when she and the rest of her geriatric posse hop on the bus and go riding off to Atlantic City. I don't even want to think about what she and her girlfriends are doing in Vegas this week."

"I like your mother," Tory said, drawing up a mental picture of the tiny, white-haired lady everyone affectionately called Nana. "We should both pray to be as spry and alert at ninety as she is. I think she can outwalk me. I know she can outtalk both of us. You were…very lucky."

"And you weren't." Peggy wheeled her chair over to the chaise so that she could take Tory's hands in hers. "I don't think they do today what they did to us more than a half century ago. Break us up that way. At least I hope to God they don't. Mom and Dad did try to find you and Stephen, you know, once I'd stopped sulking in my room like a world-class brat and told her about you. But by then it was already too late. Babies and cute little toddlers with curly black hair don't stick around in orphanages as long as skinny eight-year-old potential delinquents in pigtails, and you'd both already been adopted."

"I know," Tory said, squeezing her sister's hands, hands that always seemed cold, even out here on the balcony, with a warm June sun shining down on them. She took a deep breath, letting it out slowly, and bit the bullet. She was going to have to tell Peggy sooner or later; it might as well be sooner. "Allie found her father."

Peggy let go of her sister's hands and sat back in the wheelchair. "Oh. I haven't asked you much about her father yet, although I've been dying to dig for all the details. I figured you'd tell me in your own good time. Or, it looks like, at a bad time. So, how did that happen? Allie finding her father, I mean?"

Tory shrugged. "The internet. It seems nothing's private anymore. You can find out most anything these days if you're resourceful enough. And my daughter is very resourceful. I mean, we haven't had this discussion in fifteen years. I thought she'd believed me when I told her I wasn't sure who the father was, that she was okay with that, with me telling her that college had been a pretty…a pretty wild time for me."

Peggy smiled. "Was it? I was a nerd, always with my head in a book. Tell me more. It would be pretty nifty to think one of us had a good time."

Tory grabbed at Peggy's effort to keep the conversational tone from descending into a maudlin retelling of something Tory didn't want to talk about in the first place. "Nifty? Now you're dating both of us. When my grandson likes something, he says it's 'sick.' But, no, I wasn't wild in college. Far from it. Just the supplies for my art classes kept me pretty well below the poverty line. I had to work two part-time jobs to just barely meet my expenses. If one of those jobs hadn't been at a pizza restaurant, busing tables for a pittance and free slices of the stuff that didn't sell out by closing time, I probably would have starved to death. As it was, I think it was ten years before I could look a pizza or calzone in the face again. Sam and I used to flip a coin, and the loser got the spinach calzone because we both hated—well, never mind."

"So there was a guy. One guy. And his name was Sam."

Tory closed her eyes and could see Sam as clearly as if he were standing in front of her. "Yes. Sam. Sam Mc-Cormack."

"A louse, obviously. What happened? He was okay with the pizza, but didn't want any part of a baby? Had his school, his future to consider, and the devil with *your* schooling, *your* future?" Peggy patted Tory's hand. "Oh, I'm sorry. I'm making up my own scenarios. It's a professional failure, I suppose. It's your story, you tell it."

Tory got to her feet and walked over to the stone railing that edged the balcony. She had a clear view of the Atlantic from this vantage point, and normally she loved to simply stand here, and take it in. Right now, she could have been looking at a blank wall, for all she was enjoying the scenery.

"That's the thing, Peggy. I didn't tell it. Tell him, I mean. I just took off. I had my reasons, or at least I thought I did. At fifty-five, you don't see things the same way you did at twenty-two. But I thought Allie was okay with it, I really did. In San Francisco nobody really asks too much about who your parents are, or things like that. Families are just families, and that's the way it is. That made it all easier. But she's married, has her own family now. Maybe her kids asked her about her father. I don't know…"

She turned to look at Peggy, her eyes wide. "My God, Peggy—Sam's a grandfather! I only know Sam the premed student. I have absolutely no idea how he's reacting to what Allie did."

"And what did Allie do? Oh, God, she contacted him? She told him? Without consulting you?"

"Yes, she did. Right down to a DNA test that proved Sam is her father," Tory said, still struggling to age Sam McCormack in her mind. It wasn't easy. "Worse, she told him where I am. What am I going to do, Peggy? If he ignores what he knows, that will just hurt Allie. But if he wants to see me, the way he said he wants to see Allie—and his grandchildren—what on earth am I going to say to him? He has to hate me, and I don't blame him. I cheated him out of his daughter."

"You can't know that he won't listen to reason, sweetheart. You did have a reason for leaving, didn't you?"

"The barely twenty-two-year-old Tory thought she did, yes. She thought she had several good reasons. But what if Sam asks me why the thirty-year-old Tory, or the forty-year-old Tory, or even the Tory of today didn't tell him he has a daughter? Because I'll have no good answer for him, Peggy. None."

"Or maybe you do," Peggy suggested quietly. "Maybe you were afraid. Maybe you're still afraid. Rejection isn't something we get over all that easily, Tory. And you had plenty of it in your life, one way or another."

"Our parents died, they didn't reject us," Tory protested, wiping at her wet cheeks, wishing she could be one of those stolid people who never cried.

"No, and now that you know that, maybe things look a little different to you. But to a small child who never knew why she fell asleep in her own house one night, only to wake up in a juvenile holding facility the next morning, her sister and brother gone, her parents gone? How does that child not grow up thinking she's been rejected, abandoned?"

"Labeled 'unworthy,'" Tory added, almost beneath her breath.

"Ah, Tory…" Peggy reached into her slacks pocket and pulled out a tissue, wiping at her own eyes. "And then your adoptive mother—no, let's not talk about her again. Once was more than enough for both of us. You know what I think you should do? I think you should give it a couple of days, spend some time on the beach, thinking. That always helps me. Get your thoughts together, get your head on straight—and then call him up. Call Sam."

"And say what?" Tory asked, her heart rate moving into overdrive.

"I don't know." Peggy grinned. "I guess you could always invite him to come down to Cape May for some leftover pizza and calzone."

CHAPTER TWO

PEGGY'S HOUSE ON THE BEACH in Cape May was like something out of a storybook.

Fashioned out of pale green stucco, it rose three full floors, its seventy-three windows (Tory had counted them) of all shapes and sizes, from the two-story oriel-topped expanse of glass above the colonnaded front porch to the tall, narrow windows that wrapped the turret holding the elegantly curved grand staircase.

With the Atlantic Ocean as its backdrop, it seemed part fairy-tale castle and part defiance of the elements. From the paved stone courtyard to the sprawling rear balconies and terraces and the breathtaking infinity-edge pool, from the lush lawns and colorful gardens to the delicate wrought-iron fencing that enclosed the compound, the home had obviously been built with both skill and love.

All that was missing was the architect, Peter Longwood, Peggy's husband, who had died ten years earlier. Now the house was more than a home; it was a monument to the man Peggy had loved with all her heart.

Peggy had suffered so much heartache in her life. She'd been the only one of the siblings to really remember their parents, to really remember that five lives had been irrevocably changed that snowy night. She had found love only to lose it much too soon, and now she was in precarious health.

And I can't help her, Tory thought as she turned away from the house and headed out across the sand.

She'd been devastated when Dr. Freeman told her that she wasn't a good match for Peggy and couldn't donate her kidney to her sister. And more than a little surprised when Peggy's response to the news had been, "Good. I wouldn't have taken it anyway. Stan, try another move like that and I may have to hurt you."

Poor Stan, he was such a sweetheart. It was obvious to Tory that the doctor, an old family friend, was in love with Peggy, and wanted only what was best for her. But when Tory had tried to tease her sister into telling her how she felt about Stan, Peggy had gone suddenly quiet before saying, "I don't want his pity."

Yes, the house was like something out of a fairy tale. But the people who lived in it lived in a very real world, one not without its heartaches.

Stan had warned Tory that Peggy had refused to allow her son to be tested, had insisted from the start that since nobody seemed to know why her kidneys had failed in the first place, she wasn't about to put her son or anyone else in possible jeopardy. She was on the list, and that's where she'd stay until a kidney could be found for her, and that was the end of that discussion.

Tory didn't know whether she thought Peggy was a heroine for thinking that way, or if she wanted to try to shake some sense into her.

Either way, Peggy had shifted the conversation back to the upcoming party to celebrate her sixtieth birthday, and the family reunion it was so happily turning out to be, as well, signaling that the discussion was closed.

Peggy then went on to point out that Tory was free to fly to South Carolina if she wished, to see Allie, and then still fly back in plenty of time to help Peggy prepare for the party. The painters had already come and gone, the pool was ready for the season and the menu was being prepared by Peggy's daughter.

She had time to travel to South Carolina. She had reasons to travel to South Carolina. She had an even better reason to be anywhere but here if Sam McCormack decided he wanted some kind of a meeting, most likely some kind of confrontation.

And yet, here she was, a week after she'd learned that Sam knew about his daughter, still waiting to see what would happen next, when the next shoe might drop…probably on her head.

She should call him. Allie had given her his cell phone number, and Tory now knew it by heart. Or she could have driven up to Philadelphia to see him. She knew where he worked now, at the University of Pennsylvania Hospital. She knew the address of both his office and his condo. She knew he was a successful heart surgeon, exactly as he'd planned to become a lifetime ago.

She knew how much she had hurt him.

Tory sat herself down in the sling back beach chair she'd placed beneath the large blue umbrella she'd stuck into the sand that morning, kicked off her flip-flops and picked up the sketchbook she'd left there when she'd gone back up to the house to grab a sandwich for lunch.

She plopped her large straw sunhat on her head, adjusted her sunglasses and looked at the drawing she'd almost completed before taking that lunch break.

"Pitiful," she grumbled. "It's pitiful, and you're pitiful."

The sketch had been her umpteenth try at drawing a new superhero to be best pals with Captain Adversity, her creation, and currently one of the hottest-selling characters to hit the comic book scene in a while. But in order to stay on top, and satisfy the toy manufacturers who'd paid her a huge chunk of change to license her characters, if she didn't keep coming up with new characters to sell they'd be in danger of losing shelf space in the stores. Which, according to these marketing gurus, would be a fate worse than death.

So she'd come up with The Surgeon. Every superhero should have a doctor in the house. And the character had begun nicely. His biceps strained the sleeves of his bulletproof white lab coat, the one with the capelike look to it, which subtly floated behind him as if he was always within a few feet of some personal invisible wind tunnel. The special-powers stethoscope looked great draped around his neck, and the array of scalpels that made up his belt were, well, Tory thought they were truly inspired. As was the broken red heart on the skintight-spandex that covered his chest.

Toss in a medical bag filled with special tools, a rocket-powered armored motorcycle and maybe a sleek black jet helicopter that all the kiddies would bug their parents for, and the merchandisers would be drooling.

She even had the plot for the first *Captain Adversity Meets The Surgeon* story figured out in her head. They'd start out as enemies, but then, as the real bad guys emerged to wreak havoc on the world, they'd become not only allies, but also friends.

There remained just one small problem. Everything went just fine with each concept drawing until Tory tried to sketch The Surgeon's face. She wasn't stupid; she knew the idea for The Surgeon had pretty much come from a mind occupied almost wholly these days by one Sam McCormack. What she hadn't counted on was that *her* Surgeon kept coming out looking like the Sam she'd known more than thirty long years ago.

Worse, the man hadn't aged a day since she last saw him. She'd aged, more than she'd like to think about, but Sam would always be twenty-two in her mind. Young, handsome, sexy.

There was something grossly unfair about that.

A shadow fell across Tory's bare toes, stretching out over the sand. The shadow of a man.

"Tory? Your sister said you'd be down here on the beach. And since nobody else is on the beach, I thought…"

She put one hand on top of her hat to keep it from blowing off thanks to the breeze coming in from the water, and looked up to see The Surgeon looking down at her. Not as young as she'd drawn him time and time again these past few days, but she would always know that voice, those eyes, that one-of-a-kind smile.

As she'd drawn him!

The sunhat went flying off down the beach as Tory dropped both hands to cover the incriminating sketch on the pad resting on her knees.

"Uh…um…hi, Sam," she said, inwardly wincing at how stupid she sounded. Tongue-tied. She quickly closed the sketchpad and went to stand up, having completely forgotten the beach umbrella was over her head. Sam put out a hand too late to stop her, she instinctively recoiled, and the umbrella—already balanced rather perilously, as Tory hadn't been able to push it through the hard-packed sand all that well—toppled over, striking Sam on the shoulder before finally landing on the sand.

"And now for my next trick…" Tory said glumly, even as she surreptitiously tried to pull down the French-cut legs of her emerald-green swimsuit.

Sam didn't smile at her poor effort at humor. "Do you want me to go get your hat?"

"Oh. My hat. No, I'll get it later." *When he wasn't going to be able to watch her walk down the beach, and maybe see her jiggle in a couple of places she didn't used to jiggle in.*

"It's just going to keep on rolling along the beach, Tory, if we don't stop it now."

Great. Now he was saying things with double meanings.

At least she was pretty sure he was. He'd probably had to take some psychology courses along his way to his degree. How nice that he felt the need to practice what he'd learned on her.

"It's only a damn hat, Sam. Go get it if you want to go get it. I'll…I'll pack up here."

She watched as he trotted off down the shoreline, moving gracefully, expertly, a certain rhythm to his steps that told her he didn't spend all his time either behind a desk or standing over an operating table. He was dressed in low sneakers with no socks, a pair of khaki shorts and a navy pullover that might not fit him like a second skin, but came close enough to show that he didn't have an ounce of spare fat on his tall, wide-shouldered frame.

His hair was the same, looking as if he was overdue for a haircut, but that if he got one, you'd be really disappointed that he did, because then you couldn't fantasize about running your fingers through it, pushing it back from his forehead as you leaned in for his kiss.

Stop it, Tory warned herself as she picked up the towel she'd spread beneath the beach chair, shook off the sand and then wrapped it around her waist so that her hips and thighs were hidden beneath the terry cloth. She'd been a size six when she and Sam had been together. She was still a size six, but as the saying went, she might still have an hourglass figure, but some of the sand had shifted.

By the time he returned with her hat, which had somehow managed to land on the edge of its brim and go rolling down the beach like a great straw hoop, Tory believed she had herself somewhat back under control.

After all, she wasn't a kid anymore. She was mature, successful, her own woman. Sam was mature, successful, clearly his own man.

They'd approach this entire thing as adults. Talk, come to

some sort of a mutual understanding and then both get back to their own lives.

Sam picked up the umbrella and tucked it under his arm.

She folded the chair and he took it from her after plopping her hat back on her head. She slid the sketchpad beneath her arm, signaling that she'd carry it.

And then they both just stood there, looking at each other.

"You want to kill me, don't you?"

Sam tipped his head to one side. She remembered the movement; it meant he was considering his answer before he spoke. "I'd thought about it, yes. But I think I'm over that now. You look good, Tory. Life's been kind?"

"Life has been…life. How about you?"

"I keep busy." He employed his chin as a sort of pointer as he motioned toward the huge house in the distance. "Your sister said she'd arrange for some lemonade and cookies on the terrace."

"How very…détente-ish of her," Tory said, squinting up toward the many windows located on the back of the house as they headed in that direction, wondering which one of them Peggy was using to spy down on them. She'd be spying on Peggy if their roles were reversed. "I guess we have some talking to do."

"We have lots of time to talk. I took a room at a local B and B for the next few days. My doctor suggested I needed a vacation."

"Your doctor?" Oh, this was going well. Soon she'd be down to one-word answers, and then dwindle into only the occasional grunt.

"My friend, actually. He's the one who talked me out of killing you."

"Give me his address, I'll send him flowers." Tory winced inwardly. Better to grunt than to open your mouth and be sarcastic. *You're the bad guy here, Tory, not him,* she reminded herself.

They climbed the wide stone steps to the terrace, deposited the umbrella and chair and sketchpad next to the balustrades, and sat down at the round, umbrella-topped table already set with small plates, glasses, a leaded crystal dish of Eugenia's homemade sugar cookies and a frosty pewter pitcher of freshly squeezed lemonade.

"This is quite the place, isn't it? Allie told me you live in San Francisco. I was there two years ago for a seminar. It rained the entire three days. Do you live near the water?"

Okay, so they were going to make small talk. Yippee.

"Our winters can be pretty wet. I lived in the Sunset District when I first moved there, and it can be twenty degrees cooler than on the other side of the hill, and with a lot more wind and fog. Now I'm on the eastern side of the hills, the sunny side, but not all that close to the Bay, no, although I've got a pretty nice view of the water if I go out on my balcony and sort of lean to the left. Why are you here, Sam?"

He reached toward the crystal dish, picking up a cookie. "At the moment, I'm here to say hello, let you know I'm in town. And now I guess I'm here for the cookies. These are pretty good. I figure I can start the inquisition later, maybe over dinner."

"I do want to apologize, feeble as that sounds. I know I shouldn't have done what I did. But I did it, and then it got to be too late to take back what I did. And what I did was unforgivable. I didn't know that then, but I know that now."

Sam shook his head. "No, Tory, it's not that easy. I mean, you can apologize, and I can forgive you, I suppose, and we can both get back to our lives. Or we could, if we didn't share a daughter. And grandchildren. God, Tory. You don't have any idea what it's like to suddenly wake up one day and find yourself a grandfather. That's taking some getting used to, maybe even more than learning I have a daughter. *We* have a daughter."

"Allie looks like you," Tory said quietly, keeping her eyes on her plate, noticing that she'd reduced one of Eugenia's masterpieces to a mass of crumbs. "She has your eyes. Stay here, I'll get my wallet. I've got a few photographs."

Sam half got to his feet as Tory jumped up, whether she was anxious to show him the photographs or eager for a moment's escape from his presence, she didn't know. Probably it was a little of both.

She broke into a trot once she was inside the house and out of Sam's line of sight, and then pressed her back against the kitchen wall and closed her eyes, trying to collect herself.

He was here. He was Sam, and he was here. Like something out of her dreams, but decades too late for anything other than a "hello," an "I'm sorry," and then a "Well, it's been... interesting. See you around."

"Something I can get you?"

Tory's eyes popped open. The housekeeper was looking at her as if she had snakes in her hair, or something. "Eugenia? I didn't see you."

"That's because your eyes were closed. You don't look so good."

"I don't?" Suddenly Tory was on the move again, heading for the stainless steel refrigerator that showed every finger mark—and which Eugenia was constantly wiping at while muttering that when things had handles, you were supposed to *use* the handles—but also could serve as a makeshift mirror. She began finger combing her hair. "Oh, God, I don't. I look like I've been in the wind tunnel with The Surgeon's lab coat."

Eugenia wet a paper towel and began wiping the marble counter of the breakfast bar. "I'm sure you know what you mean by that. He's not going to go away on his own, you know. Miss Peggy says he looks like the kind that sticks."

"Did I say I wanted him to go away?" Honestly, Eugenia could really get on a person's nerves.

"You're hiding in here, aren't you?"

"I'm not—okay, so I'm hiding in here. But just for a minute, that's all. To...to collect my thoughts."

Eugenia gave the counter another swipe. "Uh-huh. According to Miss Peggy, you've been collecting them for about thirty years now. When do you think you'll have enough of them?"

Tory whirled about to face the housekeeper. A not-very-nice word almost made it to her lips, but she bit it back. "Peggy told you?"

"We talk. There's nothing much else to do while she's on the machine. Keeps her mind off things. She was pretty excited when your daughter first called her with the news."

"Of course."

"But she only told me about him today. It's not like I asked. She just told me. So, you going to run away again?"

"I did not run away. I left."

"I stand corrected," Eugenia said rather archly. "Just so I keep this all straight—what are you doing now?"

"Hiding, just like you said. And I need to stop doing that," Tory said, leaning against the refrigerator. She went over to the pantry and opened the door, reaching inside to grab her purse. "Thank you, Eugenia."

"You're welcome. You're a lot like your sister, you know. Smart—but sometimes maybe you both need a kick in the pants to get you moving in the right direction."

Tory reached into her purse and pulled out her wallet, opening it and grabbing the photos of her family. "Which direction are you kicking Peggy in these days?"

Eugenia patted her perfectly neat bun. "Let's just say that both of you might benefit from a little *medical* advice."

"Stan Freeman," Tory said, momentarily diverted from her own *medical* problem. "So you think that, too? He's in love with her?"

"Didn't I just say that? Do you want to talk about the weather now, or are you going back outside?"

Tory dropped her wallet back into her purse and headed for the terrace, not quite as nervous now as she had been— probably because she'd just realized Eugenia would make a heck of a character for her comic book series. She'd call her The Enforcer, and her weapon of choice would be the lightning bolts she kept stuck in her bun.

TORY HADN'T CHANGED MUCH in thirty years. Her hair was different, lighter all over, as if the sun had streaked it a bit, but he liked it that way. Her smile still got to him; he'd always liked her smile because it seemed to light up her entire face. He wondered if her laughter was still so spontaneous and evocative; when Tory laughed, even if you didn't see the joke, you had to laugh along with her.

She hadn't laughed yet. He guessed she'd found nothing to laugh about today.

This whole thing, from the moment Allie had called him until this very moment—it all still seemed surreal. Not really happening. He'd tried to wrap his mind around the enormity of it all, but it was probably that enormity that made the task impossible. He'd have to take baby steps; start out thirty years ago, and try to move forward to the now.

He felt as if he'd somehow aged overnight, from the still fairly young bachelor he thought himself to be, to the grand-father of three. That was going to take some getting used to, definitely. Sort of like waking up one day and deciding maybe it was time to start watching his cholesterol, taking a low-dose aspirin a day and maybe working more fiber into his diet. There weren't a lot of bennies to be found in this getting-old business....

"I'm sorry I took so long," Tory said as she slipped back into her chair. "The...um, the housekeeper had a few questions for me. Did you want to stay for dinner? I told her no, but I can always change that."

"I thought you and I were going to dinner." Sam looked at the photos she held tightly in both hands. "Those the photographs?"

She looked down at them as if she didn't realize she was holding them. "Oh. Oh, yes. Are you sure about that? Dinner, I mean."

"I try to mean what I say, Tory," he told her, not able to take his eyes off the photographs. "I'd very much like us to have dinner together. I have some questions for you, and we probably should discuss them in a public place."

"Point taken," she said, and then looked at the photographs once more. "This first one is Allie," she said, handing the top photograph over to him. "It was taken about three years ago, I think, when she and Mark did the second honeymoon thing. See? She's standing on a dock somewhere in Cape Cod. You can't tell in that shot, but she has your green eyes. And...and your smile."

Sam wasn't looking at the scenery. He was looking at his daughter, and trying very hard to imagine her as his daughter. "She has red hair. My mother has red hair."

"Well, it's auburn now, really. But it was pretty red when she was little. Molly and Megan are both redheads, too, but Quinn favors his father in his hair coloring. Here—here's another one. Allie's college graduation photo."

Now Sam was looking at a close-up of the face of a beautiful, assured and obviously happy young woman posed with a rolled-up diploma in her hand. He'd missed her graduation.

He'd missed all of her graduations—from high school, grammar school, nursery school, if she'd attended one. Her graduation from infant to toddler, from toddler to little girl, from little girl to budding teenager…to college student, to wife, to mother.

"Sam? I said, here's one of all five of them."

Sam blinked, looking at the wallet-size photograph Tory was holding out to him. He had to concentrate to keep his hand from shaking as he took it from her.

It was one of those posed, professional shots. Mother and father sitting with their children arranged between them, the boy standing with his hand on his father's shoulder, the two little girls—mirrors of each other—sitting on their parents' laps.

He didn't say anything. He couldn't say anything. The boy—Quinn, wasn't it? The boy looked a little like he'd looked at that age. Impatient to be finished so that he could get back to what was really important. Like baseball. Or maybe Quinn didn't like baseball. What were kids into these days? Soccer, maybe?

"Sam, I know this is hard…"

He couldn't do this anymore. He couldn't sit here and look at the photographs of his child, his grandchildren, and listen to another thing Tory might have to say to him. He had to get out of here, be by himself, and try to absorb the reality that had just smacked him in the face…and in the heart. So much. He'd missed so much. Tory had robbed him of so much. He gathered up the photographs, Tory had pushed a few more toward him, and stood up.

Sam wasn't the kind of man who showed his emotions. He was a heart surgeon, he had to remain clinically detached, it was the only way he could crack open a patient's chest and hold a beating heart in his hands. Over the years, maybe he'd gotten a little too detached, Sam-the-person disappearing behind Sam-the-doctor.

But not now. Not today. He wanted to rage, to scream. To throw himself onto the terrace and mourn for all the missing years, the years he'd never get back. He was holding on to his composure, maybe even his sanity, by only a rapidly fraying thread.

"Sam?"

"Not now, Tory."

She got to her feet, laid a hand on his arm, squeezed it softly. "I'm so sorry, Sam. I'm so, so sorry…"

"Yeah. So am I."

Then he deliberately put his hand on hers, removing it from his arm, and walked away, taking the photographs with him.

CHAPTER THREE

TORY HEARD THE SOUND of the rubber wheels rolling over the tile floor and lifted her head from the pillow. She hadn't been sleeping, not really. She'd been crying, and thinking, and then crying some more. For hours.

"I'm awake," she mumbled, searching beneath the pillow for one of the dozens of tissues she'd gone through, and then put her head down once more.

"You'll have to do better than that," Peggy told her. "Sam's downstairs, waiting for you."

"He's *what?*" Tory jackknifed to a sitting position, the headache she'd been nursing slamming against the back of her head like a baseball bat. "Oh, no. No. I can't, Peggy. I can't see him."

"Not looking like that, no," her sister agreed. "Not that he looks that much better. I take it things didn't go well earlier."

Tory fell back against the pillows once more. "Things couldn't have been worse. If you'd seen his face, Peggy, if you'd seen how lost he looked, how *hurt*. Oh, God, what did I do to him? To Allie? To...to all of us?"

"I don't want to stretch our newfound sisterly bond here, Tory, but maybe it's time for some straight talk. Hiding up here, having yourself a big grand old pity party, well, that isn't helping anything. You did what you did, and I think I understand why you did it. But now you have to deal with the consequences. That is one hurting man downstairs."

Tory's bottom lip began to tremble, and she put a hand to her face as if pushing back another round of tears. "I know." She sat up once more, and this time kept going, until she was on her feet, facing her sister. "Give me twenty minutes, okay?"

"I'll give you thirty. Come here." Peggy held up her arms to Tory and the two embraced, Peggy's hug strong and fortifying rather than soft and comforting...which would have totally destroyed Tory. "It's going to be all right, kiddo," Peggy whispered against her sister's ear. "It only feels like the end of the world."

Tory gave a short, rather weepy laugh, and headed off to the bathroom, first to splash cold water on her face, and then to hop into the shower.

Her hair was still a little damp when she headed downstairs, and she'd taken time for only mascara, blush and lipstick, but she was pretty sure Sam wouldn't care one way or the other how she looked. He wanted answers, and she was going to have to give them to him.

She stepped into the foyer, the cork heels of her sandals not making any noise against the tiles, and headed for the enormous living room with its two-story windows overlooking the terrace and the water. Sam was standing at those windows, his hands clasped behind his back, looking out at the view.

Peggy was nowhere in sight.

He's still Sam. Not some bogeyman. He's still the Sam you knew, the Sam you loved. You can do this. You have to do this.

Mental pep talk over, Tory took another few moments to look at Sam. He had such wonderful posture, stood so tall and straight, and yet not at all rigid. She used to love the way he walked, those long, confident strides, totally unaware that he exuded confidence and reliability, even that long ago, when they'd both been so young.

He'd had plans, grand plans. So much intelligence and ambition and drive. So much determination and dedication; it had nearly oozed out of his pores. It would have been criminal to derail the express train that was Sam McCormack on his way to his dream.

Hadn't it been his sure knowledge of what he wanted out of life that had drawn her to him in the first place? He'd seemed so centered, where she had been just floating aimlessly. He'd given her confidence in herself, pointed her in the direction of her own dream, rather than just in any direction that took her away from the thing she had wanted most to escape.

Ah, it was all so long ago. Another lifetime. But it had been her lifetime, and she'd reacted in the way she'd been trained, taught, programmed to act: she'd run.

And then it had been too late. She'd turned around one day and realized that Allie was ten years old. Much too late to turn back the clock, and years past the point where she could do things differently.

"Sam?"

He turned around slowly, and she had to bite back a gasp at the look on his face. It was as if he'd aged ten years in the few hours since she'd last seen him.

"Oh, Sam..."

He held up a hand as she instinctively took two steps toward him.

"You look twelve," he said, walking toward her.

"Hardly," Tory answered, and yet could not fight down a reflexive pat at her hair in reaction to his flattery. "Under this magic done by my colorist, my hair is just like Peggy's. Except hers is pretty, while my silver seemed to come in all striped, and made me look more like a skunk. Are you okay?"

He shook his head. "I don't know anymore what that means. Okay. I'm...functioning. Those photos? They were like a two-by-four to the head. I'd been...I don't know. Dealing in the abstract? But there's nothing abstract about seeing your daughter for the first time. And your grandchildren. Allie says they can't wait to meet me."

"She means that."

"I think she does. And I'm…hell, I'm terrified. I kept looking at those faces, those sweet faces, and thinking I'd rather perform bypass surgery on myself, blindfolded, than face them. Face Allie."

Tory couldn't understand. "But why, Sam? Why haven't you already been to South Carolina? They're dying to meet you."

"Why? You don't get it, do you, Tory? You left, yes. You didn't tell me you were pregnant. You dumped school months before graduation, you took off—and I know damn well you couldn't have had much money in your pockets—rather than tell me you were carrying my child. What kind of monster does that make me?"

Tory was so stunned she had to grab on to the back of the chair closest to her or else risk falling down. "But it was *me*. I'm the one who left. I'm the one who ran."

"Yes, and I'm the one you were running away *from*. It would be easier for me if I could blame everything on you, blame you for robbing me of my daughter, of the years I've missed. But that isn't all of it, is it, Tory? I played a role in what happened, and not just as a sperm donor. I loved you. I thought you loved me. But something wasn't right, was it? Something about me. Maybe you knew that better than I did, and that's why you ran."

Tory looked at the floor, not wanting to meet Sam's eyes. "Let's get out of here," she said quietly. "But not to dinner, unless you're hungry. I'd rather we took a walk on the beach."

THEY LEFT THEIR SHOES at the bottom of the terrace steps and made their way along the path between the dunes, walking all the way to the water's edge before turning and heading toward the lights of Cape May Point.

Their steps were slow, tiny wavelets rolling up the slightly slanted shoreline to tease their bare feet. They didn't speak, but just allowed the sound of waves breaking farther offshore and the cry of the seagulls to fill the silence.

The tip of Cape May, caught between the Atlantic Ocean and Delaware Bay, was one of the few spots where you could watch the sun both rise and set over the water, and today was no exception. The skies were still blue, but with a hint of pink in the snow-white clouds, and the slowly setting sun turned the tips and rises of the water into a sea of bright, shiny diamonds.

But Sam could have been walking down one of the narrow alleyways behind the U of P hospital at midnight for all he noticed the glorious scenery around him.

Tory stepped into a depression in the sand, and nearly stumbled, but Sam instinctively put out a hand to steady her, and then took her hand in his so that she wouldn't lose her balance again.

"Thank you."

"And you're not even chewing gum," he said, very much aware of his body's immediate reaction to the feel of Tory's hand in his. "For someone who could dance better than anyone I'd ever met, you were always tripping over things."

"It was a six-hundred square foot apartment, and you had books piled everywhere. Add in my easel, my paints, our clothes…"

"Empty pizza boxes, your latest art project, whoever was crashing on our couch that week, Harvey…"

Tory looked up at him, and he saw her first real smile in over thirty years. "I'd almost forgotten about Harvey. Did you guys finally sneak him back into the Anatomy lab?"

The skeletal remains of Harvey, or U.P.36519-C, according

to the inventory number stamped on the small metal plate attached to his left femur, had occupied one corner of the small living room and kitchen combo ever since he and Bill Helms and a couple other worse-for-drink underclassmen had boosted him from the Anatomy lab in order to study for a test.

They'd all passed the test, but getting Harvey back to the lab hadn't proved easy, so for two years he'd been passed from friend to friend for safekeeping. He'd been in residence with Sam and Tory for at least six months, and Tory had even dressed him up in a Santa hat for the holidays. It wasn't being disrespectful of a man who had died at least fifty years earlier; Harvey had been like one of the family. Or like a visiting relative who had really, *really* outstayed his welcome.

"Bill—you remember Bill Helms, don't you, classmate turned shrink? Well, he's the guy you're sending flowers to. Anyway, Bill and I took him back the day after we graduated, after we knew we wouldn't get caught and kicked out of school. Bill gave him his graduation cap. I think Harvey liked it. He was smiling when we left him, anyway, although he pretty much always looked like he was smiling, didn't he? It's funny I should remember that now. Did I tell you I had Bill in my O.R. a couple of weeks ago?"

Tory looked up at him, her smile having faded into a look of concern. "Heart surgery? Bill? Is he all right?"

"He's fine. Scared, but fine."

"So you stay in touch. That's nice. Wow, heart surgery. Where did the years go, that we're all old enough to have that sort of thing smack us in the face?"

"Old enough to be grandparents," Sam said, thinking maybe he'd finally found a way back into the conversation they'd left behind them at the house. "I'm not sure I want anyone calling me Grandpa just yet."

"I've been a grandmother seven years longer than you've known you're a grandfather. I remember the night Quinn was born, and I stood over his isolette, looking at this beautiful creature I instantly loved with all my heart, trying to find a name for myself. Nana? Grandmom? Oh, God, Sam, what am I saying? I'm so sorry. We keep tripping over minefields, don't we?"

He used his chin to point toward an outcropping of large boulders just at the edge of the beach. "How about we go sit over there for a while."

She nodded her head and let him lead the way, then climbed up onto what seemed to be a natural seat carved into the rocks by a thousand ancient storms. "I want to tell you why I left."

He sat down beside her, both of them facing the water. "And I want to hear why you left. Except that maybe I don't. It was the night I got that acceptance letter from U of P, wasn't it? The night Allie was conceived, I mean."

"I think so, yes. We were celebrating, being silly, and then…well, being stupid. Careless."

"And my responsibility. We'd discussed that at the beginning, and contraception was to be my responsibility, damn it."

"If you'd been more responsible, there would be no Allie," Tory pointed out, placing her hand on his shoulder. "And I can't imagine a world without Allie in it. Allie and the kids."

"Yes, let's talk about that. You…had options. But you decided to have the baby, keep the baby."

Tory faced forward and looked out over the water, seeing the past, perhaps, or just searching for a way to say what she felt needed to be said.

At last, when Sam thought he could stand the silence no longer, she began to talk. Not to him, not directly, but to the sea, and the sky, and the slowly setting sun.

"What I knew about myself was what my—what she told

me. My adoptive mother. She told me my *real* parents didn't want me, that I was a burden to them and they gave me away. She, uh, she said my father—my adoptive father—had wanted a child, and that's the only reason she'd agreed to adopt me. He died when I was six, and from that point on, she never missed an opportunity to tell me how unwanted I was, how much of a burden I was, how I had ruined her chances for any kind of a life now that my adoptive father was dead. Who wanted someone else's child? *She* certainly didn't. If I broke a glass, or left my jacket on the banister, or if I sassed her, dared to answer her back, she'd threaten to give me back to the orphanage, or just take me somewhere and leave me there. Not that anyone else would want me, because I was loud and dirty and ugly and stupid."

"Child abuse," Sam said quietly, his insides twisting into a knot. "Did she hit you? Hurt you in any way? Or was it all verbal abuse?"

"Hit me? No, she never hit me. Nobody called what she did child abuse in those days. But, yes, looking back on it, that's what it was. Not that knowing the term would have helped me then. She was sick, mentally ill, but I didn't realize that, either. When I hit my teens, I began running away. I'll never understand why she always took me back, but she did. Sent the police after me, that sort of thing. Finally I smartened up, studied hard and got myself a scholarship to college, along with some student loans. I turned eighteen a few days before I graduated, and that's when she packed up my belongings and put them on the front porch. I came home from graduation and there were the boxes. I was officially on my own. I stayed with friends until I could move into the dorm."

"Why didn't you ever tell me any of this? We lived together for nearly our entire senior year."

Tory shrugged her shoulders. "It was all four years behind me, the distant past. And, frankly, I wasn't proud of any of it."

She turned to look at him, her eyes dry, but filled with pain. "And maybe…maybe I was still trying to prove to myself that I wasn't worthless, I wasn't a burden, wasn't someone who could be all but put out with the garbage. That I…that I had worth."

Sam longed to take her in his arms, soothe the tenseness from her rigid posture, ease the pain in her eyes. "You would have graduated with full honors. You worked two jobs and still had better grades than anyone else in any of your classes. You took care of the apartment, of *me*. I thought you were perfect."

She nodded. "Yes, I know. Every day took me further away from my past, and I was beginning to believe my own advertising." She smiled sadly. "And then, suddenly, I was pregnant, and the past all came rushing back at me."

Sam thought he understood. "You thought I'd reject you."

"No, Sam," she said quietly. "I worried that you'd insist upon marrying me."

"And I would have. My God, Tory, what else would you have expected me to do?"

"Nothing, not then, not at that moment. But you still had more schooling, and then your internship, and then more years going for your specialty. We were already as poor as the pro-verbial church mice, and we both had a fistful of student loans, with plenty more of them in your future. I couldn't rob you of your dream, and I couldn't bear to think about the day you'd look at me, look at our child, and resent us both."

"I wouldn't have done—"

She touched a finger to his mouth. "All the pain of not being wanted, of being a burden. I'd lived it. I would not allow my child to live that, Sam. I couldn't take that chance."

Sam got to his feet, shoved his hands in his pants pockets and started walking back toward the water. He hoped Tory would realize he needed to be by himself for a few minutes.

To think. To absorb what she'd said. To look at himself as he'd been over thirty years ago.

He'd been…determined. Yes, that was a good word. Determined. Determined to graduate at or near the top of his class. Determined to succeed, get into the best school, work twenty-eight hours a day if necessary, to achieve his goals.

And he'd done it. He'd done it all. Mastered all of his classes. Survived his internship. Been named chief resident. Been asked to join one of the most prestigious cardiologist groups in the city, and then, ten years ago, opened his own practice, which now numbered seven associates.

Somewhere in there, he'd married, and almost as quickly divorced. His marriage was mostly a blur, with his wife telling him one day that if she wanted to feel like a widow, then the least he could do was die, so that she could date. When she left, he hadn't really missed her. In fact, he'd been sleeping at the hospital because of a touch-and-go surgical patient, and hadn't even known she was gone until three days after she'd left.

Rewind. Take it back to his senior year at Penn State. Add in a wife and, a few months later, a baby. An infant, crying, always needing attention. Needing food, diapers, his time. Trying to study in another cramped apartment above another pizza shop while the baby teethed, cried with colic or something. He and Tory going at each other when the money got short and the tempers shorter. Working toward his dream—no, his obsession—while being responsible for Tory and Allie.

He'd had a one-track mind back then. A clear vision of what he wanted out of life, and how he was going to get it.

Would he have had moments of resentment? Hell, yes. He wouldn't have been human if he didn't.

They'd both been young. Selfish in the way only the young can be selfish. Tory had been fighting demons she had chosen not to share, and he had pretty much been an ass actually, caring for her, sure, maybe even loving her, but with ninety percent of himself devoted to Getting Sam Ahead.

"Sam?"

He turned around to see that Tory was standing just behind him now, concern written on her features. "I want you to know something. I wasn't being a martyr back then. I loved you. The thought of ever seeing you look at me as a problem, looking at our child as a mistake that shouldn't have happened? Opening our child to even one moment of what I'd lived with growing up? I couldn't do it. I couldn't take the chance. That's why I left. Why I ran. I ran before you could tell me to go."

"Come here," he said quietly, holding out his arm so that she could step closer, so that he could draw her against him, her cheek against his chest.

They stood that way for a long time, Sam's chin resting on the top of her head, as he looked out over the water and found the forgiveness he hadn't thought he could find.

For Tory.

For himself.

As the song said, yesterday was gone. And tomorrow would be a new day...

TORY WATCHED AS SAM DOWNED an egg white omelet and some whole wheat toast, feeling guilty about the short stack of pancakes she'd ordered and enjoyed topped with butter and maple syrup, but not guilty enough to not have eaten every last bit, using the final forkful to sop up the remainder of the syrup.

She'd slept well last night, remarkably well, and felt no lingering traces of nervousness now that the two of them were sharing breakfast at one of the many Cape May restaurants that routinely opened for breakfast for the tourists. She felt comfortable, at ease, and if she sneaked looks at Sam when she was sure he wouldn't notice, and marveled at how wonderful he looked, how wonderful it made her feel to be able to look at him…well, she'd just keep that to herself.

"So, egg white omelets really taste good?" she asked him as he lowered his fork and picked up his coffee cup.

"They're an acquired taste," he admitted, smiling. "Sometimes I just eat fruit or oatmeal. How were the pancakes?"

"Nicely congealing in my arteries even as we speak, I imagine. But they tasted good. Do all heart surgeons eat healthy?"

"Most of us. It's probably an occupational hazard, since we get to see firsthand what can happen to a heart whose stomach has been making wrong choices for it. But don't worry. You're not technically family, but close enough for me to give you a professional discount. You know—would you like fries with that bypass, ma'am?"

"Har-har, very funny. And you run, too, don't you? You've got the look of a runner."

"Breathless and weather-beaten?"

"No, tanned and…sinewy. San Franciscans are very health conscious, and I see lots of runners out there in all kinds of weather. I see them while I'm sitting on my balcony, being slothful. I guess I should start realizing I'm not a kid anymore. I mean, look at Bill."

"I did, all the way inside. But Bill is also forty pounds overweight, most of that in his gut, and has a family history of heart disease."

"I wouldn't know about that. My family history, that is," Tory said, the old familiar stab of not knowing anything about her parents, her heritage, stinging her. But not as hard as it had done before she'd been reunited with Peggy. "I do know that Haswick—my real last name—is English. I hadn't known myself as anyone except Victoria Fuller until Peggy told me that. I can't explain what it feels like to know I have a sister, to know I had a brother and that our parents didn't abandon me, but were broadsided by a truck that slid on the ice that night. It's not a pretty history, but it's my history, one I didn't have until Allie got curious."

"How did she do that, anyway?" Sam asked as he paid the check and they walked out into the bright sunshine once more. He held open the door for her, and took her hand as they turned down the street, just as if this was the most natural thing in the world to do.

It felt good. His hand felt good. In just twenty-four hours, it was as if at least half of the years they'd been apart had just somehow slipped away.

"She didn't tell you? Until the twins were born, she and Mark lived in Virginia, and Allie worked for the CIA. Don't ask me what she did there, because she'd never tell me, but our daughter is one smart cookie. Since I'm nothing but a silly cartoonist who got lucky, I always figured she got her brains from you."

"Really? Thanks for the compliment, and I only hope she didn't also get my overbite. My dad never let me forget how much he put out on teeth braces."

"Oh, so that's how it happened," Tory teased him. "In that case, you owe me four thousand dollars for her orthodontic work. Pay up, buddy."

"Keep eating pancakes, and you can take it out in trade. Come on, let's go in here," he said, drawing her toward the door to a shoe store. "We're going to get you some running shoes, and tomorrow morning we're going to run on the beach before I introduce you to a healthy breakfast."

"Oh, no, we're not," Tory protested, pulling back her hand. But it was no good, as he was stronger, and she wanted to please him, anyway. "And you'd have to tie me to the chair and force-feed me before I'd eat eggs that are nothing but the…the icky colorless parts."

"That can be arranged," he told her as he pulled open the

door and the bell hung above it jangled, bringing them to the attention of a freckled teenage boy dressed in a running suit complete with glow-in-the-dark green headband. "What size are you?"

"That, sir, is a secret that I'll take with me to the grave, thank you. My feet are horribly out of proportion to the rest of me. To my height, I mean."

"There isn't anything about you that's out of proportion, Tory," Sam told her, shocking her and pleasing her at the same time. "And I speak from experience."

"Well, my body has had a lot more *experience* since last you saw—I mean, that is…"

He gave the tip of her nose a slight flick with his index finger. "You can still blush. I like it. Now, your shoe size."

She told him.

SAM WAS AMAZED AT HOW QUICKLY he and Tory had moved from awkwardness to a sort of mature compatibility he wouldn't have believed when he remembered how angry he'd been with her only a single day earlier.

Maybe it was because she'd tried to let him off the hook, as if her decision not to tell him about her pregnancy had all been her mistake, and he'd been an entirely innocent victim.

When he'd known that wasn't possible. There were always two sides to every story, he'd understood that, but by acknowledging that fact, it also became a foregone conclusion that blame is never one-sided, either.

Now he had a daughter. Grandchildren.

And Tory was back in his life.

There weren't any downsides in his present, and that was a great feeling.

The only questions remaining were what would happen next for both of them, and if the past should stay in the past, that they'd had their chance, their *moment,* and now the most they could hope for was friendship.

"Why San Francisco?" he asked her as they continued their walk through the neatly arranged shopping area in the center of Cape May. "I mean, is that where you went immediately?"

She nodded her head, and didn't say anything for a few moments. "You talked about it a lot, remember? California, land of opportunity, and San Francisco in particular. It seemed like a good place to make a new start. I...once in a while I'd wonder if I'd see you there one day, just the two of us bumping into each other on the street or something. Why did you stay on the East Coast?"

"My dad took ill during my residency. He fought for nearly four years before he passed, and then I couldn't envision leaving my mother, being on the other side of the country if she needed me. Philadelphia was as far from Scranton as I got, but I've never regretted it."

"I'm sorry to hear about your father. I only met him that one time, but he seemed like a lovely man."

"He was hard as nails and stubborn as a mule. I still miss him. My mother remarried two years ago, at seventy-four, and she and Harry live in Florida now. She's taken up golf. Life is strange, isn't it? And funny."

"And hopeful," Tory said quietly. "Do you like Harry?"

"He sends me a huge box of cigars for my birthday and at Christmas. I hate cigars. But I do like Harry."

Tory laughed, that free, unaffected laugh he remembered, and any lingering ice Sam had held inside his heart shattered and melted away.

"ARE YOU SURE SHE'LL LIKE IT?"

Tory rolled her eyes in mock exasperation. They'd been

inside the crystal shop for nearly an hour so that Sam could pick out a present for Allie.

At the moment, he was hesitating over a simple teardrop crystal hanging from a delicate silver chain.

"Do you do this to your operating-room nurses?" she asked him facetiously. "I'll take the number two scalpel, nurse. No, wait, maybe the number four. No! How about that long silver one on the end? Honestly, Sam, she'll love it. It's elegant, it's just the sort of necklace she'd wear, and it's her very first gift from her father. She'll be over the moon. Now buy it and let's go back to the house and see how Peggy's doing. The cast was supposed to come off today."

Sam nodded to the clerk, who caught Tory's eye and mouthed a silent "thank you," and then quickly bustled away with the necklace and Sam's charge card before he could change his mind yet again.

"I'm not usually so indecisive, you know," he said.

He looked so embarrassed. And so adorable. And she felt much more his equal than she had when they'd been living together. She was surprised to realize that she'd felt that way back then—not quite his equal, rather in awe of his drive and ambition. How different their lives would have been if she'd told him about Allie and they'd married then and there.

And she felt fairly certain that they wouldn't have made it. She'd had too many insecurities back then, too many problems still to work out in her head before she could truly see herself as a partner in any relationship, rather than just the supportive handmaiden, the supplicant, always looking for approval and acceptance.

"Considering what you do for a living, I'd say that's a good thing," Tory responded, and then acted without thinking. She went up on tiptoe and gave him a quick kiss on the mouth.

"What was that for?" he asked her, putting his hand to her cheek. "No, never mind answering. Just let me say thank you." He leaned in and kissed her, just a brief touch of their mouths, and then stepped back. "Thank you."

The clerk brought him his package and a receipt to be signed, so he probably didn't hear Tory when she whispered, "You're welcome."

CHAPTER FOUR

BY THE TIME THEY'D WALKED BACK to the house and climbed the stairs to the front porch, Tory was more than ready for a chair in the shade and a tall glass of Eugenia's homemade lemonade.

Instead, as she and Sam were only halfway up the stone steps the door opened and Eugenia appeared in the doorway, her expression caught between exasperation and worry. "Finally! What did you two do, walk every street of Cape May? I was about to send out a search party. Miss Peggy's in the living room. It isn't good. She came home from the hospital and now she won't talk, she won't tell me what's wrong, and it's Kinsey's day off and she's not here."

Tory was immediately on the move, Sam close behind her.

Her sister was in her wheelchair, facing the wall of windows overlooking the terrace and the shoreline. Her shoulders were slumped, her head down and she had a blanket drawn over her lap and legs, something she'd never done before, saying she didn't want to look like an invalid. Tory felt an instant cold shock of panic, her mind immediately going to the state of the woman's health. She knew so little about what could happen to a person with total kidney failure, but she was sure if she did know she'd be even more panicked.

Sam put a hand on her back, as if to steady her, and she was so grateful he was there with her. "Peggy? Peggy, honey, what's wrong?"

Her sister's answer was low, muffled. "I don't want to talk about it. And tell Sam to go away. Eugenia, too, as I'm certain she's still back there, hovering. Just bring me the black marker from the drawer on my nightstand. I would have asked Eugenia, but then I never would have heard the end of it."

"You'll never hear the end of it anyway, Miss Peggy," Eugenia said with a sniff. "Acting like a two-year-old."

"Eugenia, please, do as she says." A black marker? Was Peggy delirious? Tory looked at Sam, shaking her head *no* even as she asked, "Sam? Would you also please leave us alone?"

"Sure, but I think I'll stick around," Sam said cheerfully enough. "Out of sight, but not out of earshot. Maybe Eugenia has more of those sugar cookies." He leaned in to whisper, "Just yell if you need me," and then followed the clearly upset housekeeper to the kitchen.

Tory approached the wheelchair and laid a hand on her sister's shoulder. "How bad is it? Where do you hurt?"

"Hurt? I don't hurt," Peggy said. "I just feel like an idiot. Look!"

The blanket was thrown back and Tory walked around to the front of the wheelchair to see Peggy's pink toe-to-knee cast covered in black graffiti.

Begone, devil!

Pink is for sissies!

Onward and upward!

This cast for rent, cheap.

There once was a cast from Nantucket... Tory decided not to read the next three lines of that particular bit of poetry.

There was a long dotted line and the words *cut here*.

There was a clearly drawn skull and crossbones.

And a few words not usually heard in polite company.

"Oh, Peggy," Tory said, sinking to the floor, laughing so

hard she had to hold on to her sides or maybe risk cracking a rib with her giggles. "What did you do?"

"I think it's obvious what I did," Peggy said, a small smile at last playing around her mouth. "The cast was coming off this morning. Everyone said so. I've been good, Tory, I haven't complained—"

"Much. You haven't complained much," Tory corrected. "But clearly there was some pent-up hostility champing to get out."

"Clearly." Peggy glared down at the cast. "It's this damn renal failure. I don't heal as fast as other people. The cast stays on at least another two weeks. I'm stuck in this chair at least another two weeks. And now I'm not only hobbled, I'm *obscene*."

"You look like a wall that's been attacked by rabid spray paint artists, yes," Tory conceded, and then broke into another round of giggles as Tory lifted her leg and the words *bite me* became visible. "Why didn't they just give you another cast? Or cover it up somehow, or something?"

"I know," Peggy sighed. "I even tried bribes, but they wouldn't do it. Stan says it serves me right. I'll get even with him for this, I swear it. Now please go get the black marker and…and paint this thing."

"In a moment," Tory promised, and then pulled her cell phone from her pocket and took three quick pictures of the cast. "For posterity, you understand, and in case I ever find a reason to blackmail you."

"Statements like that prove we're sisters more than any DNA test," Peggy said, lowering her leg.

"You think so? Good. And you know, with just a little imagination, I think I can do much better than just turn your pink cast into a black cast. A few flowers to cover up that business about the devil, for starters. How do you feel about superheroes?"

"I think I love you more every day, that's what I think."

"Good. Hold that thought. I'll be right back."

Tory retrieved the black marker and then went to the kitchen, where she told Sam and Eugenia that Peggy was fine, just a little upset that the cast hadn't been removed as she'd hoped.

"It's those kidneys of hers," Eugenia said, nodding her understanding. "They play havoc with everything."

This statement served to produce a raised eyebrow from Sam, and Tory realized she'd not told him about Peggy's medical problems. "I'm going to be a while," she told him. "Would…would you like to have dinner later?"

"I like to have dinner every night," he told her. "Having dinner with you could only be seen as a bonus. I'll pick you up at six." He leaned in and gave her another kiss like the one they'd shared in the crystal shop, and then saw himself out, calling a farewell to Peggy as he passed through the living room and getting a more cheerful goodbye than the nongreeting he'd had from her only ten minutes earlier.

"Do I get to know what's going on here?" Eugenia asked once the front door had closed behind Sam.

"There's nothing going on, Eugenia," Tory said, feeling her cheeks growing hot. "We've…we've come to an understanding, that's all. We're…friends."

"I don't need you to tell me what I can see for myself, and *friends* isn't what you want to be, either of you. Anyway, I'm asking about what's going on with Miss Peggy."

"Oh." Tory had a momentary urge to sink into the floor, but it passed. "That's a sisterly secret, Eugenia. I'm sorry. But she's all right, I promise."

The housekeeper made a *harrumph* sound in her throat and headed for the pantry.

And Tory smiled, hearing the words *sisterly secret* once more in her head. They sounded good.

Life at the moment was so good, in fact, that Tory's next reaction was to worry how long such happiness could last.

THEY ATE DINNER AT A restaurant that looked out over the Delaware, lingering over dessert, coffee and after-dinner drinks in order to watch the sun set over the water.

Tory watched the sun set. Sam watched Tory watching the sun set.

He still had his moments, he couldn't deny that. The photographs he'd kept, those of his daughter, his grandchildren? Each time he took them out and looked at them, and he probably did it hourly, he remembered something else he'd missed. Christmas morning. Allie's first two-wheeler; having her trust him enough to allow him to let go and watch her steer down the sidewalk. Her first date, and how he would have put the boy through hell before he'd let him take his baby away to the movies.

Tory had denied him those moments.

Sitting up half the night when his child was feverish, imagining all sorts of terrible illnesses that could happen to children. Helping her choose a college; he would have liked it if Allie had gone to Penn State, but she'd been in San Francisco, and graduated from Stanford.

Walking her down the aisle when she'd married Mark.

These were memories he'd never have, moments he'd never get back.

"What was it like," he asked Tory now, "raising Allie alone?"

She kept her gaze on the horizon for long moments before turning to look at him. She cupped her chin in her hand and studied him, as if trying to gauge why he'd asked, what he might want to hear.

"It was difficult, at first, anyway. There was no storybook kindly female neighbor in the apartment building where I lived, nobody to mother both of us or sit with Allie when I went to work. That only happens in the movies, I guess. There was a succession of jobs, waitress jobs mostly, a succession of not really nice apartments. Too many sitters I had to leave her with, wondering if she'd be all right when I got back."

"You should have called me. Damn it, Tory, even if you didn't want to marry me, I could have helped somehow. Financially."

She gave him a half smile. "Really? You mean you were holding out on me all those years ago, and we didn't actually have to exist on pizza and calzone?"

"You could have lived with my parents," he offered, knowing he wasn't exactly being reasonable. "There were things you could have done, we could have done."

"I can't change the past, Sam," she said, blinking rapidly, obviously close to tears. "My decision, good or bad, was my decision. I'm not even certain I regret it, not on the whole. Or haven't you wondered where we'd be, both of us, if I'd let you do the right thing, as I'm sure you would have seen it?"

"I'd have been with you," he said, shocked to hear his own words, knowing he had to say them. "I would have had my daughter. Maybe even other children. You said I would have resented you and the baby, that I would have thought you were holding me back. Maybe you're right, and I was a selfish bastard back then, with my eyes only on school and my career. But maybe you aren't, maybe we would have made it. You didn't even give me a choice, let alone a chance. You just left. I understand about your past, about your adoptive mother, why you ran. I do, intellectually. But then I think about my daughter, and about you, *us,* and I feel so damn cheated."

"Sam, I'm sorry. I know *sorry* is just a word, but it's the only one I've got." She picked up her purse and stood up. "Maybe you should take me back to Peggy's now. Or I can probably call for a cab."

"No, I'll take you." He'd already paid the bill. He stood up, dropped some bills on the table for the tip and followed Tory back in through the restaurant and out to the street. "Let's walk a little first," he said, pulling her arm through his.

They headed down the sidewalk toward the beach as all around them tourists window-shopped and the streetlights came on, barely yet needed in the warm dusk. Tory was nervous; with her arm tucked through his he could actually feel her trembling. He'd said some hard things, hurting things, and he couldn't take them back any more than he could recapture the lost years.

"I was married, you know," he said at last. "About two years after I finished my residency. Bill told me he'd always thought she looked a lot like you."

Tory kept her head down, as if suddenly she'd been promoted to Chief Sidewalk Watcher. "Did she?"

"I don't know. I don't think so." He hesitated and then added, "Maybe a little. It didn't take. The marriage, that is. It wasn't her fault. I wasn't a good husband."

Finally, Tory looked up at him.

"I was everything you said I was," he admitted. "Selfish, driven, oblivious. All I wanted was to be in the operating room. That was my whole goal, my entire focus. You were right to leave."

She leaned her head against his shoulder. "No, I wasn't. You had a right to know you were going to be a father. I had no right to make choices for three people, only for myself. We were both still so young, Sam. The older I get, the younger twenty-two becomes."

"My parents were married at nineteen, had me seven months later," he said, and then smiled. "Not that I was ever supposed to know that. Mom deliberately spilled something on their marriage certificate, to blur the date, just in case I ever had a reason to go looking at it. Dad told me when I left for Penn State, somewhere in the lecture he was giving me about safe sex and the danger of getting sloppily drunk at keg parties."

"Well, look at it this way, Sam," Tory said, a small smile lighting her features, "you never got drunk at a keg party, at least not as far as I know. So maybe one out of two isn't bad."

"There it is, that perverted sense of humor. You could always make me laugh, even when I was bone tired, facing another warmed-up spinach calzone and stuck pulling an all-nighter, studying for exams. God, I've missed you, Tory," Sam told her, sliding his arm around her waist. "I had no idea I've been missing you so much."

"I missed you most when Allie smiled," Tory admitted softly, once again doing her sidewalk-watcher move.

Sam didn't know what to say to that, so he said nothing.

They reached the end of the sidewalk and turned around, heading back to the restaurant parking lot.

He opened the car door for her and then went around and slid in behind the steering wheel. He put the key into the ignition but didn't turn it, instead just sat there, looking through the windshield at absolutely nothing.

"I don't want to take you back to Peggy's yet."

"Okay," Tory said quietly.

What did that mean, *okay? Okay,* let's go somewhere else. *Okay,* hey, how about a movie? Or *okay,* let's go back to your B and B and see if what we once had was as good as I remember it.

He decided to take a chance on door number three.

TORY TRIED TO TELL HERSELF that they were just going to talk.

But she knew she was lying to herself.

Neither of them said much on the drive back to the B and B,

which turned out to be one of the lovely old Victorian buildings Cape May was so famous for, a three-story confection of tricolor paint and magnificent woodworking.

Sam's rental was on the top floor, a converted attic that absolutely reeked with charm…and much more lace than she was sure he was accustomed to, especially on the canopy of the huge bed that pretty much dominated the room.

"Lots of pink in here," she said, trying not to smile as she took in the flowered wallpaper and the lace curtains that matched the canopy and bedspread. "I never saw you as the lace and rosebud type."

"I booked online," he explained rather sheepishly. "You look good here, though. There's a small refrigerator in that cabinet over there. Would you like some juice?"

Her mouth was feeling rather dry. "Sure, thanks." She looked around again, hunting for someplace safe to sit, but there really wasn't much; just a single pink-and-white striped armless thing she was pretty sure was called a slipper chair, good only for sitting on while you put on your slippers, she guessed.

And the bed. There was the bed….

"Here you go," Sam said, handing her a small bottle of orange juice.

Orange juice? How…healthy.

He'd had wine at dinner, and hadn't shied away from the browned butter for the clams they'd shared, so it wasn't as if he was some total health nut. Still, she had a long way to go if she wanted to live up to his healthy ways, considering the fact that her idea of exercise didn't extend beyond climbing the two flights to her condo, and she remained a big fan of white sugar and rich chocolates. She might live in health-conscious San Francisco, but her heart still belonged to the doughnuts and cheesesteaks of Pennsylvania.

She sat down on the slipper chair and took a sip of orange

juice. "Do you really expect me to go jogging on the beach tomorrow? Because, you know, I think maybe I should sort of…ease into that sort of thing."

He remained standing, leaning one elbow on the mantelpiece of the fireplace that sported a spray of colorful flowers instead of logs ready to be lit. "Ease into it as in first we walk a little, run a little, or ease into it as in you'll think about it for a couple of years, and then maybe give it a shot?"

"I'd say the second one, but then you'll probably give me a lecture."

"Not me. Okay, yes, I probably would. It comes with the territory, I suppose. But you don't know your family history, Tory, the way Bill did. He ignored that, and look where it got him. Now, are you going to tell me what else is going on with your sister's health besides the broken foot, or am I going to have to ask her?"

Tory took another drink from the bottle, a little surprised at how good the orange juice tasted, when she would have normally reached for a sugary soda. And then she told Sam about Peggy, about her frustration at not being able to donate a kidney to her, and then asked Sam several questions she hadn't dared to ask Peggy. Sam was blunt, forthright and by the time he was done Tory felt a lot better.

"She refuses to face her condition," she said at last. "That really worries me."

"No, I think you have that wrong," Sam told her, taking the empty bottle from her and putting it, along with his, on one of the small doily-covered tables. "She's not allowing her condition to define who she is. She's Peggy Longwood the woman, the mother, the sister, the author, not Peggy Longwood, the kidney patient. And I'd say she's also a survivor. She takes what life dishes out, and moves on. We could all probably learn from her."

"Move on," Tory repeated gently. "Yes, I suppose you're right. But that's not always easy, is it, Sam?"

"No, I suppose not." He stood in front of her and held out his hands, so that she put her hands in his and stood up, facing him, her body thrillingly aware of their closeness. "Not if we try to do it alone."

"This could be a big mistake," she told him, searching his eyes as if their expression might tell her something more about his mood, his intentions. "We're not twenty-two anymore, Sam. We've been apart for more years than we'd even lived when we met, when we…were together. We're two very different people than we were back then."

"I know. Maybe time has made our memories more rosy than the reality of that year we lived together. Maybe we'd be smarter to leave the past in the past. Or maybe, just maybe, we'd be making a second mistake if we didn't act now on what we feel. What I feel, at least. Maybe you feel differently."

"I don't know what I feel," she whispered, sensing the threat of tears moving closer.

"Then maybe this will help," Sam answered just as quietly as, their hands still clasped, he leaned in and put his mouth to hers.

There had been other men. Not many, but a few, one or two of them who might have been more than temporary additions to her life. If she'd let them be. But she'd always held back, always been the one to break things off gently, walk away. Why? Because of Sam? Because of what she'd believed was the one true love of her life? What had none of those other men, good men, lacked that Sam had in such abundance?

Maybe it was his kiss….

He let go of her hands and slipped his arms around her even as she raised her hands to his shoulders, drinking in the feel of him, the taste of him…that wild, familiar taste of him.

The years fell away as he picked her up, carried her to the

bed that someone had already turned down for the night, and laid her gently down, followed her, their mouths still melded, their bodies touching in that old familiar way.

She'd thought she'd be shy, nervous about the changes age and a pregnancy had made to her body. But there was no shyness as he unbuttoned her blouse, slid a hand inside her bra to cup her breast. There was only Sam, and the slowly building passion his touch aroused.

Like muscle memory, that brain-to-nerve connection that knew how an elbow should bend, a heart should beat, took over and Tory raised her hand to slide her fingers through Sam's hair, then cup the back of his neck as she signaled that she needed him closer, closer.

Their clothing fell away, melted into nothingness, and now Sam's hands, those sure, steady surgeon's hands, those long, strong fingers, moved over her, relearning her, smoothing away any lingering shyness, so that she gloried in her body, in the way that it reacted to him.

His chest was still his chest, his strong shoulders were still the shoulders she'd depended on, clung to so long ago. She knew how he liked her to touch him, what his soft sighs meant, when his need would have him moving over her, into her, so that they weren't two people, searching. They were one person, found.

"So good," he whispered, close beside her ear. "Why, Tory? Why has there never been anyone else who made me feel this way? Like I'm home, I'm where I belong. Where you belong."

He cut off her soft moan of pleasure with his mouth, his tongue sliding between her lips in a stirring mimicry of the way he moved inside her, the two of them effortlessly falling into the old rhythms, her hips rising to meet his every strong thrust.

She knew the signal, the one he waited for, and lifted her

legs up and over his back, locking their bodies together as she opened to him, gave to him, took from him.

They were beneath the lacy canopy. They were on the lumpy mattress in the apartment above the pizza shop. They were in the backseat of his old car, parked under the stars. They were everywhere and nowhere, here and now and long ago; it had all melded, blended together, their passionate, reckless youth, their more sober, mature middle age.

As if they'd been apart, as if the years had never flown.

"Now, Tory," Sam said as he reached down, cupped her buttocks, his breathing shallow, quick. "Now?"

"Yes… Oh, Sam, yes. Now…"

He plunged into her one last time, holding her tight against him, and she went willingly over the edge, her body clenching and releasing, her blood singing in her veins, her entire body transported to someplace where only Sam had ever been able to take her.

Her hands were on his back, her fingernails digging into his muscles as his release came to him, as his body shuddered in her arms and then finally went still, his weight a burden she welcomed.

He kissed her again, rolled off her and brought her against his side, her head automatically finding that special dip just below his collarbone where she'd often slept the night away— and only then did Tory begin to cry.

"Tory? What's wrong? Oh, cripes, I did it again, didn't I? No protection."

She sniffled, a laugh bubbling in her throat even as the stupid tears continued to fall. "And you call yourself a doctor. I don't think there's much chance of you getting me pregnant, Sam. I'm a grandmother, remember?"

"You're too young and beautiful to be a grandmother."

"And now I'm supposed to say you're too young and handsome to be a grandfather?"

"I wouldn't mind if you said it, no," he told her, then kissed the top of her head and smoothly levered them both up against the pillows, still with his arm around her waist. "Are you going to tell me why you're crying?"

"I'm not cry—okay, so maybe I am, a little," she protested, and then made a liar of herself by wiping at her wet cheeks. "I don't know…"

"You used to cry at fast-food commercials, as I remember it. How did that song go? Something about people deserving a break today? And that one where kids away at school were reminded to call home and talk to their mothers—ah, damn. Why didn't you ever tell me about your mo—your adoptive mother?"

"My home life wasn't exactly something I was proud of, or wanted to remember, for that matter. And I guess I might have worried that I wasn't, I don't know—worthy? I'd spent a lifetime being told I was inferior, unwanted. You seemed to want me, to overlook all my many flaws. Why would I have told you that you might have misjudged me?" She twisted slightly in his arms, to look up into his face. "I know how ridiculous that sounds now, but at the time, I was still pretty insecure."

"I never would have applied that description to you. I always saw you as strong, confident, sure of what you wanted."

"Then you were looking in a mirror, not at me," Tory said, wiping at her cheeks once more as she sat up, suddenly feeling naked in more ways than the usual. "But thank you."

Sam didn't try to pull her back down to him, for which she was grateful, as she was grateful that only one small lamp burned in a far corner of the dim room. "Isn't there some old saying about youth being wasted on the young?" he asked her as the two of them dressed, he on one side of the bed, she on the other.

"Yes, I think there is. And another one about how we only

go around once in this life. Maybe we had our *once,* Sam. Maybe we're tempting fate, trying for a second chance."

He came around to her side of the bed and laid his hands on her shoulders. "Do you really believe that?"

"I don't know. I don't know why I felt so good, making love to you, with you, or why I cried when it was over. I've been alone for a long time, Sam. Now suddenly I have a sister, and suddenly you're here, back in my life. It's one thing to share a daughter, our grandchildren. It's quite another to think we can just pick up where we left off. I don't want to make any more mistakes."

"And tonight was a mistake?"

Tory couldn't speak. If she said a word the tears would start again, and crying was the last thing she wanted to do. So she simply shook her head.

"I'll take you back to your sister's," Sam said. "I didn't mean to rush you, Tory. I don't even know if I was trying to prove something to myself, or to both of us, or what the hell I was thinking. But I don't want to lose you now, I don't want you to feel you have to run again."

"I'm past running, Sam. Having a child, well, it grows you up in a hurry, teaches you responsibility. No matter what happens or doesn't happen between us, I wouldn't do that to Allie. She needs her father in her life, and she needs to see the two of us getting along."

Sam shot a quick look toward the bed, the tumbled covers, and then smiled that special smile that could curl her toes in her shoes. "Well, then, I guess we can consider tonight proof of that, at least. We do get along." He held out his hand to her. "Come on, let's get you home."

"You're an even better man than I remember," she said, placing her hand in his, her trust in him.

"I can be even better, if you give me a chance. I was a little out of practice, but I think my recuperative powers haven't suffered too much in thirty-two years, especially if you keep complimenting me like that."

Tory looked at him in confusion for just a moment, and then gave him a quick punch in the arm. "Great, I've just been to bed with a dirty old man."

They playfully argued the merits of experience over youth all the way back to Peggy's house, and parted with plans already made to drive to Philadelphia the following day for dinner. While they were there, they'd take a drive past the childhood home Tory had been too young to remember, because Allie had asked for photographs, and Sam would make arrangements with his office to take another few days off, and the two of them would travel to South Carolina together, where Tory would introduce him to his daughter.

They hadn't declared a truce; there could be no truce when there'd been no actual fighting. But there was a new sense of calm between them, as if a hurdle had been cleared and they could now close the door on the past and move on.

Where that might be, Tory didn't know, and she doubted Sam did, either. But, for now, that was all right....

CHAPTER FIVE

"THIS CAME IN THE MAIL yesterday, but I didn't see it until last night, after you and Sam had gone to dinner."

Tory took the large manila envelope Peggy pushed across the breakfast table and looked at it with some trepidation. "Oh. That's an Australian postmark, isn't it?"

"Yes. It's from Adam Hunter, the man Stephen willed his construction business to before he died. There's a photograph of Stephen inside."

Tory looked at the envelope again and sighed. "This is hard. I never knew I had siblings, not for certain. I certainly didn't remember having a baby brother. And now he's gone, without ever knowing either of us existed or that he'd been adopted, if what this Hunter man told us is true."

"I know. All I remember is this small, noisy, messy thing that took up too much of my mother's time. Go on, take a look."

The eight-by-ten-inch photograph was of a smiling man standing on the deck of a rather impressive sailboat, perhaps even the one he'd been sailing the day he died. He was tall, slim, outrageously tanned and he held his hat in his hand, so that his thick salt-and-pepper hair had been blown about by the wind. If she looked hard, Tory thought she could imagine the color of his eyes, and didn't have to imagine the cleft in his chin that marked him, as well as the color of his hair. Stephen Matteo had been her brother.

"He looks so happy," she said on a sigh, tracing her fingertip over the photograph. "I feel better, believing he had a good life."

"Imagine, Tory, Stephen grew up believing he was Italian. Even learned the language, according to Adam Hunter, and played soccer for a local Italian team. Italian to his core, that's what Hunter says in his letter. Life's funny, isn't it?"

Tory had been quickly scanning the enclosed letter from Adam Hunter. "He says he's coming here," she said, looking across the table to her sister. "You invited him to your birthday party?"

"Yes. He'd seemed reluctant at first. I suppose I don't blame him, since Stephen never knew he'd been adopted. Maybe he wants to take a good look at the both of us and satisfy himself that we aren't fortune hunters. Whatever the case, he promised to bring more photographs."

"I think I knew you'd invited him, but I never thought he'd take you up on it. After all, Australia isn't just a short commuter flight away, it's halfway around the world. This could be awkward, don't you think?"

"He knew Stephen better than anyone else. I want to hear how our brother lived, don't you?"

"Yes, of course. Will he stay here, at the house?"

"Yes, I hope so. Lord knows we have the room," Peggy told her, taking back the envelope and putting it in the side pouch of the wheelchair. "Now, tell me about your date."

Tory rolled her eyes. "It was hardly a date. We went for dinner."

"I'm in a wheelchair, sweetheart, I'm not stupid. You went to bed with him, didn't you? You've got that *glow,* as Mom would call it, embarrassing the hell out of me, as I remember it. Just thank your lucky stars she and her Gamblin' Grandmas are still in Vegas. Well, good for you. Good for both of you. Now what?"

"I haven't the vaguest idea," Tory told her honestly. "I still can't believe he doesn't hate me."

"And I give him credit for that. I'm really just wondering now why you two haven't gone to see Allie."

Well, that was a nice opening for what Tory had to tell her sister. "We are going to go, maybe as early as tomorrow. We're driving up to Philadelphia this morning and then flying out of the airport there. If, of course, that's all right with you."

"Me? Since when do you and Sam have to run your plans by me?"

"But…but you're my sister, and you're…you're right. Eugenia's here, Kinsey's here. You don't need me hovering over you, as well."

"Exactly. And you forgot Stan. God, does Stan know how to *hover*. I'm not an invalid, you know. Wait until you see me go, once I'm out of this damn cast."

Tory walked around the table and leaned down to kiss Peggy on the cheek and give her a fierce hug. "You're remarkable, Peggy. I'm so proud and lucky that you're my sister."

"Yeah, yeah, now go upstairs and pack a bag and get out of here. Eugenia and I are going to begin working on menu ideas for the week of the party that is rapidly turning into one heck of a family reunion. Allie and her family will still come up for it, even though you and Sam are going down there?"

"I can't speak for Sam, but I know Mark has already reserved plane tickets. Don't worry, it's going to be just what you wanted. A real reunion. Even with this Hunter guy standing in for Stephen."

"Don't forget David, he's promised to, and I quote, 'clear his calendar.' My son, the stick-in-the-mud. It's embarrassing. And of course, Laurie will be here, since she's taken on much of the party planning, plus the catering. Eugenia is already girding her loins."

Tory laughed. She'd met Peggy's daughter a few times, and liked her very much. But Laurie was just on the other side of a divorce and although she lived only a two-hour drive from Peggy, she'd had her hands full with her two teenage children and hadn't been able to visit very often. But now that school was out for the summer, she'd promised to come and stay for a week at the least. Since Laurie owned her own catering business, she was bound to have definite ideas on the menus for the party.

"So that's why you and Eugenia are planning the menus now? To sort of head Laurie off at the pass?"

"Not really. I mean, Laurie is officially catering my party, but at least Eugenia will feel a part of things this way. It's a delicate balance sometimes with Eugenia. And see? I'm far from alone, not with Laurie showing up to join the crowd hovering around poor, sick Peggy. Now, are you going to sit here all day, or are you going upstairs to pack?"

TORY GOT MORE STIFF AND QUIET in the passenger seat the nearer they got to Cherry Hill and the childhood home she couldn't remember.

"You okay?" Sam asked, reaching over to take her hand.

"Yes, I'm fine. I just can't understand why Allie didn't send me a copy of the newspaper article when she sent me everything else. Or maybe I do."

Sam nodded, squeezed her hand.

He'd called his daughter early this morning and she'd told him how and where he could find the information on the accident that had robbed Tory of her parents, and then warned him that the story contained a photograph of the twisted, burnt-out wreckage that had been all that was left of the family station wagon once the tractor trailer truck had mowed it down.

"She was trying to shield you a little, I think," he said, putting on his turn signal as the voice on the GPS informed him that he was to make a right turn in one hundred feet, onto Bonneymeadow Lane.

The news story itself had concentrated on the fact that Mary and Stephen Haswick had gone out to dinner to celebrate their tenth wedding anniversary, leaving their three children in the care of a neighbor, Ruth Baxter, only to perish in a violent, fiery collision caused by icy conditions on the Schuylkill Expressway. The three children, Margaret Mary, age eight, Victoria, age three, and an infant son, Stephen, were removed to a juvenile care facility pending notification of next of kin.

Except there had been no next of kin.

There had been one further notice Sam and Tory had found, leading them to a small cemetery beside an old church, and the graves of Mary and Stephen Sr. But that was all.

"I'm not sure I want to do this," Tory said as Sam slowed the car, looking for the house number on a narrow street lined on either side by semidetached brick houses that had probably seen better days. "It's not as if I'm going to remember anything."

"Peggy might. And since she's not here, she might want to see photographs. Ah, here we are."

They got out of the car and stood on the pitted sidewalk, facing the redbrick structure marked by two doors leading to mirror-imaged houses joined by a common wall.

"Three-forty-two," Sam told her. "The one on the right. Damn, I forgot my camera. I'll be right back."

Tory only nodded, the soles of her shoes seemingly glued to the sidewalk until he'd grabbed the camera from the backseat and hurried back to her.

"Those steps," she said. "Those cement steps up to the porch. I can almost feel myself sitting on the top step, impatiently waiting for someone. I…oh, Sam. I don't remember. It's like Peggy. I remember Mar-Mar. The words. But I don't remember her."

"May I help you? Are you looking for someone?"

Sam turned to see an older woman pushing a baby stroller toward them, turning it onto the concrete walkway leading up to the house attached to number three-forty-two.

"I don't think so," he answered her. "My friend used to live here, but that was a long time ago."

"Really? Well, I've lived here all my life," the woman said. "My husband and I took care of my parents until they passed, and the house came to me. Now my daughter lives here with me. This is her boy, Charlie."

"Hello, Charlie," Sam said to the toddler as Tory took a step back, as if ready to run. "I'm Sam, and this lady is Tory. Victoria, actually."

The woman set the brake on the stroller and held out her hand. "Ruthie Newman. Used to be Ruthie Baxter, but that was really a lot of years ago." She smiled, and then looked past Sam, to Tory. "Oh. Oh, my goodness. Are you one of Mary's children? You look just like her." The woman shivered. "Kind of like seeing a ghost. Except for the hair, of course. Hers was all black and silver. Prettiest hair I ever saw. You're her, though, aren't you? Victoria. Well, isn't this something! I used to change your diapers."

SAM WATCHED TORY AS SHE SLEPT on his bed. After two hours spent with Ruthie Newman, they'd come back to his condo. Tory had asked if he'd mind if she laid down for a while. She'd needed to be alone, just for a little bit.

Ruthie had told them small stories she remembered about the family, including how Margaret Mary and Victoria would sit on the front steps each night, waiting for their father to get home from his job at a local foundry, how the two girls would argue over who would take his lunch pail and carry it into the house.

Sam had watched Tory's face, seeing the torture there,

of not remembering, of just the shadow of that one memory staying with her…sitting on the top step, waiting.

Before they left, Ruthie had promised to go through her old family photographs, to see if there were any of the Haswick family, and Sam had given her his address.

Bits and pieces of Tory's first three years were falling into place. She knew how her parents had died, she knew where they'd been buried. She'd seen her childhood home. At fifty-five, after surviving her adoptive mother, having a child on her own, finding a career that was both financially and personally rewarding, Victoria Haswick finally knew who she was.

Sam wondered if that would change anything, for either of them.

He sat down on the side of the bed and began stroking Tory's hair back away from her face, watching the slow, easy rise and fall of her chest as she slept.

He'd loved her once. Believed he loved her. Did he love her again now, or simply love her still?

And did it matter?

"Hey, sleepyhead," he said, leaning over her. "I've got reservations at seven. Aren't you hungry?"

Tory rolled over onto her back and opened her eyes. For the first time, he saw no shadows in those lovely blue depths, no fear, no uncertainty. Only the reflection of his own face.

His heart, the one that had always beat so sure, skipped a couple of beats.

"Yes," she said, lifting her arms to wrap them around his neck, pull him down to her. "Yes, I am. And then, later, if you're very, very good, I'll scramble us a couple of eggs…"

THEY HELD HANDS DURING the flight, this time Sam the one filled with apprehension, needing reassurance Tory was more than willing to offer.

She deliberately kept up a light chatter about how she'd

created Captain Adversity and Cybor The Super Dog, and even told him about her work in progress, The Surgeon. That last part got her the only smile he'd produced all day.

"Honestly, Sam, our daughter doesn't bite," she said at last, when the rental car was only a few blocks from the rambling redbrick colonial Allie and Mark had purchased after the twins were born.

"She might if she figures out I've been sleeping with her mother," he answered, lifting her hand to his lips. "She's had you all to herself for a lot of years. Wanting to know who your father is, that's one thing. But maybe this will be too much for her, too fast."

"Oh, and what, exactly, is *this?*" Tory asked, her heart beating faster.

Sam pulled the car to the curb and put the transmission into Park. He turned on the seat and took her hands in his. "I don't know. I know what I don't want it to be. I don't want it to be you going back to San Francisco and me going back to my nonlife, the two of us alone on separate sides of the country. I know I only thought I was alive until I saw you sitting on the beach that day. I know I truly understand now what Bill was saying, that second chances don't come along that often, and we should take advantage of them."

"I…I've already decided to put my condo up for sale. I want to be here, closer to Peggy, closer to Allie and the children. San Francisco used to feel safe. Now it's just someplace too far away from everyone I love."

"We'll take it slow," Sam promised her, not wanting to scare her away. "Maybe you can stay on with Peggy for a while, and I could come down to visit, or you could come stay with me…"

The corners of Tory's mouth began to twitch a bit, until she had to let the smile out, had to let it go, let everything go, all of the past, all of the heartaches behind them.

"Sam McCormack," she said firmly. "We're fifty-five damn years old, and not getting any younger. Exactly how slow do you want to take this?"

"God, I love you," he said, pulling her into his arms, kissing her long and hard until she was at last able to catch her breath and tell him that she loved him, too—had always loved him, and didn't intend to ever stop loving him.

He kissed her again then, several times, until a car filled with teenagers passed them, the driver blowing his horn, the boys on the passenger side of the car hooting and yelling encouragement.

Five minutes later, they stepped onto yet another sidewalk, this one not a view to the past, but a look to the future.

Sam slipped his hand into Tory's and took a deep breath. "Ready, Doctor?"

"I'm The Surgeon, a superhero. I was born ready," he said with noticeably nervous bravado, squeezing her hand. And then, suddenly, he let it go, audibly drawing in his breath. "Oh, God, Tory…she's beautiful…"

The front door had opened and Allie had stepped out onto the small porch, Mark behind her, holding on to the twins' hands, Quinn standing close beside him. Allie hesitated for only a moment, a single heartbeat, and then came flying down the walkway to throw herself into Sam's waiting arms.

Allie was Tory's daughter. She'd been a good child, a miracle of a child, and she'd grown into a strong, intelligent woman, a mother in her own right.

But right now, Tory thought as she let her tears fall unheeded, Alexandra Samantha Gibbons was at long last her daddy's little girl….

SAM FLEW EVERYONE TO LAS VEGAS three days later, and they drove to the hotel with little Megan and Molly still sparring as to which one of them got to sit beside Grandpa Sam in the limousine, so that Quinn had ended up with the honor.

Over the course of the next five days the family got to know each other. Sam took all three children to an amusement park and let them ride too many rides and eat too much junk food, earning himself a stern look from his daughter when Megan dutifully recited everything they'd had to eat once they'd returned to the hotel.

Megan's red curls were tighter than her sister's, but Sam was also able to tell them apart because Megan was the more serious of the two, Molly more carefree. Quinn...well, Quinn was something special. At seven, he already knew he wanted to be a doctor when he grew up, but not the kind that gave you shots, but the kind that found cures for "all the bad things that can happen to people."

Sam and Mark talked sports, politics and shared a love of running and physical fitness, which caused both Tory and Allie to excuse themselves to go to the lobby restaurant with the expressed intention of ordering hot fudge sundaes. With double fudge.

Allie and Sam drove out to Red Rocks, just the two of them, and spent a day hiking and sightseeing, but mostly sharing a bench overlooking the vista, talking. It was impossible, during the length of one sunny afternoon, to catch up on thirty-two years, but they made a start. A good beginning; one they could build on.

He asked Allie, just before their drive back to the city, if she'd mind very much if he married her mother, and Allie showed herself to be her mother's child when she'd responded, "Well, to quote Quinn at his worst, 'duh.' Or did you think I thought you brought us all out here just for a vacation? I did work for the CIA, you know. I've also already bought the cutest little white dresses for the twins to wear at the wedding." And then she'd hugged him.

And at night? Ah, at night. That's when Sam and Tory retired to their own suite of rooms and worked on their current project: making up for lost time.

On the afternoon of the sixth day Peggy showed up, still in her wheelchair, still with her now wonderfully psychedelic cast on her leg, and with her mother in tow, snatched from her Gamblin' Grandmas group to attend the wedding in the hotel chapel.

Nana took Sam aside, grilled him on his intentions, and then winked and motioned for him to bend down and kiss her papery cheek. Sam loved her in an instant. If only Tory had been so fortunate as to have been adopted by someone like Nana Longwood. How different would all of their lives have been?

But it wasn't the past he was thinking about as he stood at the front of the small chapel, waiting for his bride. It was Tory, and their future.

Quinn stood beside him, standing very straight in his tuxedo, trying to look taller and older than he was as he performed the duty of best man, pretending that a plastic Captain Adversity action figure wasn't sticking halfway out of his pocket.

The canned organ music began filtering through the speakers, and Megan and Molly appeared in the white dresses their mother had picked out for them, Molly's circlet of pink rosebuds tilted rather precariously over one eye as the two marched down the short aisle and were shepherded to their seats by their father.

Allie followed, her smile wide, her eyes bright with happy tears, looking young and beautiful, almost a bride herself. Sam's heart swelled with pride and love.

If anyone had told him a short month ago that he would be standing here today, that he would be a proud father and grandfather, he would have thought them insane. Now he couldn't imagine his life any other way.

But his new family, much as he loved them all, instantly faded away when the organ music changed into the distinctive "Wedding March" and Tory appeared in the doorway, Peggy beside her, balanced on the walker she'd graduated to as long as she used it only sparingly, for it was Tory's newfound sister who would give the bride away.

His bride walked toward him slowly, keeping pace with Peggy, her eyes never leaving Sam's face. He knew she looked beautiful, her gown something soft and dreamy and a pretty pale ivory, but it was her smile that caught at his heart, that told him that all their yesterdays were gone, and their future started now....

* * * * *

With thanks to Marsha and Karen
for thinking of me, and to the other
Reunion writers for their support and creativity.
It was a blast working with you, ladies!

ALL OUR TODAYS

Sarah Mayberry

CHAPTER ONE

"THERE'S BEEN SOME KIND of mistake."

The delivery man checked his clipboard. "You're Laurie Sutcliffe?"

"Yes, but—"

"And this is 29 Walker Street, Vineland?"

"Yes. But I didn't buy a dog." Laurie glanced at the pet carrier resting beside the delivery man's feet. "I mean puppy. I didn't buy a puppy."

The carrier shook as the puppy stood and began to wag his tail. Big brown eyes peered up at her beseechingly. Despite the fact that she was running late with a long drive and an even longer day ahead of her, Laurie's mouth curved into a smile. Whoever had chosen this dog had chosen well—he was adorable, with features vaguely reminiscent of both a labrador and a beagle. In fact, if she was to guess she'd say he was a mix of the two breeds, with his floppy, silky-looking ears and neat muzzle and—

"It says here that the goods were dispatched by Guy Sutcliffe."

Laurie's focus snapped back to the man with the clipboard.

"Guy?"

"That's what it says here."

Laurie frowned. Why on earth would her ex-husband send her a puppy? Especially when she and the kids had campaigned for one on and off throughout their seventeen-year marriage and he'd never once softened his antipet stance. Was this some bizarre form of apology from him? Some acknowledgment of the pain he'd inflicted when he'd walked out on their marriage?

Her lips thinned as another thought occurred. Guy never did anything without a reason. And there was only one reason Laurie could think of for him to give her such an emotionally loaded gift: things had gone wrong with The Strumpet and he wanted to come home.

She crossed her arms over her chest. "I'm sorry, but I can't accept it. I mean, him."

The delivery man sighed. "You're sure? Because the little fella's already been in the van for a couple of hours, and it's gonna be another half day before I get back to the depot."

Laurie looked at the carrier again. A small, shiny nose pressed through the gap between the bars. Brown eyes pleaded with her.

Her ex-husband was a manipulative weasel. Pure and simple.

"Give me a second," she said.

She'd been literally on her way out the door when the delivery man knocked. Her purse was still sitting on the table in the entry hall. She grabbed her cell phone and dialed. She tapped her foot impatiently as the phone rang.

She was going to let Guy know in no uncertain terms that his gift was not welcome, and neither was he. She would not be manipulated like this. He'd opted out of her life the moment he started having an affair with their neighbor. Giving her a puppy didn't even come close to gaining him admission again.

The call connected and she launched into her speech.

"Congratulations on reaching a new low, Guy. If you think that dangling a puppy in front of me is going to make up for everything, you've been drinking way too much red wine. If you have something to say to me, at least have the courage to pick up a phone and say it yourself, instead of sending a furry envoy to try and soften me up."

She paused for breath and realized Guy had been speaking at the same time.

"…and I'll get back to you as soon as I can," a familiar, cultured voice said in her ear.

A beep sounded.

She'd wasted her ire on Guy's message service.

Aware of the delivery man's interested gaze, she tried to regain momentum as she left a message.

"Guy. This is not good. Not good at all. I don't know what you were thinking, but you need to call me. Urgently. Please."

Not quite the same as her original blistering reprimand, but it was hard to recapture the same outrage on the second take—especially with an audience.

The delivery guy checked his watch, clearly impatient to be gone.

"So, what am I doing, lady? Is he going or staying?"

Surely it was obvious? No way could she accept something as personal and significant as a puppy from her ex-husband. She opened her mouth to say as much then made the mistake of glancing at the pet carrier again.

The puppy had given up on gaining her attention and had dropped to his belly. His head rested on his paws, his expression doleful as he gazed off into space.

Was it just her, or was he the saddest, most dejected-looking puppy in all the world?

The words of rejection died in her throat. She closed her eyes for a long beat.

Then she opened her eyes and held out her hand. "Where do I sign?" she asked resignedly.

Fifteen minutes later she was in the car on the way to

her mother's house on the New Jersey coast, the pet carrier strapped into the backseat. Every few minutes she glanced in the rearview mirror and frowned. Guy was in for the tongue-lashing of a lifetime when he returned her call.

He knew how busy she was right now, with her mother's sixtieth-birthday-party-cum-family-reunion coming up. Definitely he knew that her company, Laurie Cooks, was catering the event—she'd asked him to take Josh and Amy for the week so she would be free to stay at her mother's place during the lead-up. And yet none of those considerations had stopped him from pursuing his own agenda and saddling her with a living, breathing millstone.

Yep, Guy was in big trouble. As for his secret agenda, whatever that may be… Their marriage was over. No matter what he said or did, no matter how charming he could be when he wanted something.

She was running a full forty minutes late when she drove up the long, curving drive to her mother's house and parked in front of the three-car garage two hours later. Laurie had called from the road to let her mother know she'd been delayed, but she could see her mother peering out the window of her second-story office, alerted to Laurie's arrival by the sound of the car engine. Laurie gave her a wave as she exited the car, then tapped her watch and pointed to the side lawn to indicate she had things to do outside and wouldn't be coming straight into the house. Her mother gave her an "okay" signal, and Laurie turned to get the puppy out of the car.

She could feel her mother's interested gaze as she released the puppy from his carrier, and, right on cue, she heard the sound of a window opening.

"When did you get a puppy?" her mother called down.

"Guy sent him to me via courier this morning."

"Why would he do something like that?" her mother asked.

Laurie gave her a speaking look.

"You think something has happened with The Strumpet?" her mother asked.

"Maybe. I don't know. But he wants something."

Her mother looked worried. "Well, I'm here if you need to talk. Or stick pins in a voodoo doll."

"I know, Mom." Laurie gestured toward the side lawn. "I've got the tent guy coming any minute and I need to go pace out the tent site. We can talk about how big a rat Guy is later, okay?"

Her mother waved her on her way. "Go. Do what you have to do. I'll be here. As always."

Frustration was rich in her mother's voice. Laurie gave her a sympathetic smile before grabbing her purse and herding the puppy onto the lawn. Her mother had been confined to a wheelchair for six weeks since breaking her foot slipping on the marble floor in the foyer, an injury that was complicated by the fact that her mother suffered from chronic kidney disease. While Laurie was aware that the constraint of the wheelchair and, more recently a walker, was driving her mother nuts, privately she was grateful that the injury had forced her mother to slow down a little. Despite requiring home dialysis three times a week, her mother refused to make allowances for her condition, claiming life was about quality, not quantity. While Laurie agreed with her mother philosophically, she was nowhere near ready to say goodbye to her parent yet. The enforced rest required by the accident, in Laurie's opinion, had been a godsend.

A cool sea breeze lifted her hair off her forehead as she rounded the house, squinting as she walked into full sun. The puppy gamboled about her feet, his tongue hanging out, his bright eyes inviting her to stop and play with him.

She glanced down at the little guy. There was no getting

around it—he was utterly adorable, almost irresistible—just as Guy had intended.

"It's not going to work, you know," she told the puppy as they crossed the lawn to the place she'd decided to site the tent. "It's not personal—I'm sure you're a lovely dog. It's a principle thing."

Gratified to be the focus of her attention, the puppy leaped onto his hind legs and put his paws on the cuffs of her navy capri pants, his tail wagging so fast it was almost a blur. A smile crept onto Laurie's mouth.

The moment she registered it, she pulled her phone from her pocket and dialed Guy again.

Only to get voice mail once more. She left a second message, then stuffed her phone back into her purse. She glanced back toward the driveway. The tent guy was late. Just what she needed. If things started to go wrong at this end of the day, she could only imagine how the afternoon was going to look.

She had an appointment with a seafood supplier in town in an hour, and another with the local baker. She also needed to liaise with the florist and the company she was hiring linen, crockery and flatware from. She didn't have time for other people's slipups.

She killed a few minutes by pacing out the site and stopped the puppy from digging up one of her mother's prize rose bushes. She made a few phone calls, then checked her watch again.

Okay. Tent guy was officially twenty minutes late. And he hadn't bothered to call to let her know what was going on, either. A big no-no in Laurie's book.

Another five minutes crawled by. Her stress level kicked up a notch as she stopped the puppy from digging up the roses for the third time. She didn't have time for people who didn't honor their commitments. She didn't have time for an untrained, unexpected dog and tradespeople who couldn't keep their word.

There had been more than one occasion over the past three years when Laurie had doubted her mother would make it to sixty and Laurie wanted this party to be perfect, in every way. She wanted to create a warm, memorable celebration of her mother's life, to give something back to the mother who had always been there for her. If this was the last birthday her mother had—

She pushed the thought away. No. She refused to go there. Her mother was a fighter. Always had been, always would be.

She was scrolling through the calendar on her phone in search of a contact number for the tent company when she glanced up and saw a dark-haired, broad-shouldered man striding toward her across the grass.

A hot surge of anger washed over her, tightening her throat. How dare he waste her time like this? Who did he think he was? She had a good mind to tell him where he could stick his tent, even if it would effectively leave her high and dry.

Shaken by the intensity of her reaction, she ducked her head, using the excuse of fiddling with her phone to give herself a chance to pull herself together. Rationally, she knew that her anger was way out of proportion with the tent man's crimes. It was Guy she wanted to rip shreds off—along with fate for saddling her mother with an incurable disease.

She could see the tent man drawing closer in her peripheral vision. She took a deep breath, determined to deal with him firmly but fairly. She lifted her head.

"Listen—" The rest of her speech evaporated as she found herself staring into a pair of rich caramel-brown eyes set in a rugged, tanned, very masculine face.

The oddest feeling came over her, a feeling of familiarity

and recognition. But she knew that was impossible—she'd never met this man before. She was sure of it.

She blinked. Swallowed. Tried to remember what she'd been about to say.

"Listen. I—I appreciate that life's full of the, um, unexpected, but a simple phone call…"

She shook her head, unable to remember the rest of her speech.

"Do I know you?" she heard herself ask instead. She sounded as bewildered as she felt.

"I don't think so."

He had an accent. English, maybe. One of the regional ones she wasn't familiar with.

"Right." She glanced down at the phone in her hand. Its shiny plastic surface helped ground her, reminding her of where she was and what she was doing. "Well, you're late. I was about to give up on you."

She didn't give him an opportunity to respond, gesturing toward the swathe of lawn in front of them in a vain attempt to cover how flustered and off-kilter she felt.

"I want the main tent sited here, facing the water. I think an exit point closest to the house would be smart, in terms of people having access to the facilities. And I was thinking the catering tent should be back a little, to the left. Unobtrusive but practical."

She was aware of her focus being split the whole time she spoke, part of her brain concentrating on the business at hand, the other half cataloging how tall he was and the fact that he needed a shave and that his worn denim jeans fitted him very nicely, thank you very much.

There was a short beat of silence before he spoke.

"I think we might have our wires crossed. I'm Adam Hunter. I'm here for the party."

For a moment she still didn't understand. Then the penny dropped and a rush of embarrassed heat warmed her face.

"Adam. From Australia," she said stupidly.

The man her mother had invited to her party in lieu of the recently deceased brother she'd been separated from in childhood. The man her mother was counting on to give her some insight into the brother she would never now have a chance to know.

"Yeah," he said. "I'm guessing you're Peggy's daughter?"

"That's right. Laurie. Laurie Sutcliffe."

She offered him her hand automatically. He took it in his, his palm rough and warm against hers.

"You're early," she said, her sluggish brain finally catching up. "More than a week early."

She sounded rude. The heat in her face intensified.

He shrugged. "I wanted to get in a little sightseeing."

Behind him, she saw that the puppy had started in on her mother's roses again.

"One second," she said.

She ducked past him and bent to pull the puppy away from the garden bed.

"Not the roses, okay? Anything but the roses," she told the puppy before she let him go again.

Adam was watching her when she turned around and she realized that she'd offered him an untrammeled view of her backside when she bent over.

Very ladylike. As first impressions went, this was a doozy.

"Nice dog," he said.

"Yes, he's cute." She gestured toward the house. "Why don't I take you up to meet Mom?"

She started walking, the puppy dancing around her feet.

"It'd be a mistake to put your tent here, you know."

She glanced over her shoulder and realized Adam Hunter hadn't budged an inch.

He gestured toward the other side of the lawn. "You'd be better off putting it over there."

She gave him a polite smile. Men. Why did they always think they had a monopoly on logistical issues?

"I've been planning this for weeks. This is the best site for the tent," she said confidently. "Have you just flown in today? You probably want a shower and something to eat."

Again she started walking. Again he didn't follow her.

"This is the best site for the view, sure. But you're in a dip here. If it rains, the ground will get waterlogged. Land's higher over there."

"I'm sure it will be fine," she said coolly, hoping he'd take the hint that his advice, well-intentioned or not, was not required.

But apparently Australian men weren't so great at picking up on subtle conversational cues.

"It's not just a drainage issue. You're exposed to the crosswind here. It's more protected on the other side of the house."

Some of her earlier irritation returned. She crossed her arms over her chest.

"I've catered more than two hundred events over the last few years, and I know a good site when I see one. This is perfect for views and access to the house."

"But not so great if it rains."

She narrowed her eyes. This man gave new meaning to the word *stubborn*.

"You work with tents do you, Adam?" she asked pointedly.

"I work in construction."

His gaze drifted down her body.

"Well, with all due respect, I think we're going to have to agree to disagree on this one."

She was pleased with how firm and authoritative she sounded. Cool and calm and in control.

"I guess we are." He paused for a small moment. "You should probably know, your dog just peed on your shoe."

"I beg your pardon?"

Laurie's gaze shot to her feet. Sure enough, a dark stain was spreading over her left shoe, the dampness only now beginning to register.

A whole lawn, and the puppy had to choose her foot as a watering post. What were the odds?

"Looks like you've got your hands full down here. Why don't I see myself up to the house?" he said.

He set off across the lawn before she could form a coherent thought, let alone verbalize it. She tugged her wet shoe off, feeling more than a little stupid. When she glanced up again, he was halfway to the house, his stride long and easy.

She stared at his back, aware that she'd come off a definite second best in their encounter.

Why that mattered, she had no idea, but it did. It definitely did.

CHAPTER TWO

ADAM WAITED UNTIL HE WAS about to step onto the wide, gracious front porch of Peggy Longwood's house before allowing himself to glance back over his shoulder.

Laurie had taken both shoes off and appeared to be talking to her puppy. Giving him a lecture on toilet etiquette, no doubt. Adam watched as she bent to give the puppy a scratch behind his ears, then forced himself to look away.

She was…unexpected. He'd spotted her on the lawn when he'd pulled up in his rental car and assumed she was Peggy, his deceased mentor and friend's long-lost sister. He'd started across the lawn, determined to relieve her of any misapprehensions she might have regarding her brother's estate before another minute passed. It was only when he was within a few feet of her and she'd lifted her head that he'd realized that she was far closer to thirty-five than sixty, with her small, fine-featured face and dark pixie haircut.

He'd had the craziest feeling as he stared into her clear slate-blue eyes—as though he could drown in those blue depths, losing himself forever with not a single regret…

Adam grunted, embarrassed by the schoolgirl diary slant his thoughts had taken. He'd never drowned in a woman's eyes in his life—nor did he want to. He was a practical man, down to his bones. Eyes were for seeing stuff. End of story. And he was here with one purpose, and one purpose only—to ensure the trust was safe. A nice pair of eyes—okay, a stunning pair of eyes—didn't change any of that.

He rang the ornate doorbell, taking a step back to survey the facade of the house as he listened to the sound echo inside. His limited research had told him that Peggy was a successful children's book author, but he'd had no idea how successful until he'd pulled into the long, curved driveway of her estate a few minutes ago.

The trappings of wealth on display went some way to addressing the concerns he'd harbored since she'd made contact with him a couple of months ago, but not all the way. He'd built plenty of houses for people who looked the part but couldn't pay the bills at the end of the day. Appearances weren't everything.

The door swung open and he found himself facing a middle-aged woman in an austere black dress, her dark hair pulled into a severe bun on the back of her head.

"Can I help you?" she asked, her expression coolly polite.

She was the hired help, of course. No one with a house this big answered their own door.

"I'm Adam Hunter. I was wondering if Peggy was available?" he asked.

The woman's eyebrows rose toward her hairline briefly. "Come in, please. I'll just let Mrs. Longwood know you're here."

"I know the party's a way off, but I arrived early and I wanted to touch base," he explained, addressing her obvious surprise.

"Of course."

She stepped aside to allow him to pass and he entered a tiled foyer with a soaring ceiling that rose three stories high. An elaborate chandelier glittered high overhead and a round mahogany table supported a huge display of exotic flowers.

"I won't be a moment," the housekeeper said before ascending the curving flight of stairs to his left, her pace and posture positively regal.

He killed the time inspecting the antiques and art on display on the glass shelves lining one wall. His eyes felt gritty from lack of sleep and he rubbed them tiredly. A shower was going to be very welcome when he finally hit his hotel.

Footsteps heralded the return of the housekeeper.

"Please, come upstairs. Mrs. Longwood is in her study."

She led him upstairs and they emerged onto a spacious, airy landing. She gestured toward the nearest open door. He entered the room and couldn't stop himself from staring as an elegant, slim woman with dramatic cheekbones and vibrant blue eyes rolled her wheelchair toward him.

"Adam! What a lovely surprise."

She held out her hand and he kept his face carefully blank as he stepped forward to take it. Her resemblance to Stephen was uncanny. And his research hadn't revealed that she was disabled.

"I didn't think we'd be seeing you until next week at the earliest. I would have had a car meet you at the airport if I'd known," Peggy said as she shook his hand.

"I grabbed a rental car, since I figured I'd do a bit of sightseeing while I was here."

She beamed at him. "Please, take a seat." She waved a hand at the couch against the wall.

He sank into soft cushions, only then registering what looked like a bright pink cast covered with elaborate illustrations peeking from beneath the hem of her long black skirt.

She noticed his interest.

"I slipped in the foyer, broke my foot. Not something I'd recommend, believe me. When we were building the house, those marble tiles were the one thing me and my late husband fought over. He wanted them, but I thought they were dangerous. Twenty years later, I finally proved my point."

"I broke my leg when I was a kid. Longest six weeks of my life."

"Then you know how I feel—like a caged tiger. Not that I was ever particularly wild or fierce, you understand, but still. The big concession lately has been that I'm allowed to use a walker. I almost skipped the first time Kinsey—she's my physiotherapist—let me walk up the hall. My doctor's promised me faithfully that the cast can come off in a few more days. Just in time for the party. Needless to say, I cannot wait!"

It was disconcerting how much she looked like Stephen when she smiled. It was the eyes, mostly, but there was also a strong echo of Stephen's face in her cheekbones and the straightness of her nose.

He shifted in his seat, keen to cut to the chase. He wasn't a fan of confrontation, but this had to be done.

"You're probably wondering why I've turned up so early."

He leaned forward so he could pull the folded check from the back pocket of his jeans. He offered it to her, and after half-a-second's hesitation she took it.

"That's repayment for the plane ticket you sent me. I wanted us to start with a clean slate before we got into anything else," he said.

She frowned, placing the check on her knees. "I intended the plane ticket as a gift. You're doing me a favor, after all, coming all this way just to indulge my curiosity."

"I can pay my own way. Between us, Stephen and I built up a good business. Money's not an issue."

The frown remained in her eyes.

"Why am I getting the feeling that something else *is* the issue, though?"

The tilt of her chin was achingly familiar—Stephen used to lead with his chin whenever his hackles were up, too.

"I think it's important that we understand each other. I

know you've done your research—you wouldn't have tracked me down if you hadn't. So you know that your brother left a pretty healthy bank account behind when he died. What you may not know is that every last cent of his estate is tied up in the Ground Up Trust the two of us established a few years ago."

"You're right, I wasn't aware of that."

"I figured that might be the case. And I figured you should know straight up that Stephen's will was rock solid, and that my legal advice is that if you attempt to make any claim on his estate the only thing you'd get out of it would be a big fat legal bill."

There was a short, loaded pause before she responded.

"I'm going to guess that no one ever accuses you of beating around the bush, Adam."

"Not recently, no."

"Well, I'm going to be equally frank in return. I don't need or want my brother's money. I understand your concern. I'm aware of the good work your trust does with disadvantaged teens, and I understand why you want to protect it. But you don't have anything to worry about where I'm concerned, I can assure you."

She smiled sadly.

"All I want is to know a little about the brother that I lost all those years ago. That's all."

She held his eye, and he could see she was sincere. Some of the tension left his chest and belly. The trust was going to be all right, which, in turn, meant his kids would be all right, too.

"Like I said, I just wanted to make sure we were on the same page before things went any further," he said.

"I appreciate that." She glanced down at the check in her lap. "I don't suppose that now that we've gotten the difficult part out of the way that you might reconsider allowing me to pay for your travel expenses? After all, the only reason you're here is to indulge my need to have some connection with Stephen."

"One of the first things your brother taught me was to take responsibility for myself."

"Did he? You know, the last memory I have of Stephen was when he was a colicky baby. It's hard to imagine the kind of man he grew into."

"He was a good man. The best man I knew." His voice caught unexpectedly and he cleared his throat, embarrassed.

Peggy leaned across and patted his knee.

"Something tells me you're not a bad man yourself, Adam Hunter. I'm also guessing you're a man who desperately wants to unpack and catch up on his sleep. Why don't I get Eugenia to show you to your room, then we can meet a little later in the afternoon and I can start driving you crazy with questions? You'll find we've got a pretty full house here at the moment—my mother lives with me, and my son has taken up residence in the guesthouse. Although he assures me that's only temporary. My sister is also in and out—she got married last week, so she's splitting her time between here and her husband's home in Philadelphia. Then there's Kinsey, an old friend of the family whose good nature I am ruthlessly exploiting since she's also—as I've already mentioned—my physiotherapist. And, of course, my daughter, Laurie, is staying in the leadup to the party…"

She laughed.

"That's a long list, isn't it? Eugenia's going to be in her element at meal times. That woman loves cooking up a storm."

Still smiling, she swung the chair toward her desk.

"Thanks for the offer, but I booked a room in town," he said.

"But I thought we'd agreed you were going to stay here?"

"It's a generous offer, but as I said, I prefer to make my own way."

Peggy looked as though she wanted to argue her case some more, but after a moment she simply shook her head slightly.

"Can I at least lure you back here for dinner tonight?"

She was too well mannered to say anything, but there was hurt and disappointment in her eyes. Guilt bit him but he pushed it away. It was only smart to keep his distance, even if they had cleared the air over Stephen's legacy. He didn't know these people, after all.

"Dinner sounds good. What time should I be here?"

"Why don't we say seven?"

They talked a little more, then she shooed him toward the door, insisting he get some rest.

He was surprised by how much lighter he felt as he took the stairs down to the foyer. Ever since he'd picked up the phone two months ago and heard an American voice come down the line, he'd lived with a niggle of tension between his shoulder blades. Right from the start Peggy had indicated that she was simply seeking information about the brother she'd tracked down too late to meet in person, but only a fool would take her at her word when there were millions involved. More than a dozen former street kids relied on him and the Ground Up Trust to keep them safe and help them find a future that didn't involve drugs, violence and the prison system. He owed it to all of them to be protective, but now that he'd met Peggy himself and looked into eyes so like Stephen's, and heard her state her case, he knew that there was nothing to worry about on that score.

She was a nice woman, a genuine woman. Which meant the business part of his mission was accomplished. As of this moment, he was officially on vacation. The first he'd had in over seven years.

The housekeeper appeared as he hit the foyer, escorting him to the front door. He took his leave, striding toward the circular drive. Of its own accord, his head turned and his gaze swept the lawn, searching for a slim, dark-haired figure and a bouncing puppy.

She was where he'd left her, barefoot, talking to a guy in jeans and a plaid shirt. As Adam watched, she gestured toward the sweep of lawn in front of her, then pointed back toward the house. Even from a distance Adam could see the tent guy nod an affirmative. Shoes dangling from her fingertips, Laurie strode across the grass toward the higher ground he'd recommended earlier, the tent guy and her puppy hard on her heels.

Despite his tiredness, he grinned. He'd thought she was too stubborn to take his advice, but apparently she'd been listening after all.

As if she sensed his regard, Laurie glanced over her shoulder. Their gazes locked across a swathe of green. Her step faltered. Then she whipped her head to the front and kept walking.

He watched the sway of her hips for far longer than was sensible before turning away and continuing toward his car.

He was jet-lagged. That was the only possible explanation for the crazy thoughts that popped into his head every time he looked at Laurie and she looked back at him. The sooner he caught up on the sleep he'd lost on the long flight, the better.

CHAPTER THREE

BY THE TIME LAURIE FINISHED briefing the real tent guy, she was twenty minutes late for her next appointment. Fortunately she'd already phoned the seafood supplier and pushed their meeting back to later in the afternoon, but she hated the feeling that the day was slipping out of her control.

She glanced down at the roly-poly bundle of fur trying to trip her as she climbed the stairs to the second story. If she was being honest, she'd lost her grip on the day the moment she'd signed for the puppy. Something she must remember to thank her ex-husband for when he finally returned her call.

Her mind flashed to the other memorable moment of slippage she'd enjoyed this morning, complete with goggle-eyed staring, stupid questions and even stupider blushes. Whatever slide the puppy had started, Adam Hunter had finished. She couldn't remember the last time she'd been so incoherent and gauche with a man. The memory alone was enough to make her bare toes curl into the carpet.

Her mom was having a cup of tea with Nana when Laurie popped her head into her office.

"I don't want to interrupt—I just wanted to let you know I'm heading to main street and won't be back for a while."

"You're not interrupting. Come and give me a kiss," Nana said. She held out an imperious arm, cocking her head for Laurie's kiss.

"Love your new hairdo, Nana," she said as she followed orders and kissed her grandmother's soft, powdery cheek.

Instead of her usual tight-set curls, her grandmother's head was covered with loosely combed-out waves.

"Thank you. I'm auditioning a new stylist," the old lady said, patting her hair. At ninety-one she still wore makeup and perfume every day. Appearances were important to her.

She pushed herself to her feet.

"I'm going to leave you two to talk party business. My walking group is meeting in half an hour and I need to go change."

She bustled off, and Laurie and her mother exchanged amused looks.

"I hope I'm half as good at her age," Laurie said.

"Don't we all. How did it go with the tent people?" her mother asked.

"Apart from the guy being late, we're all good. But you should probably know we opted for the north side of the house instead of the original site we'd discussed."

It had been galling to hear the tent guy agree with Adam's assessment of the site, but Laurie wasn't stupid. She wasn't about to put her pride above the success of her mother's party.

"Okay, if you think that's best," her mother said with a distracted smile.

Laurie frowned. "Are you okay?"

"Of course."

There was no of course about it. Now that she was really looking, Laurie could see her mother was upset. All the telltale signs were there—the fingers of one hand fiddling with the rings on the other, the small wrinkle between her eyebrows, the distracted look in her eyes.

"How did things go with our early arrival?" Laurie asked, despite the fact that she really needed to get moving if she was going to claw back some sort of control of her schedule.

"Well, I think. He's coming for dinner tonight. He seems like a nice man."

Nice. Hardly the word Laurie would use to describe the man she'd met on the lawn half an hour ago. Then she registered the rest of what her mother had just said.

"I thought he was supposed to be staying here, at the house?" she asked.

Her mother shrugged. "He was. But he said he'd prefer to stay in town. I think he's concerned about feeling under an obligation."

"An obligation?"

Her mother held up a check. "He repaid me for his plane ticket, too."

Something her mother clearly wasn't happy about.

"Did he say why?"

"I think he was concerned that I might have my sights on Stephen's estate."

For a moment Laurie was so blown away she was lost for words.

"He actually said that to you?" she finally asked.

"Oh, yes. He's very straightforward. Doesn't mince words at all. I wonder if all Australian men are like that?"

"Mom! I can't believe this. I hope you told him where to get off?" Because if her mother hadn't Laurie had a good mind to. She'd never heard anything more insulting in her life.

"No, I told him I understood. And I do. A lot of people would be seeing dollar signs if they knew a relative had died and left millions behind."

"You're not exactly on the breadline yourself," Laurie said. Her late father, a successful architect, had left her mother very well provided for, and her mother was very successful in her own right. "It's insulting that he automatically assumed you were after something he considered to be his."

The whole notion left a bad taste in Laurie's mouth. She'd

never been a big fan of self-interest, especially not where money was concerned. There were a lot of things higher on her list of priorities than the quest for the almighty dollar.

"Oh, I don't think he was circling the wagons to protect himself. I'm not sure I told you this, but before he died my brother set up a philanthropic trust aimed at supporting disadvantaged teens," her mother said. "Adam told me today that Stephen left his entire estate to the trust, not to Adam, as I originally believed. I think today was simply about Adam ensuring Stephen's legacy is left as he intended it. Adam's clearly very passionate about the work they do."

"Still. There was no reason for him to insult you," Laurie said, even though her mother's explanation had taken much of the heat out of her initial reaction.

Her mother smiled faintly. "It was a little confronting, I'll admit. But I couldn't help wishing a few more people were so honest. Life would be a lot less messy."

Laurie's thoughts immediately flashed to Guy and the web of lies he'd spun in the lead-up to their divorce.

"That doesn't mean he had to throw your hospitality in your face, as well."

Her mother shrugged. "I could hardly tackle him to the ground and force him to stay."

Laurie knew exactly how much her mother had invested in regaining the family she'd lost when she was eight years old, and how devastated she'd been when she'd learned that Stephen had died in a sailing accident two years ago. Getting to know him via his friend and business partner was a poor substitute for the real thing, but she'd been prepared to accept it. And now Adam Hunter was trying to take that away from her mother, as well.

Unless someone did something about it.

"We can talk about this some more later, okay?" Laurie turned for the door, her mind already whirring with plans.

She barely heard her mother's parting words as she started down the stairs.

She had no idea where Adam was staying in town, but she figured it wouldn't be too hard to track him down—it wasn't as though Cape May was Vegas, after all, with a gazillion hotels to check.

And once she'd found him…well, she was going to do her damnedest to make sure he understood how important this reunion was to her mother. No matter what it took.

THE HOTEL WAS NOISY. Adam had requested a room away from the elevator, but the sound of the housekeeping staff vacuuming and talking to one another as they worked leaked under the door and into his room anyway.

Nonetheless, he made a bold attempt to get some sleep. Images and impressions from the day slipped across his mind as he hovered on the verge of dropping off. The crowded airport…the grandeur of Peggy's home…the moment of suspended time when Laurie Sutcliffe had lifted her head and he'd found himself staring into her eyes.

He rolled onto his back. He wasn't a masochist. He'd learned a long time ago that it was useless to want something he could never have. She was probably married—women like her always were. She probably had a husband and children and a home that Martha Stewart would be proud of.

A knock sounded at the door. He sighed heavily.

Clearly, he wasn't meant to sleep this afternoon.

Rolling out of bed, he grabbed his jeans and tugged them on, sans underwear. Then he grabbed the first shirt from the top of his case and pulled it on as he walked toward the door. He had one button through the hole of a very wrinkled white shirt when he opened the door to reveal Laurie standing in the corridor, a determined set to her face.

For the third time that day he locked eyes with her, and

for the third time he forgot everything else for a long, sticky moment. He didn't understand what it was about her that slipped under his guard so completely. She was attractive, but not beautiful. Her body was slim and curved in all the right places but hardly provocative.

And yet he couldn't look away, not for the life of him.

She was the first to break the contact, her gaze dipping below his chin to his chest for half a beat before quickly glancing away.

"Um. I hope I didn't wake you…?" she asked, her gaze aimed firmly at his chin.

"I'll survive. Is everything okay?"

"Can I come in for a moment?"

He hesitated a second. Because he was a man, a handful of scenes plucked straight from a teen boy's fantasies slipped into his head before he rejected them with a mental eye roll. Laurie Sutcliffe did not strike him as the kind of woman who tracked a man down to his hotel room in order to proposition him.

More was the pity.

He stood to one side and gestured for her to enter. "Come on in."

She walked past him and he caught a waft of her perfume, a crisp floral scent that made him think of freshly cut grass and citrus blossom. He shut the door. She turned to face him, her hands gripping each other in front of her in a way that told him she'd been working herself up to whatever she was about to say.

"I came to ask you to reconsider staying out at my mother's house," she said. "Mom explained to me that you wanted to be independent, but you'd be absolutely free to come and go as you like up at the house, and I know you'd be at least as comfortable because Eugenia is wonderful and although you wouldn't have room service on command, there's always plenty to eat in the kitchen…"

He frowned, surprised by the request. He'd known Peggy was disappointed he wasn't taking up her offer to stay, but she'd appeared to get over it quickly enough. He'd figured she had plenty of other guests staying over to keep her occupied.

"I didn't realize it was that big a deal."

"I don't know how much she's told you, but she was devastated when she was separated from her sister and brother. She was only eight-years-old, but she felt responsible for both of them and I think she's always blamed herself for not being able to keep the family together. Personally, I think that's why she never tried to track them down herself—I think she was afraid that they might blame her, too. If my cousin Allie hadn't taken matters into her own hands… And now that delay has cost her the opportunity to know her brother. Having you stay with her, having the chance to talk to you and learn what she can of Stephen means so much to her. She would never tell you these things herself because she never asks for anything that might inconvenience or hurt anyone else. So, Mr. Hunter, *I'm* asking you—please, reconsider your decision."

She blinked rapidly and he realized she was fighting tears. His frown deepened. Was it just him, or was there something else going on here? Something deeper than a daughter trying to help her mother reconcile with her past?

"Like I said, I didn't realize it was so important to your mother," he said slowly.

"She doesn't want to waste any more time," Laurie said. "She was shattered when she found out Stephen had died. I can't tell you…"

She shook her head and half turned away from him, clearly trying to gather herself. He turned and walked into the bathroom, returning with a box of tissues.

The look she gave him was deeply chagrined as she plucked

a tissue from the proffered box. She obviously didn't relish becoming emotional in front of him.

"Thanks." She blew her nose, then took a deep breath. "So, Mr. Hunter, what do you think?"

"I think that if you call me Mr. Hunter again I'm going to have to go buy myself a fob watch and a horse and cart. It's Adam. And I'm happy to cancel the rest of my booking and come up to the house if that's what you want."

Her shoulders visibly sagged with relief.

"Really? Oh, that's wonderful. Mom will be so happy." She smiled, the corners of her eyes crinkling attractively. "You know, I was sure you were going to be a lot more stubborn about this."

"Me, stubborn?" He kept his expression absolutely deadpan and was rewarded with a deepening of her smile.

"I know. You're probably wondering where I got a crazy idea like that from."

"Maybe it's a case of takes one to know one?"

"Perhaps."

They were both smiling now. Because he couldn't help himself, his gaze dipped to her hands. There was no wedding band on her ring finger.

Thank God.

When his gaze returned to her face she was watching him, a wary expression in her eyes. Which was fair enough, given the sorts of thoughts that had been bouncing around inside his head since she'd walked through the door.

"I need to go. I guess I'll see you back at the house…?" she said.

"You will."

"Well…"

She started toward the door. He shifted so she could get past, but not before he registered the warmth of her body heat as she passed by.

He didn't think he'd ever been so aware of a woman before.

She offered him her hand as she faced him in the corridor.

"Thanks again, Adam. You're about to make my mother a very happy woman."

He shook her hand, tightening his grip when she would have ended the contact. Startled, her gaze flew to his.

"Don't make me out to be a saint, Laurie, because I can assure you, I'm not."

Her gaze dipped to his chest again. "I didn't think you were. Far from it."

He released her hand, a smile curling the corner of his mouth.

"That put me in my place."

"The question is, will you stay there?"

He leaned his hip against the door frame and crossed his arms over his chest, thoroughly enjoying himself.

"What are the odds, do you think?"

"Not good, from what I've seen so far."

He wracked his brain for something else to say, something that would keep the smile on her face and the glint of challenge and interest in her eye, but she checked her watch and frowned.

"Oh, I'm late. I really have to go. I'll see you up at the house, though, okay?"

That quickly she was gone, striding up the corridor, one hand pulling her phone from her purse. And like the fascinated fool he was, he watched her every step of the way until she disappeared around the corner.

CHAPTER FOUR

IT WAS LATE WHEN LAURIE returned to the house. She was hungry and bone weary—and she wasn't the only one. She glanced in the rearview mirror, checking to see if the puppy was still asleep in his carrier. He was—lucky hound.

She'd made the mistake of taking him with her when she went into town, more because he seemed distressed to be parted from her than out of any inclination of her own. He'd proven to be a great icebreaker with all her suppliers, but she'd quickly learned that toting a puppy around à la Paris Hilton was not all it was cracked up to be. Keeping him entertained and out of trouble had been a mission in and of itself for the bulk of the day.

She added another mark against Guy's name as she gathered the drowsy dog in her arms and let herself into the house via the side door. He still hadn't returned her calls—a cynical attempt, she suspected, to force her to bond with the puppy before she could make him take it back.

Well, it wasn't going to work. She wasn't a pushover. Even if the puppy was cute, and even if she'd felt an odd little prickle of pride every time someone crouched down to pet the dog today. What Guy had done was unforgivable. Literally.

The house was dark, except for a stray lamp in the downstairs living room. She set the puppy down and headed for the kitchen. If he was anywhere near as hungry as her, he would be ready to scarf down anything she put in front of him. Which was just as well, because she hadn't thought to stop for dog food anytime today. He was going to have to make do with whatever she could scrounge from the fridge.

She glanced up the darkened stairs as she passed by, wondering how her mother's guest had settled in. She'd fielded a call from her mother midafternoon and had been quietly pleased by the delight in her voice when she'd reported Adam's change of heart. Which was all terrific, except for the fact that it was only just dawning on Laurie now that with Adam in residence, the two of them would be living under the same roof.

Normally, not a big deal—if only she could get the memory of him answering his hotel room door all rumpled and sexy and half-dressed out of her mind. Images of his tanned, firm-looking chest and belly had been slipping into her head all afternoon. She told herself it was because she'd been caught off guard by his near-shirtless appearance, but she wasn't buying.

The truth was, whether she liked it or not, and whether she was ready for it or not, Adam Hunter reminded her that she was a woman, an awareness she'd pretty much successfully pushed to the background for the past eighteen months.

There hadn't been time to be a woman once Guy had walked out. She'd been too busy being a mother and a business owner to think about her own needs—especially the kind that involved raised heart rates and tangled sheets.

Frankly, she hadn't been in the mood, either. She'd loved her husband, and his betrayal had made her both angry and sad. It had taken her the better part of a year to grieve and accept that the partnership that had borne two great children and navigated seventeen years of sometimes stormy seas was a thing of the past.

At forty, she was suddenly single again, the last thing she'd imagined happening at this stage in her life. And even though the notion of signing up for a dating website or whatever it was that single women with two teenage kids did these days had crossed her mind, it hadn't stuck. She simply hadn't been ready. Or she hadn't been interested. Or some combination of both. But then Adam had opened his hotel room door in bare feet and faded denim and a shirt that revealed almost more than it concealed, and her belly had tensed and her heart had knocked against her chest. She'd felt almost dizzy with the heady awareness that he was a fit, healthy male in the prime of his life and that there was a perfectly good bed going to waste just a few feet away.

The memory was enough to make her stop in her tracks. Standing in the darkened hallway, she pressed her hand to her chest, aware that her heart rate had kicked up a notch.

It had been a long time since she'd been this hot and flustered over a man. A long time.

She wasn't sure if she liked the feeling or not. Certainly, it was nice to know that part of her life wasn't over. But the timing was definitely on the sucky side.

Her stomach contracted with hunger, the growl echoed by the small furry shape at her feet.

"Yes, I know you're hungry. So am I," she said.

She bent to scoop the puppy into her arms again and continued up the hall to where a faint wash of light spilled out into the hall. Eugenia usually left the light on over the range hood at night to guide anyone in search of a midnight snack, so she didn't think anything of it until she stepped into the room.

He was standing at the counter, stacking a thick slice of bread on top of what looked like a tower of sandwich fillings. He was barefoot again, in those jeans that fitted him so well, but this time he was wearing a plain white T-shirt, the fabric a sharp contrast to his tanned complexion.

His profile was to the door, but he must have sensed her

presence because he glanced toward her as she hesitated on the threshold.

"Hey. You just getting in?" he asked.

"For my sins," she said, doing her best to ignore the hammer of her excited heart against her breastbone.

She was worse than a teenager, getting all silly simply because the object of her lust was in the vicinity.

She covered her confusion by ducking and setting the puppy down. The dog made a beeline for Adam, his little claws clicking on the tiles.

"Careful. He's probably going to try to challenge you for your sandwich," she said.

"I think I can handle him." Adam's tone was dry. "What's his name, by the way?"

"He doesn't have one."

He raised his eyebrows.

"It's a long story. And I don't want to keep you from your snack."

Her gaze gravitated to the tower of bread and fillings he'd created and her stomach growled again, the sound echoing off the hard surfaces of the kitchen.

"Have you eaten?" he asked.

She considered fibbing, but she figured her stomach had already given the game away.

"No, but I'm about to."

Without saying a word, he reached for the bread knife and neatly cut his sandwich in two. Then he slid one half onto the plate he had at the ready and offered it to her.

She stared at it blankly for a moment, surprised by the simple gesture.

"I can't take your sandwich."

"You're not, you're taking half. It'll probably only give me indigestion, anyway."

He was being polite—she bet he'd never had indigestion in his life. But she was so hungry she was past caring.

"Thank you," she said, accepting the plate.

She rounded the island counter and slid onto one of the stools ranged there. Then she remembered the puppy and glanced toward the sandwich makings still piled by the cutting board.

"I don't suppose there's any ham left?"

"The first rule of the midnight raid is to never deplete all the stores," he said, pushing a paper-wrapped parcel her way.

"Sounds like you're talking from experience."

"Yep. I mastered the art when I was a kid."

She slid off her stool and grabbed a bowl for the puppy.

"There's a lot of salt in that ham. Not the best thing for him," Adam said as she placed the bowl on the ground.

"It's just for tonight. I forgot to pick up puppy food."

She washed her hands, then returned to her stool, very aware of him watching her all the while from the other side of the island counter.

"So you have a puppy, but he doesn't have a name and you don't have dog food to feed him…?"

He was curious, and she didn't blame him—she'd be curious, too.

"My ex-husband had him delivered this morning. Without telling me."

"Right."

He took a bite of his sandwich and she followed suit. Half-a-dozen flavors battled for supremacy in her mouth—pickles and cheese and mayonnaise and double-smoked ham. Man, but Eugenia knew how to stock a fridge and this man knew how to pillage it.

"This is a great sandwich," she said once she'd swallowed.

"How long have you been divorced?"

The question wasn't a complete surprise. In fact, a part of her had been half expecting it. She might have been out of the dating game for seventeen years, but she knew when a man was aware of her.

"Heading toward two years."

He nodded. She licked some mustard off her fingers.

"What about you? Married, kids?"

"No to both."

She cocked her head. "Let me guess—you're one of those lone wolf types?"

"Nope. I want a family. I've had a couple of long-term girlfriends, but I guess I just haven't found the right woman yet."

He said it simply, with no inflection at all, but for some reason she could feel warmth climbing into her cheeks. She grabbed her sandwich and took another bite.

"I take it you're planning on giving the dog back?" Adam asked.

She nodded, then swallowed. "Have to. There's no way I can keep him. It's a matter of principle."

They both glanced over to where the puppy was licking the bowl hopefully.

"Pity. He's a nice dog."

"Yeah."

There was a short silence as they both polished off the remainder of their meals.

"Your mom tells me you're catering the big party," Adam said.

"That's right. I've got my own catering business, so I insisted Mom let me take care of it all. It's my present to her."

"How many people are you expecting?"

"Close to four hundred."

He whistled.

"We've handled bigger numbers, don't worry," she said, aware of the defensiveness in her tone but unable to do anything about it.

"I wasn't."

She sighed and rubbed the bridge of her nose.

"Sorry. It's just that my ex was always really patronizing when it came to the business. Called it my 'little hobby.' Then, when I started bringing in real money, he complained that it took up too much of my time."

She shut her jaw with a click, just in time to stop herself from telling him about Guy's affair with the neighbor—aka The Strumpet—and how he'd blamed Laurie's lack of availability for his infidelity.

She'd already revealed more than enough.

"You want some juice?" Adam asked.

Probably because she'd embarrassed him with her little confession.

"Sure. Thanks."

She watched him open the fridge, mentally planning a dignified escape. She'd make some excuse about having to be up early—which, as it happened, was no lie—then retreat to her room in order to salvage what was left of her dignity.

He poured two glasses then slid one across the granite counter toward her.

"Starting a business is pretty tough, but statistically if you survive the first year you're doing better than most." He lifted his glass. "Congratulations, Laurie. You're officially a survivor."

His words were so unexpected, for a moment she could do nothing but stare at him. How many years had she waited for Guy to say something similar? To acknowledge all her hard work and creativity and perseverance?

"Thank you." Her voice came out croaky and she swallowed noisily as she leaned across the counter and clinked glasses with him. "Thank you."

He was probably only being polite, but she felt explicably shaken. As though he'd seen something inside her that no one else had.

"So, does that mean you started your own construction business?" she asked.

Suddenly she had a burning need to know more about this tall, broad-shouldered man. Beyond the fact that he had a killer body and warm caramel eyes.

"Yeah, you could say that. I apprenticed with Stephen, then I went out on my own. But once you get to a certain size, it pays to have someone you can rely on by your side, someone who's as invested as you are. Stephen and I officially became partners about ten years ago."

"So where does the trust fit into all this? Mom said something about you helping troubled teens?"

"We train them through the construction business, and give them housing and anything else they need through the trust. At the end of the process, if they stay the course, they wind up with a career and a chance at a fresh start."

"Sounds like a win-win for everyone."

"It can be. When it works. We've had our fair share of successes, but we've also had a few notable failures. But it is what it is, and in the end the kids have to want to change, too."

He yawned, then immediately apologized.

"Don't apologize—you must be exhausted. You should go to bed. And I need to hit the sack, too. Lots going on tomorrow."

She stacked the dishes in the washer, then worked alongside him to stow the food and fixings back in the fridge. Then she stooped to collect the puppy to take him outside for a last toilet break.

"Where are you going to put him for the night?" Adam asked.

"I hadn't really thought about it. The laundry room, I guess."

Although she couldn't help thinking he'd be lonely down here all on his own.

"Probably a good idea if you're not planning on keeping him. If you don't mind a bit of advice, you might want to think about leaving something of yours with him. Something with your scent on it. It'll help reassure him."

"Oh. Okay. That's a good idea. You obviously have dogs."

"I did. I lost Diesel last year."

"I'm sorry."

"He had a good life."

She was about to ask what sort of dog he was, then realized she was making excuses to hang around.

"Well, good night. And thanks again for sharing your sandwich."

"My pleasure."

She ducked out into the hall before she came up with another excuse to linger. Then she took the dog outside.

Standing in the cool night air, she wrapped her arms around herself and stared at the stars.

Her mother was right—Adam Hunter was a nice person. It seemed like such an innocuous description for such a dynamic, compelling man, but it was right on the money. He was honest and decent and considerate.

And hot. Don't forget that. Really, really hot.

Not that any of the above made any difference to her. She might be attracted to Adam, but she was hardly going to make a move on him.

For starters, she was woefully out of practice with all that sort of stuff and he struck her as being the kind of man who knew his way around a bedroom. Second—and most important—he was only here for a week or two, and she'd never been a casual sex kind of woman.

"Which pretty much resolves that," she told the garden.

Except she didn't feel resolved as she put the dog in the laundry—with a T-shirt of hers, as Adam had suggested—before climbing the stairs to her room. She definitely didn't feel resolved when she reached the second story and noticed the slit of light beneath the door to the guest room opposite hers.

Which was crazy. She had more than enough on her plate right now without slicing herself off another big hunk of trouble. Even if that hunk of trouble looked incredible in jeans and had an accent that made her toes curl.

Go to bed. Get some sleep. When you wake up tomorrow, this will all be a fading memory and you can get on with business as usual.

With a bit of luck.

THERE WAS NO SIGN OF LAURIE when Adam came downstairs for breakfast the next day. He figured she was either sleeping in or long gone. From what he'd seen of her so far, he suspected it was the latter.

He grabbed some toast and coffee, sharing the morning paper with Peggy's son, David. Peggy's elderly mother put her head in halfway, inviting any takers to join her regular morning Tai Chi workout. He declined on the grounds that he had some business back home to take care of via the internet.

Once he'd finished dealing with work, he went in search of Peggy, tracking her down in the kitchen.

"I wanted to let you know I'm around if you had any questions," he said. "And I wanted to give you this."

He handed her the box of photos he'd unpacked last night. Peggy set it in her lap, her palms pressed flat against the faded cardboard lid.

"These are Stephen's?" she asked. She sounded a little breathless.

He nodded. "I found them in the closet when I cleaned out his place. He wasn't exactly sentimental, so there's not a lot of stuff…"

He didn't want her getting her hopes up too high.

"Anything is wonderful. Oh, I should see if Tory's around. She'll want to be a part of this."

Five minutes later, Tory had been summoned and both sisters were huddled around the box as Peggy lifted the lid, their faces unreadable as they studied the odd assortment of letters, postcards, photographs and film negatives filling the box.

Peggy offered the box to her sister.

"You go first."

"No, you go."

Adam had to look away from the hope and sadness in their faces. He understood now why Laurie had been so determined that he return to the house. This clearly meant a lot to both sisters.

Peggy reached into the box and pulled out a photo—an old, faded Polaroid of him and Stephen from years ago. He was so young it was almost embarrassing, his posture filled with the defensive brashness that had been his hallmark before Stephen had taken him on. Beside him, Stephen stared down the barrel of the camera with the same steady good humor that he approached everything.

"How long ago was this taken?" Tory asked. Like Peggy, she had a strong resemblance to his deceased mentor.

"Over twenty years ago," Adam said.

"He looks happy," Peggy said.

Tory looked to Adam for confirmation.

"He was a pretty easygoing guy. So yes, I'd say he was happy a lot of the time."

"I just realized—this is you, isn't it?" Peggy asked, tapping a nail over the image of his younger self.

"'Fraid so."

"I didn't realize you were so young when you first met," Tory said.

There was a question in her voice, if not her words.

"Yeah, and I wouldn't have gotten much older if it hadn't been for Stephen."

Both sisters raised their eyebrows and cocked their heads. It was uncanny that two siblings should have such similar body language when they'd been raised apart.

"I wasn't exactly a model kid, if you know what I mean," Adam explained. "I was train-surfing with a few buddies when we first met. You know, jumping on the back of the last carriage, hanging off the back hitching a free ride. Stephen saw us when we were stopped at one of the stations and went nuts. Dragged me off before I could bolt. I thought he was going to shake the life out of me he was so angry."

"It sounds as though you scared him," Peggy said.

"Yeah. And he scared me, too. Made me tell him where I lived, then took me home to my mom. I can still remember standing there while he told her everything and she cried her eyes out. Then he offered me a job helping out on his latest work site after school."

Peggy smiled. "The beginning of a beautiful friendship."

Adam gave her a wry look. "Believe me, it wasn't so beautiful to begin with. But by the time he'd saved me from juvenile detention by offering to be my court-appointed mentor, we had each other figured out."

"Ah—that's why the two of you started the trust," Peggy guessed.

"Yeah. We'd been helping kids out informally all along, but we decided we needed to do more. The trust means we can have a voice, lobby for services, get involved more."

They kept talking, Peggy and Tory drawing out photos from the box one by one, asking him what he knew about them, trying to piece together the story of their brother's life. Adam did what he could, but there were inevitable gaps and he could feel the sisters' frustration.

When lunchtime rolled around he made sandwiches for them all and they sat together at the kitchen table while Tory told him about the new series of comic books she was working on.

He heard a light step on the tile as they were winding up and glanced up just as Laurie entered the room. She was dressed in a pair of slim-fitting jeans and a red T-shirt, a pair of sunglasses pushed high on her head. Her furry shadow followed a few seconds later, head shifting from side to side, tail wagging, as he scanned the room for interesting new smells or potential food scraps.

"Good morning. Afternoon, I mean," Laurie said, her gaze skittering away from his after the barest of contacts.

Interesting.

"You were up early. I missed you at breakfast," Peggy said.

"Things to do, people to see."

"Did you at least *have* breakfast?" Peggy asked.

Laurie rested a hand on her mother's shoulder affectionately.

"I'm fine."

Tory gave Adam a look. "That means no, in Laurie-speak. Even I know that after just a couple months."

Adam stood and crossed to the fridge. Laurie's eyes widened with surprise as he handed her the sandwich he'd made for her earlier.

"You made me lunch?"

"I had a hunch you'd need it."

Peggy laughed. "He's got your number, Laurie. She always forgets to eat. Especially when she's busy."

Laurie hadn't taken her eyes off him. "You really made this for me?"

She looked so arrested, so wary that he was tempted to lie and say he'd made a spare in case he got hungry later. But she struck him as being a woman who appreciated honesty, so he simply lifted a shoulder in a casual shrug.

"I had the bread out."

Her eyes dropped to the plate in her hands for a long beat. Then she lifted her gaze to his again.

"Thank you."

There was so much surprised gratitude in her face. Just as there had been last night when he'd toasted the success of her catering business. It made him wonder all over again what kind of a jerk her ex had been. This woman—this warm, generous, capable woman—should not be surprised at praise. And yet she was.

"Look, Adam's brought us Stephen's treasure box," Peggy said.

He stood at the counter and teased the puppy with the toe of his shoe, watching as the three women put their heads together over the photographs. Laurie ate her lunch, occasionally looking his way as he answered Peggy's and Tory's questions or added detail to a story. Every time his and Laurie's eyes met, he felt it in the pit of his stomach.

If they were in Australia, he would be storming her barricades with more than sandwiches, he realized. He'd be pulling out all the stops to capitalize on the attraction between them.

But they weren't. They were here, in her home country, and he was a visitor. A very temporary visitor.

All of which meant that he probably shouldn't be making

her lunch, and that the next time she looked at him, he should look away.

She looked up again, and their eyes met and held.

He didn't look away.

CHAPTER FIVE

LAURIE SPENT THE DAY WRANGLING the puppy, dealing with the myriad last-minute problems of hosting a party for four hundred people and trying to pretend to herself that she wasn't on the constant alert for the sound of a certain deep voice or the sight of a particular pair of broad shoulders as she moved around her mother's house and grounds.

Any notion she'd had of being sensible and keeping her distance from Adam had gone out the window when she'd walked into the kitchen at lunchtime and he'd calmly handed her the sandwich he'd made for her.

Every time she remembered that small moment of generosity she felt the same wash of incredulity and warmth. It said so many things—that he'd been thinking of her, that he understood she was sometimes too busy taking care of everything and everyone else to take care of herself, that he cared about her comfort.

Perhaps she was reading too much into two slices of bread, but she didn't think so.

She reminded herself that his thoughtfulness didn't change the essentials of the situation. He lived on the other side of the world. Once the party was over and he flew back home, they'd never see each other again. He probably wouldn't even remember her name in a few months' time.

It didn't make any difference. Intellectually she knew she should give their mutual attraction a wide, wary berth, but her brain pretty much shut down when Adam was around.

The truth was, she was very badly smitten with her mother's Australian guest. She wasn't sure what she was going to do about her feelings yet, but she was beginning to understand that whatever was going on, it wasn't going to simply fade away because she gave herself a good talking to.

She allowed herself to range over the possibilities as she stood on the lawn in the fading afternoon light, watching the crew erect the tent.

Adam was here for now. His room was opposite her own. A bold woman would seize the day and say to hell with the consequences. She'd slept alone for nearly two years, had been dead to passion and need and want for all that time. She'd been a devoted mother, a tireless worker, a good daughter. She deserved something for herself. Even if it was a small and fleeting something, destined never to be more than a handful of nights with a man she'd never see again.

Adam would be a wonderful lover. She wasn't a wildly experienced woman. She and Guy had married straight out of college, and while she hadn't been a virgin, she might as well have been. But she still knew instinctively that things would be good between them.

So why not? Why not do something a little reckless? A little daring?

She glanced toward the house, imagining. Her, in something silky and sexy, slipping across the hallway to tap on Adam's door. Him answering the door in nothing but those well-worn jeans. What might she say to him? "I was waiting for you?" Or maybe a simple "Can I come in?"

The strident ring of her phone cut across the fantasy, startling her. She pulled her phone from her pocket, glancing at the screen to check the caller ID.

Guy.

Finally.

She walked a few feet away from the tent site and took the call.

"Nice to hear from you, Guy," she said coolly. "Yesterday would have been even nicer."

He laughed. "I was giving you time to calm down. Can you blame me?"

She hated the confidence in his voice. The knowing. He thought he had her down pat, that all he had to do was click his fingers and she'd come running now that he'd recovered from his midlife crisis or whatever it was.

"Do you have any idea how busy I am right now? Mom's still in the cast and I've got a million things to tick off before the party. The last thing I need is an untrained puppy arriving on my doorstep."

"Puppies are like children—you adapt," Guy said.

She glanced across to where the puppy was sleeping in a sunny spot on the lawn. He'd been amusing the tent crew all afternoon, earning himself multiple tummy rubs and scraps from people's lunches.

"You can't sweet-talk me on this, Guy. A puppy isn't a bunch of flowers that you deliver to someone on a whim."

"Okay, okay. I'm sorry, all right? I was walking past the pet shop and I saw him and I remembered how much you always wanted a dog…. But maybe it was a little impulsive. I should have checked with you first."

"Don't B.S. me, Guy. I don't care what's happened with you and Prue, gifting me with a dog isn't going to change things between us. You wanted out of the marriage, and you got it. You can't weasel your way back in with a puppy, cute or not."

She was proud of the firmness in her voice. The certainty.

There was a short pause and she imagined Guy trying to regroup.

"Prue and I haven't broken up," he finally said.

She tightened her grip on the phone. "So you just sent me a puppy out of the blue because you're a lovely guy and you thought of me? I'm not an idiot, Guy. I was married to you for seventeen years, remember. I know you. You never give without expecting something in return."

"Okay. I did want to talk to you about something. But it's not… Prue and I are fine." He sounded awkward. Uncomfortable. "Maybe the kids haven't told you, but I've resigned from the agency. I'm going out on my own. I know Roland has been your mother's literary agent for years now, but I've put together a great deal for her and I wanted to ask you to put a good word in for me before I make my approach."

Heat swept up her chest and into her face as the full import of what he was saying hit her.

The puppy had not been a sweetener because he regretted the loss of their marriage and wanted her back. No, his emotionally loaded bribe was all about his career as a literary agent, his bank account, his success.

He was waiting for her response. She tried to gather her thoughts, but she kept hearing the echo of her own words in her ears. *Gifting me with a dog isn't going to change things between us.* She felt as though her whole body was flushing with mortification at the assumption she'd made.

Guy didn't want her. Correction—Guy *still* didn't want her.

"Mom and I never talk about business. You know that," she said.

Her voice sounded strained, even to her own ears.

"I respect that. I do. But this is a huge deal for me. Make or break, you might say."

Vaguely she wondered what had happened at the agency to force Guy out on his own. There had always been power plays and politics amongst the senior partners in the business.

Maybe Guy had pushed too hard one too many times. Or maybe this was all part of the new life he was creating for himself, Guy Sutcliffe Version 2.0.

It didn't matter. It was nothing to do with her. Nothing.

"What happens between you and my mother is between the two of you," she said. "It's none of my business."

"Great in theory, Laurie, but you know she's still pissed with me because of the divorce. I need to know you won't be in her ear, campaigning against me."

Laurie shook her head. Had he always been this arrogant? This selfish?

"I have to go, Guy."

"Laurie, wait—"

She ended the call. The phone rang again immediately but she let it go through to voice mail. Then she switched her phone off and started walking. She didn't stop until the house was well behind her and the silvered wood of her mother's private dock was beneath her feet. She walked to the end, then sat, gazing out at the ocean.

She told herself that it was mostly her pride that was hurt. She didn't love Guy anymore, but she'd gained a very real sense of satisfaction from the idea that he regretted leaving her. Salve for her bruised ego, perhaps.

Whatever. She'd been wrong, and she felt stupid and exposed. Even now Guy was probably thinking that she was still pining for him—poor, lonely Laurie.

He was wrong, but there was no way she'd ever prove it to him.

So, yes, it was absolutely her pride that was stinging right now. But that didn't make it any easier to bear.

A small, cold nose pressed itself against her arm and she glanced down to see that the puppy had followed her onto the dock. He nuzzled his snout against the side of her hand, his tail wagging tentatively.

She reached out to pull him onto her lap. His small, sharp nails dug into her belly through her T-shirt as he circled once and then settled.

Belatedly it occurred to her that she'd ended the phone call before she'd told Guy to arrange to take the puppy back.

She stroked his soft fur and he sighed his approval. She lifted her gaze to the horizon. She would call Guy again tomorrow and talk to him about the puppy. She'd had enough of her ex-husband for one day.

More than enough.

She stayed on the dock for half an hour, then her conscience began to prod her. She had a list of calls to make, things to go over with her mother, plans to make for tomorrow... She didn't have time to sit around feeling sorry for herself.

She set the puppy on the deck, laughing at his outraged look.

"You've just had the world's longest tummy rub. Don't give me that look."

She headed back up the slope. She could see that the tent guys had finished erecting the main pavilion and had packed up for the day. She switched her gaze to the house. She wanted to start installing the party lighting tomorrow, and there were a few minor maintenance issues she wanted to cover off with George, her mother's gardener and jack-of-all-trades.

A shadow detached itself from the wall beneath the first-floor balcony as she approached the house.

Adam. She'd recognize his big, broad frame anywhere.

He stepped into the sunlight. He was wearing a pair of dark glasses. A beer bottle dangled from the fingers of one hand. He looked supremely at ease, a man in command of his world.

The fantasy she'd had earlier flashed across her mind— her approaching him, propositioning him. The two of them indulging in a few days of no-strings passion.

She almost laughed out loud. Talk about kidding herself.

No way could she pull something like that off. She was a forty-year-old mother of two with too many commitments and no idea how to negotiate the treacherous waters of singledom. She couldn't even read her ex-husband properly—what chance did she have with a sexy, confident guy from the other side of the world?

Instinctively she changed her tack, veering away from the house so that she wouldn't have to engage with Adam.

She didn't feel together enough to deal with his clear-eyed regard right now. He was too perceptive, too tuned in to her.

Head down, she walked past the house.

ADAM WENT TO BED WITHOUT seeing Laurie again, a circumstance he was fairly sure was intentional on her behalf. Something had happened to upset her today. He'd known it the moment he wandered out onto the rear terrace with a beer in hand and spotted her sitting at the end of Peggy's private dock. He hadn't needed to see her face to know she was struggling with something—it was there in the tight line of her shoulders and the downward tilt of her head.

And then, of course, she'd avoided running into him by changing her trajectory as she approached the house.

He'd been sorely tempted to go after her and ask what was wrong, but he knew that would be overstepping, big-time.

She didn't need or want a virtual stranger sticking his nose into her life.

He spent the evening going through Stephen's photo box with Peggy and Tory and answering more of their questions, then he spent half an hour online checking in with the business.

He was a little surprised at how smoothly things were running without him at the helm. He'd never taken time out from the business or the trust before. So far, however, his second in command, Syd, seemed to be on top of things. She was one of the trust's success stories—their star graduate, in fact, and one of the best cabinetmakers he'd ever worked with. She had a firm grasp of the day-to-day operations of both the construction company and the trust, and if her calm demeanor when they video conferenced was anything to go by, she was well and truly on top of things.

Which left him with nothing to do except chill out. And, of course, think about Laurie.

He set his alarm for early the next morning. She was downing the last of her coffee when he entered the kitchen.

"You're up early," she said with a small smile.

She was wearing a pair of navy shorts and a dusky blue tank top that was a near match for her eyes.

"So are you."

"I always get up early."

"So do I." Although, technically, he was a big fan of the sleep-in whenever he could sneak one in.

He helped himself to coffee, then refilled her cup without asking. She gave him a look.

"Are you under the impression I need feeding or something?"

He gave her a slow head-to-toe, cataloging her small, firm-looking breasts, slim waist and athletic legs. She had a runner's body and while she wasn't carrying any extra weight she wasn't greyhound-thin, either. Certainly she had curves in all the places that interested him.

Her cheeks were pink when his gaze returned to her face.

"You look pretty good to me," he said. "I just thought the caffeine might come in handy."

She fiddled with the handle of her coffee cup, flustered. She was fresh from the shower, her hair still damp. Her mouth was pale, nude of lipstick. He eyed her full lower lip, wondering what she'd taste like. Coffee? Or something uniquely Laurie?

He was betting on the latter.

"Were you planning on seeing any other parts of the country while you're here?"

She spoke quickly. A little nervous, he guessed. She made him nervous, too. Although maybe that wasn't the right word for it. She made him feel young again. Uncertain, in a way he hadn't felt for a long time.

"I might visit New York for a couple days after the party. Seems dumb to come all this way and not take a look around," he said.

"Then it's back home, I suppose?"

His gaze met hers. "Yes."

For a moment neither of them said anything, then she gulped her coffee down and took her cup to the sink.

"I'd better get going," she said.

"Much on today?"

"Oh, yes." She looked rueful.

"Anything I can do to help?"

She lifted her eyebrows. "On your vacation? I don't think so."

"I'm one of those people who don't really do vacations."

Her gaze flicked down his body then back to his face again.

"I can believe that."

"So is there anything I can do to help?"

She eyed him for a beat, clearly wrestling with her conscience.

"You'd be doing me a favor, putting me out of my misery," he cajoled.

Her mouth quirked into a half smile. "I don't know if I should believe you or not."

"What have you got to lose?"

"You really want me to answer that?"

He laughed. She grabbed her phone from the counter.

"Come find me in the garden when you've finished your breakfast and I'll put you to work, if that's what you want."

"Done."

He wolfed down two pieces of toast, then tracked her down inside the main tent.

"You were really serious," she said when she saw him.

"I don't make offers I don't intend to keep."

For the next few hours he worked alongside Laurie and four of her staff members setting up tables and chairs inside the big tent. There was a lot of laughter and good-natured teasing as they labored, and it was clear that Laurie was genuinely liked by her team. It wasn't hard to understand why—she was a good boss, clear and direct with her instructions and quick with praise.

By midmorning they'd moved on to setting up fairy lights in the garden, hampered only slightly by the puppy's insistence on getting involved. Adam returned from fixing a run of lights along the balustrade surrounding the terrace to find Laurie perched on top of a ladder on the front doorstep, her hands full of tangled fairy light cable.

His immediate impulse was to grab the ladder and insist she come down, but she wasn't his to protect. Not even close. He settled for placing a steadying hand on the side of the ladder and giving it a quick once-over to ensure it was sound.

"All good up there?" he asked.

Laurie glanced down at him, seeming to register his presence for the first time.

"Oh, hi. Is the terrace finished already?"

"Yep. I can take over here, if you like." He eyed her precarious perch on the second-from-top step.

"Wow. Maybe I should hire you permanently. You're making the rest of my guys look bad. Don't be surprised if they take you aside for a little chat to ask you to slow down before the end of the day," she joked.

"I can live with that."

What he couldn't live with was the sight of her up a ladder.

"I think I should have untangled these before I came up here," Laurie said as she plucked at a knotted run of cable.

"Great idea. Come on down and we'll sort it out."

He could hear the strain in his voice. She gave him a curious look.

"Don't tell me you're one of those men who gets worried about women changing tires and climbing ladders?"

"Guilty as charged, Your Honor."

"You know that's really sexist, right?"

"Again, guilty. You want to come down now?"

She laughed. "Here, catch."

She dropped the fairy lights into his arms. He tossed them to one side as she started down the ladder. For the life of him he couldn't stop himself from placing a steadying hand on the small of her back as she descended, just in case she slipped.

She offered him a slightly disconcerted smile when she finally stepped off the last rung.

"Thanks."

"My pleasure," he said.

But he didn't move away, and now that she was facing him, his hand was on her hip. She swallowed, her gaze dropping to his mouth.

Time slowed.

If he took a step forward and lowered his head, they'd be kissing.

His fingers curled into her hip. She felt good, warm and strong.

"Laurie—"

The low throb of a car engine effectively silenced the rest of what he'd been about to say. He glanced over his shoulder as a sleek, black Aston Martin Vanquish swept up the driveway.

Laurie stepped away from him. He let his hand fall to his side.

"Who is it?" he asked.

She shot him an indecipherable look.

"Guy. My ex-husband."

CHAPTER SIX

LAURIE'S FACE LIT UP AS SHE saw the two other occupants in the car.

"And that's Josh, my son, and my daughter, Amy."

She moved forward to greet her children, clearly delighted to see them. Adam stayed where he was, watching keenly as her ex-husband climbed out of his low-slung car.

Guy Sutcliffe had the sleek, well-fed look of a man who'd never had to struggle for anything in his life. His brown hair was peppered with gray and he was starting to thicken around the middle. Good tailoring ensured it wasn't blindingly obvious but the signs were still there.

One glance was all it took for Adam to understand the kind of man Laurie had married. The brightly striped designer tie, the glint of gold at his cuffs and pinky finger, the hand that rose to smooth his hair as he watched his ex-wife embrace her children.

No wonder Laurie had looked so surprised when he'd raised a glass to her success the other night—this man's ego would take up all the air in the room and then some.

Adam shifted his gaze to Laurie's children, both of whom had had the good fortune of taking after her—dark hair, dusky blue eyes, athletic builds. The daughter, Amy, was going to be beautiful like her mom one day, and Josh looked as though he'd be getting his fair share of attention from the ladies, also.

"This is a surprise." Laurie laughed as she hugged first her son then her daughter.

"Dad said he was coming up here and we told him we wanted to come along for the ride," Amy said. "He's got a meeting with Grandma, then he's going to go off and do other stuff and come back to pick us up later. If that's okay with you?"

"Of course it's okay. It's great."

"Where's the puppy?" Josh asked.

Laurie gave her ex a dirty look and the other man shrugged as if to say the matter was beyond his control.

"He's with Justin and Leonie," she said after a short, tense silence.

Her son rolled his eyes. "Right. And where are they?"

Laurie gave him a light shove on the arm. "Don't roll your eyes at your mother. They're around the side of the house, working in the main tent."

"Cool."

Josh was about to take off, but Laurie caught his arm.

"Whoa there. You want to remember your manners?" She turned to Adam. "Adam, this is my son, Josh, and my daughter, Amy. And this is Guy. Adam's come all the way from Australia for Mom's birthday."

"Nice to meet you," Josh said politely before looking at his mother. "Now can I go?"

"If you have to."

He took off across the lawn.

"Australia? Does that mean you know Hugh Jackman?" Amy asked eagerly.

"Sorry, no. But I sat next to Cate Blanchett in a restaurant once. Does that count?" Adam said.

"That's pretty good," Amy conceded.

Guy was frowning, his hand smoothing his hair again. Now

that he was closer, Adam could see the other man was a little thin up top.

Probably explained the car.

"You're a little early for the party, aren't you?" Guy asked.

"He's visiting with Mom first," Laurie said.

There was a definite edge to her voice and a tightness to her posture. Did that mean things weren't as over as she'd said with her and her ex? Or was she simply wound up over the dog?

"I see. And what line of work are you in back home, Adam?" Guy asked.

"I'm a builder."

Out of the corner of his eye, Adam saw Laurie give him a sharp look.

"Construction? Things must be pretty tough at the moment, then, with the downturn and everything," Guy said, tweaking the cuffs of his shirt and buttoning his suit jacket.

"Things are a little different in Australia. We pretty much sidestepped the recession," Adam said easily.

"Right. I remember reading something about that." Guy's gaze shifted to Laurie, and Adam understood he'd been dismissed. "I've got an appointment with your mother. I'd better not keep her waiting. You want to walk me inside?"

"You know the way," she said coolly.

Guy frowned and looked as though he wanted to say more, then he obviously thought better of it and strode toward the house.

Adam kept his focus on Laurie, pleased to see that she didn't waste another second on her ex, instead turning to her daughter and giving her a little squeeze.

"A pop-in visit," she said. "Does this mean you miss me?"

"I miss your cooking. Prue can't cook to save her life."

"Lovely. I *am* good for more than food and laundry, you know."

"I know," Amy said, resting her head briefly on her mother's shoulder. "But I don't want you to get a big head about it."

"Just for that, I'm going to put you to work. You can help me untangle these fairy lights so we can make the front of the house pretty for your grandma's birthday."

Amy shrugged good-naturedly. "Josh said you'd rope us into working."

"He's a smart boy."

Adam watched as the two of them put their heads together over the tangled cable, tugging fruitlessly at various loops and strands.

"If I might make a suggestion…?" he asked after a few minutes.

Laurie arched an eyebrow. "You may. Especially if it's a good one."

"Only kind I know." He reached out and grabbed the plug. "Start at the end, work your way in."

"Ah. Man logic. I love it," Laurie said.

"We occasionally have the odd good idea," he said, deadpan.

"Right. Like war and the atomic bomb and high heels."

"And the toilet, the telephone and the electric light."

Amy's head was bobbing back and forth as she followed their banter.

"Are you guys fighting?" she asked.

Laurie gave her a startled look. "No."

Amy's lips curved into a smug, knowing little smile. "I didn't think so. I'm going to go meet the puppy."

With a wave of her hand, she set off around the side of the house.

Laurie dropped her gaze to the fairy lights, fiddling pointlessly. Avoiding looking at him, if he was to guess.

"Amy's young. She, um, reads into things sometimes, you know, things that aren't—"

"It's okay, Laurie. I didn't think we were fighting, either."

He shocked a laugh out of her.

"You're pretty smooth, aren't you?" she said.

She glanced up at him then, and he saw the uncertainty and vulnerability in her eyes even though she was still smiling.

"There are plenty of people back home who'd laugh their heads off if they heard you say that."

"Hmm. I'm not so sure about that."

Her gaze slid over his shoulder and she frowned. He turned and saw Josh and Amy crouching down to pat the puppy, their delighted smiles apparent even from a distance.

"I can't believe Guy told them about the puppy. He knew I was unhappy about the dog. It's going to be impossible to send him back now."

"That was probably the point, don't you think?"

"Yeah." She shook her head. "Here's a tip for you, Adam. Never marry someone who negotiates for a living. It's asking for trouble."

"Noted."

She handed him the cable plug. "Come on. Let's at least solve one mess today."

There were a lot of things he'd like to do for Laurie, chief among them being setting straight her smug fat cat of an ex and doing whatever it took to get rid of the small, worried frown that had formed between her eyebrows.

But since he had no right to do any of those things, he bit his tongue and bent his head to their task. It was both the least and the most he could do.

"Okay, omelets are up," Laurie said as she pulled the first of a series of omelets she'd whipped up for dinner out of the oven. It was Eugenia's night off, and even though Josh had campaigned for pizza, Laurie had insisted on cooking. At least that way she knew he got some vitamins and minerals into his body.

Her mother, Josh, Amy, Kinsey and Adam were ranged along the other side of the island counter, cutlery at the ready, and the last rays of the setting sun were staining the sky outside the kitchen window a rosy apricot.

Josh immediately reached for the first omelet and she gave him a dark look.

"Guests first, Josh. Please try to behave as though you weren't raised by wolves."

"I'm a guest, too. I'm only visiting for the day," Josh complained.

"We're family," Amy said, making a big deal out of passing the salad to Adam first.

"Thanks," Adam said, hiding his smile.

Laurie had to hide her own smile. He'd handled her kids just right all day, talking sports with Josh and answering Amy's questions about which way the water went down the drain hole and other antipodean curiosities as they worked to decorate the tent and garden.

If ever she'd had any doubts on the subject—and she hadn't—today had proven that Adam Hunter was a good, decent man. He'd pitched in with her staff, teased her children, wrangled the puppy and calmly dealt with the myriad of minor crises that had popped up during the day.

He was officially a keeper, and some lucky Australian woman—his "right woman"—would one day be very happy to come home to him at the end of each day.

"Laurie, your omelet's getting cold," her mother said.

Laurie blinked and realized she'd drifted off for a moment.

"Come and sit down. You've been running around all day," her mother said.

Laurie allowed herself to be shuffled onto a stool. Amy loaded her plate up with salad, and Josh slid a piece of garlic bread onto her plate while Kinsey handed her a glass of wine.

"It's okay, everyone, I'm not about to fall over." She laughed. "This is what I do all the time. It's my job."

"Then you need a business partner and twice as many staff," her mother said. "I can't believe you don't collapse at the end of each day."

"I'm tough. It's the Longwood genes," Laurie said.

"I'm serious, Laurie. I don't like to see you looking so tired," her mother said.

"I want to do this for you, Mom. It's my gift to you," Laurie said.

Not her gift of choice, but that was a taboo subject.

Her mother frowned.

"So, Josh, I guess they've got you doing a lot of practice drills in the lead-up to the play-offs?" Adam said.

It took Josh a moment to understand he was supposed to help provide a diversion.

"Um, yeah. Yeah, lots of practice sessions. Coach is a real hard-ass about training."

"Josh. Could we at least save the profanity until dessert?" Laurie said dryly as Kinsey snickered into her napkin. Laurie gave her an admonishing nudge in the ribs.

"You're supposed to be an adult, remember? One of us."

"I keep forgetting. Thanks for the reminder," Kinsey said.

"Sorry, Mom. He's a really hard*case,*" Josh said with an unrepentant grin.

"I guess he's shown you the old Thompson drill then, for improving ball handling?" Adam asked.

Josh frowned. "Thompson drill? I don't think we've ever done that one."

"Yeah? Huh. I can show you now if you like…?"

"Sure," Josh said eagerly.

Adam grabbed his water glass, then reached for Amy's. "Do you mind?"

"Go for it."

Adam stood and walked to where Josh was sitting.

"Put out both your hands, palms down. Actually, maybe you should stand, so you can really get a feel for it."

Josh nodded, sliding off his stool eagerly.

Laurie narrowed her eyes. Was it just her, or was there a certain mischievous light in Adam's eyes? There definitely was a smile lurking around his mouth.

He caught her looking and lifted both eyebrows in a classic "who, me?" expression. She shook her head slightly to let him know she wasn't buying.

He was up to something. She could tell.

He grinned, then returned his focus to her son.

"Okay, keep your hands stiff, no matter what I do," he instructed Josh.

He placed one of the water glasses on the back of Josh's left hand, then quickly slid the other onto his right.

Josh's face was intense as he focused on the glasses. "Okay, what do I do next?"

"Whatever you like. But you have to put the glasses down first," Adam said.

Laurie bit her lip as she watched the realisation of his predicament dawn on her son's face.

"No way!" Josh said, clearly equal parts chagrined and delighted to have been suckered.

The others laughed.

"Speaking professionally, you are totally toast, Joshy,"

Kinsey said, clearly delighted. She took advantage of his inability to move by ruffling his hair.

"Not the hair!" Josh complained, arching his head away from her roving hand.

"I've seen kids hold those glasses for over an hour, trying to work out a way to put them down without asking for help," Adam said.

"If I was fast enough, I could drop them and catch them before they hit the floor," Josh speculated.

Laurie shook her head. "I don't think so, my little ninja."

After a few more minutes of teasing, Amy finally took mercy on her brother and took one of the glasses away.

"My turn now," she said.

By the time everyone had proven to themselves that, yes, it was indeed impossible to safely put down the two glasses, they were all a little silly from laughing too much.

"I guess maybe I should have left it a little later before I swung by. Looks like you're having a good time."

Laurie swung around on her stool to find her ex-husband standing in the kitchen doorway.

"Guy. We didn't hear the doorbell. Would you like a glass of wine?" her mother asked graciously.

"No thank you, Peggy. I really need to hit the road," Guy said politely.

Laurie glanced back and forth between the two of them. Her mother hadn't said anything about their meeting after Guy had left, and Laurie hadn't asked. She didn't need to—she knew in her heart that her mother would never throw her lot in with Guy, no matter what the inducement. Frankly, Laurie was surprised Guy had even considered it a real possibility.

"Do we have to go back already?" Amy asked.

"I told you, I have things on tomorrow. And we've got a long drive ahead of us," Guy said.

Amy and Josh grumbled as they collected their coats and

various electronic gadgets. Then Amy dropped to her knees and pulled the puppy close for a hug goodbye.

With the sometimes canny instinct of children, neither she nor Josh had pushed the issue of the puppy all day, but the look her daughter gave her now over the puppy's head spoke volumes.

If she stuck to her guns and returned Guy's gift, her children were going to think she was Attila the Hun's first cousin.

"I'll see you guys next week, okay? And I'll call you tomorrow night," Laurie said as she kissed Josh and Amy goodbye.

"Sure. But not during *Next Top Model,* okay?" Amy said.

"I know, I know," Laurie said.

Amy surprised her then by crossing to Adam and giving him a quick kiss on the cheek.

"If you ever get Hugh Jackman's phone number, you have to promise to let me know, okay?" she said.

"Cross my heart and hope to die," Adam said.

Amy rolled her eyes, aware he was teasing her, but couldn't keep the smile from her face.

Following his sister's lead, Josh offered Adam his hand.

"Thanks for the trick. I'm going to try it out on my buddies."

"Pleasure. Remember—the fuller the glass, the greater the peril," Adam said.

"Yes, and the bigger the mess," Kinsey pitched in.

"Come on, guys, we need to get moving," Guy said from the doorway, jingling his car keys impatiently.

Laurie walked them to the door, one hand on each of her children's backs.

"I want to thank you both for your hard work today. I really appreciate it and I know your Gran did, too."

"It was no big deal. Especially if we get to keep the puppy," Josh said with a sideways look.

"Can we name him, Mom?" Amy asked. "I think we should call him Toffee because his coat is the color of melted toffee."

Josh pulled a face. "Get real, Amy—he's a boy. He needs a tough name."

"What, something ridiculous like Tiger or Wolf or Killer?"

Laurie held up a hand before World War Three erupted.

"I haven't even decided to keep the dog yet."

"What?" both her children said at once.

They stared at her incredulously.

"But, Mom, he's ours now. He's bonded with us," Amy said.

"You can't just take him back and ask for a refund," Josh said.

Laurie was aware of Guy sliding into the driver's seat in the background, his expression carefully neutral.

The rat.

"Deciding to take on a dog is a big decision. Puppies are a lot of work," she said.

It would be so easy to just give in and say yes and let the puppy become a part of their family, but every time she looked at him she'd think of Guy and why he'd given the puppy to her. She didn't want to give her ex-husband that much of a presence in her life, and she certainly didn't want to allow him to manipulate her into a corner.

"Mom—" Amy said.

"We'll talk about it tomorrow, okay?" Laurie said. "I promise."

It was merely delaying the inevitable, but at least it gave her some breathing room.

"We won't forget, if that's what you're thinking," Amy said.

The car roared to life and Guy opened his window.

"Kids, come on."

As though it wasn't his fault that his children were haranguing her and holding him up.

Josh slid into the rear of the car, but Amy lingered a beat before following him.

"Amy, we'll talk tomorrow, I promise," Laurie said, pre-empting her.

"It's not about Toffee." Amy lowered her voice conspiratorially. "I just wanted to say, I think you should go for it."

"I beg your pardon?"

"With Adam. He's hot and he likes you, so I think you should go for it."

Laurie laughed awkwardly, very aware of her daughter's close scrutiny.

"Amy, I hardly think—"

But Amy simply patted her on the arm. "You don't have to deny it, Mom. See you next week, okay?"

She slid into the car and Laurie lifted a hand in farewell as Guy put the car into gear and took off with a spurt of gravel.

She hesitated a moment before reentering the house. Was the tension between her and Adam really so obvious? She wasn't sure if she should be embarrassed or reassured. Or, perhaps more sensibly, scared.

Kinsey was helping her mother navigate the move from her stool to the walker when Laurie returned to the kitchen.

"Bedtime for me. I have a big day tomorrow—it's finally C-day!" She hit her cast with the flat of her hand. "Not that it hasn't been fun, buddy, but you are so out of here."

"I forgot. Do you need a lift to the clinic?" Laurie asked, already starting to rearrange tomorrow's schedule in her head.

"Hey, stop trying to make me look even more superfluous than I already feel," Kinsey said with a grin.

Laurie threw the other woman a grateful look. The whole family had lucked out when Kinsey had been available to manage her mother's recovery. No other physical therapist would have been as patient or as thorough, let alone have been prepared to live in-house for the duration—although Laurie's mother had dropped a few hints that Kinsey's long stay wasn't entirely about her recovery. Laurie suspected that her mother was playing cupid, hoping for something to happen between her brother and Kinsey. It was a nice idea, but David was so tightly wound that Laurie found it hard to imagine the two of them together. Still, stranger things had happened.

"I hope you're turning in early, too, Laurie," her mother said. "Please tell me you're not doing more work this evening."

"I'm not. A little bit of paperwork, then I'm hitting the sack, too," Laurie fibbed.

Her mother's lips thinned but she didn't say anything else. Laurie kissed her good-night, very aware of Adam's tall figure in her peripheral vision.

She started clearing the counter once they were alone.

"You have a tell, you know," Adam said as she ran water in the sink.

"Sorry? A tell?"

"A giveaway. When you're lying. Most people have one."

"Oh." She shot him a look from under her lashes. "What's mine?"

"You widen your eyes," he said, demonstrating.

"Huh. I didn't realize."

"I figured you didn't. But I think your mom might be on to you."

"You're probably right."

He passed her a stack of plates and she rinsed them before slotting them one by one into the dishwasher.

"Thanks for your help today," she said as she worked. "You made a big difference."

"I like being busy."

"Well, you came to the right place at the right time."

"I'm beginning to think that."

She glanced up. He was watching her steadily. She smiled uncertainly.

"Do you believe in fate?" he asked.

"No."

"Me, either. But I've been trying to work out what's been going on the last couple of days, and that's the only answer I can come up with."

"I'm not sure I know what the question is," she said.

"Don't you?"

He closed the distance between them. Laurie took an instinctive step backward and felt the square edge of the counter against her lower back. She was still holding one of the plates when Adam reached out and slid it from her fingers, putting it down on the counter behind her.

"I can't get you out of my head, Laurie Sutcliffe," he murmured.

Then he lowered his head and kissed her.

CHAPTER SEVEN

HIS LIPS WERE FIRM AND WARM against hers. His hand slid up to cup her jaw, his fingers curving against the sensitive skin beneath her ear. She could feel her heart racing out of control, could feel the blood rushing through her body as he moved closer.

You shouldn't be doing this, a small voice said in the back of her mind. *You really shouldn't be doing this.*

Adam's tongue teased the seam of her lips and she hovered on the edge of decision, torn between the need in her body and the caution in her heart. His thumb brushed across her cheekbone, the barest whisper of contact, and the tenderness of the small gesture broke the last shreds of Laurie's resistance. She parted her lips and she felt his mouth quirk into a quick, victorious smile before his tongue swept inside.

Hot need washed over her as they tasted each other. He threaded both hands into her hair, tilting her head back as he deepened the kiss. She clutched at his shoulders, welcoming the firm press of his hips against hers.

He tasted good and strong, like coffee and dark chocolate, and his body felt hot and hard and real against hers. It had been years since she'd felt so on fire for a man. So reckless and needy.

She wanted…

She wanted too much. The feel of skin on skin. The intimacy of shared passion. The knowledge that no matter what happened, someone had her back. That she didn't have to stand alone to fight life's battles, and that there would always be someone to share her laughter and tears and desires.

But that's not what this is about. This is just sex. That's all it can be.

It didn't feel like *just sex,* but she knew the voice in her head was right. It gave her the strength she needed to break their kiss, turning her head away from his mouth, her hands pushing his shoulders away now instead of drawing them closer.

She could feel his breath on her face, could feel the rapid rise and fall of his chest. Knew he was as aroused as she was, and probably wondering what the hell she was playing at, kissing him like that and then pushing him away.

"I'm sorry," she said after a long, tense moment.

"You don't have to apologize."

"I wasn't leading you on. I just…I can't do this."

He took a step backward. She risked a look at his face. His gaze was intent, but she saw no anger or frustration in the depths of his warm brown eyes.

"I pushed. I shouldn't have," he said.

"No. I wanted… But, Adam, you live in *Australia.*"

He gave a single, tight nod. They were both well aware of the geographical impossibilities standing between them.

"I haven't dated since Guy left. Not even a bad date," Laurie said. "I haven't wanted to. And then you suddenly appear in my life and all of a sudden it's like I'm sixteen again—"

"Tell me about it." He sounded rueful.

"But I'm not the kind of person who can handle casual sex," she continued. "It's always been about more than that for me."

"This isn't about sex."

Her gaze dropped pointedly to the front of his jeans where his body gave the lie to his words.

He shrugged a shoulder, his mouth curling up at one corner.

"Okay, it's about sex, but it's not *only* about sex. I really like you, Laurie. I liked you the moment I laid eyes on you. Even though you didn't have a clue where to site a tent."

She smiled faintly at the reminder of their first encounter. Hard to believe it was a couple days ago. She felt as though she'd been resisting Adam's gravitational pull for weeks. Months.

"I like you, too, Adam. But it doesn't change anything. And us sleeping together will only make things worse."

He ran a hand over his hair. "Yeah."

She could tell he was frustrated, even if he agreed with her. Hell, she was frustrated, too. But as she'd said, sex wasn't going to solve anything.

She slid out from between him and the counter and put some distance between them.

"I'm going to go to bed."

"Okay."

She turned toward the door, took a few steps. Swung back to face him.

"For what it's worth, I had a great day. And even if this didn't quite come off, I'm glad we at least tried. If you know what I mean. I wouldn't want to die wondering."

"Good night, Laurie," he said, his voice very low.

"Good night, Adam."

Then she turned and made a run for her room before she changed her mind and did something they'd both regret.

ADAM STARED AT THE CEILING, arms folded behind his head. Never in his entire life had he regretted being born under the Southern Cross, but apparently there really was a first time for everything. If only he was an American....

But he wasn't.

You can't have her. You know it, she knows it. There's no point even thinking about it.

He knew it was true, but it hadn't stopped him from going over those few minutes he'd had her in his arms again and again. The taste of her, sweet and warm. The feel of her skin beneath his hands. The shape of her head in the palm of his hand, the firm push of her breasts against his chest…

She was incredible. Hands down the most desirable woman he'd ever met. But as he'd said to her, it wasn't just about desire. He'd spent the day watching her laugh. He'd talked with her, shared stories about the trust and her uncle and her kids and her business. He'd watched her with her kids, seen the soft, proud light in her eyes, her deep love evident in the small excuses she found to touch them—brushing Josh's hair out of his eyes or tugging at the hem of Amy's T-shirt and telling her it was time they went shopping again.

Any man would want her, but he felt as though he'd been looking for her all his life.

Which was crazy. But it felt true. Like the truest thing in his life.

Which left him…nowhere.

His life was in Australia. Hers was here. They'd shared one kiss. The math was pretty simple.

They weren't meant to be. Right person, wrong place, wrong time.

Life was full of near misses, and apparently he and Laurie Sutcliffe were one of them. In a few days' time, he would go back to Melbourne and pick up the threads of his life and Laurie would become a faded what-if in his mind, the woman who got away, the big could-have-been of his life.

He swore under his breath. He knew it was the only answer, the only rational, smart way to go. But, man, it felt crappy. Utterly, completely wrong.

Rolling onto his belly, he buried his head in his pillow and tried to find some peace in sleep.

IT WAS RAINING WHEN HE WOKE, a steady drizzle that pattered softly against the window. He got out of bed and checked the sky, noting the dark, angry clouds to the west. Being on the coast, he suspected Cape May probably scored its fair share of summer storms. He hoped they weren't in for one now. Both the main and catering tents were well pegged and braced, but no rope in the world was proof against a really vicious storm.

He booted up his computer and did a quick weather check. His frown deepened as he checked the satellite photographs. It didn't look good to him, but he wasn't a local.

He showered, pulled on jeans and a polo shirt, then went in search of Laurie. Not because he wanted to see her, but because he wanted to make sure she knew about the weather report.

That's what he told himself, anyway.

He found her in the ground floor living room, sitting on the couch, her laptop balanced on her knees as she tapped at the keyboard. She glanced up when he entered the room.

"Oh. Good morning." Her smile was a little shy, but her eyes were warm.

"Hi."

She was wearing jeans and a raspberry colored sweater. She looked good, and for a moment all he could think about was how she'd felt in his arms, how she'd tasted.

Pointless self-torture. He shoved his hands into the pockets of his jeans.

"Have you seen the weather report?"

"Yes. I'm hoping the bulk of the bad weather is going to miss us, but the storms can be fierce this time of year. Especially when they come from inland."

She looked worried.

"We can make a tour of the tents, if you like. Make sure everything's watertight."

She gave him a grateful smile. "That's a great idea. Maybe if I see everything's okay I'll be able to concentrate on this damned schedule."

She shut her laptop and slid it onto the couch beside her, then pushed herself to her feet.

"Paperwork not your thing?" he asked.

"Definitely not."

"How'd you get started with the business, anyway?"

She waved a hand dismissively. "It's not a very exciting story."

"I'm interested."

Adam wasn't simply being polite—he wanted to know everything about her, whatever she was willing to share in the limited time they had.

Which just went to prove he really was a sad case.

"Well, okay, but you've been warned. If you slip into a coma, I'm going to deny all responsibility."

She told him her story as they collected an umbrella and made their way to the side door, explaining how a love of food and cooking had grown from a hobby helping out friends with parties into a fully fledged business.

"The funny thing was, I hadn't even realized that I was ready to work full-time again until I found myself loving it so much," she said as they left the house.

"What did you do before you had kids?"

"Oh, this and that. I studied Arts at college—nothing that was very applicable in the real world. So I wound up doing a bit of marketing and a bit of admin work once I'd graduated. Then I got pregnant and Guy was keen for me to stay home with the kids so that was pretty much it until I started up the business."

She glanced across at him.

"What about you? How did you get into the construction business?"

"Your uncle offered me an apprenticeship, and I decided I'd rather learn how to build a house than spend time in juvenile detention."

She was in the middle of opening the umbrella but she paused and gave him a speculative look.

"Ah. I thought I detected a hint of bad boy beneath all that easygoing charm."

He took the umbrella from her.

"You keep telling me I'm charming and I'm going to take it the wrong way."

"Which way is that?"

"As encouragement."

"Oh."

It was the first time either of them had even come close to addressing what had almost happened between them last night. He watched the color climb into her cheeks as she dropped her gaze to the toes of her shoes, a small, pensive frown appearing between her eyebrows.

God, he liked her. And he really wanted to kiss her again.

But he'd already decided that was never going to happen.

The umbrella opened with a flourish of red silk. He held it overhead.

"You ready to do this?" he asked.

"Sure."

She kept her gaze on the ground as they stepped out into the rain. They fell into step with each other easily and he inhaled her perfume and didn't even try to keep his distance when his shoulder inevitably brushed hers. He might not be able to kiss her or pursue her as his instincts urged, but he could have this moment and he was damned well going to enjoy it.

They walked in silence across the lawn. With anyone else, it might have been awkward, but not with Laurie. It simply felt…good. As though they were both in the right place, with the right person, doing the right thing.

He reached out to hold back the tent flap for her when they arrived at the site and she gave him a small, fleeting smile of thanks as she ducked under his arm. He followed her inside, shaking the umbrella out.

"Everything looks okay," she said, glancing around.

"Yeah."

They did a quick circuit, then made their way to the smaller tent and repeated the exercise.

"Well, unless this gets really ugly, it looks as though we're all good here," she said.

He opened the umbrella again and they stepped out into the rain. They were halfway back to the house when Laurie slipped on the wet grass. She grabbed his forearm instinctively to avoid falling and for a moment they were locked together, her body pressed against his side. Then she released her grip and gave him an apologetic look.

"Sorry. That was pretty stupid. No need for me to take you down with me."

"I can think of worse things."

She stilled, gazing up at him.

"Adam…" She broke off, shaking her head, clearly unable to articulate her frustration.

"It's okay, I get it. Sorry. I won't bring it up again."

He knew he was being a dick, pushing things when they'd made a mutual decision to be sensible.

"No! That's not what I was going to say." Her blue eyes were full of regret. "If you had any idea how long I lay awake last night, thinking about you. About what almost happened…"

He didn't say anything. He didn't need to.

"I wish…I wish things could be different," she said quietly. "I think it would be a real privilege to know you properly."

He reached up and ran his thumb along the curve of her jaw. She was as soft and smooth as silk.

"Ditto."

She took a deep breath, then closed her eyes for a long second.

"Okay. We need to start walking or I'm going to be stupid again," she said.

He was tempted to call her bluff. Instead, he started walking. After half a second she fell into step beside him.

A small moment of silence passed.

"Think I might head into town today, take a look around," he said, keeping his gaze trained on the house.

"You should check out the Cape May Courthouse. And the Arts Center is pretty good, too."

"Thanks. I'll be sure to look them up," he said.

It wasn't what he really wanted to say, just as checking out a bunch of tourist sites wasn't really how he wanted to spend his day. But there wasn't much he could do about that.

Once they were inside the house, Laurie took the umbrella off him.

"Have a good day," she said.

"You, too."

Then they went their separate ways.

CHAPTER EIGHT

LAURIE WAS AWARE OF AN unsettled feeling within herself as she went about her business for the rest of the morning. Twice she snapped at her crew, both times apologizing and blaming a bad night's sleep for her mood.

But it wasn't lack of sleep that was responsible for her snappishness—although it definitely played a part, since she'd spent more time than she wanted to acknowledge staring at her ceiling last night, thinking about the man sleeping across the hall.

She was frustrated. Not sexually. Well, not *just* sexually. She felt as though the universe had dangled a wonderful gift in front of her and then snatched it away the moment she reached for it.

She'd never been so drawn to a man, to any *person,* as she was drawn to Adam. When she was with him, she felt as though she was a magnet and he was true North. She felt confused and excited and hyperconscious of her own body and of where he was in relation to her and what he might be thinking about the things she was saying, even if she wasn't talking directly to him. She wanted desperately for him to like her children, and for them to like him. Most of all, she wanted him to like her—and last night he'd told her he did, then he'd shown her with the most soul-searing kiss she'd ever experienced.

And he lived in Australia.

It was like a bad joke. Only she felt like kicking something instead of laughing.

She knew it would pass. It had to. After the party his visit would be done and he'd head home. And she would go back to her home, back to her business and her children. Life would go on.

And she would never see him again.

A strange, dizzy sensation hit her as she contemplated the concept of never talking to Adam Hunter again. Never seeing his smile. Never hearing his low, deep voice. Never looking across the room and straight into his eyes *ever again*.

It took her a moment to recognize the feeling as panic.

Don't be stupid. You hardly know him. You're forty, not fourteen. Snap out of it.

But the feeling sat on her chest, a heavy, dull weight, for the rest of the morning. It wasn't helped by the fact that the weather got steadily worse, the wind picking up and the rain driving against the windows. More than once she peered out at the tents, but they seemed to be holding their own against the storm. She wished she could say the same.

She headed upstairs to talk to her mother after lunch, wanting to sign off on a few last-minute things. It was Friday, a dialysis day, and she found her mother in her bedroom, sitting in the recliner chair she'd bought especially to accommodate her home treatment. Two tubes ran into her arm, both filled with the brilliant red of oxygenated blood. A bag of clear fluid hung from a drip stand. The home dialysis machine sat to her left, a lifesaving miracle the size and shape of a home printer.

Her mother was reading, and she glanced over the top of her glasses when Laurie knocked on the door frame of the half open door.

"Okay to come in?" Laurie asked.

"Of course. You're better than a book any day, sweetheart."

Laurie sat on the visitor's chair her mother always kept at the ready.

"I wanted to discuss the menu with you…" she said.

They chatted for a few minutes, her mother agreeing easily to all of Laurie's suggestions. Finally Laurie gave her mother a steady look.

"Mom. Stop being such a pushover. You're allowed to have an opinion, you know."

"I do, and you've obviously listened to it. But you're the expert. All I want is to give my family and friends a great day, and it seems to me that everything is well in hand for that to happen. True?"

"You're going to ruin me for my real customers, you know that, don't you?"

Her mother laughed, the sound rich and low. Laurie was filled with a warm rush of love as she looked into her mother's so-familiar face. Her mother had always been the type of person to laugh instead of cry if given a choice. She always had time for others, no matter what the hardships or demands in her own life. And she'd always made sure her two children felt loved and safe, no matter what. She wasn't a saint—she had a temper when roused and she could be as stubborn as a mule sometimes—but she was utterly unique and precious to Laurie.

"I love you, Mom," she said, reaching out to capture her mother's free hand.

"Oh! I love you, too, Laurie Bear," her mother said, using her childhood nickname.

Heat stung the back of Laurie's eyes, and even though she'd promised she'd never bring it up again, the words were out her mouth before she could stop them.

"Please reconsider, Mom. I want to do this for you. I'm healthy, and I want you to be well so much…"

Her mother's smile dropped away. "You know how I feel about this, Laurie. I've made my decision. Please respect that."

"You've seen the statistics. The odds of me needing that other kidney are so remote—"

"Laurie, please. Stop. I don't want to have this fight with you again."

Laurie's throat worked, but she didn't say anything. She couldn't—she was too busy trying not to cry.

"Laurie," her mother said, her voice softening. "It's not that I'm not grateful, but I can't take something so precious from you. You have your children, your whole life ahead of you still."

She squeezed Laurie's hand. Laurie nodded, then slid her hand free and stood.

"I'm sorry. I know I promised not to bring it up again…"

Her mother's eyes were warm but determined.

"I won't change my mind on this, Laurie. You're going to have to accept it one day."

Laurie nodded again, then strode for the door.

Only when she was down the hallway, well away from her mother's bedroom, did she stop and close her eyes. A single tear slid down her cheek but the need to shed more pressed against her chest.

She took deep breaths, letting them out slowly, deliberately calming herself.

Getting upset wouldn't make a difference to anything. Neither would yelling or bargaining or threats—she knew, because she'd tried everything in her quest to make her mother see sense and accept her offer of a kidney.

A transplant would give her mother her life back and, all going well, guarantee that she would be around for many years to come. Laurie already knew she was a tissue match, and yet her mother refused to even discuss the possibility of accepting her gift. It was a battle that had been simmering between them for over a year now, and the last time it had flared up her mother had insisted that Laurie respect her decision and refused to enter into any discussion on the topic whatsoever. That had been three months ago, and even though it had made her jaw ache sometimes, Laurie had bitten her tongue and respected her mother's wishes.

But she was only human. And she loved her mother dearly. The day she was prepared to give up the fight entirely would be the day her mother died, and not a second sooner.

Laurie started down the stairs, wiping her face dry with the back of her hand. The rain was slashing violently at the window when she returned to the living room. She bit her lip, then made her way to the side door and stood beneath the overhang, squinting out at the tents through the driving rain. Outside, she could feel the power of the wind for herself, see the way it whipped at the trees, bending them almost to breaking point.

A small shape darted past her legs and out into the rain. Laurie groaned.

"Come back here!" She bolted out into the rain, grabbing the puppy just before he disappeared beneath a dripping shrub.

"You are nothing but trouble, you know that, you furry pest? Getting into things, tripping people up. You think I don't have better things to do than to run around after you?" she told the puppy as she ducked back into the house. Her voice was hard and sharp, and the puppy flinched in her arms.

In the back of her mind she knew she was heaping more blame on the puppy's shoulders than he'd earned, but all the stress and emotion building inside her had to find an outlet somewhere, and the puppy had just volunteered himself with his foolish dash into the elements. She dumped the puppy on the tiled floor.

"Stay!" she said firmly.

The puppy gave her a puzzled look. She leveled a stern finger at him.

"Bad dog. Bad dog!"

The puppy dropped his head, avoiding her gaze. His tail tucked firmly between his legs, he slunk away.

Guilt tugged at her, but she shrugged it off. She wouldn't even be having this problem if Guy hadn't dumped the puppy on her. No way would she have taken on another responsibility at such a busy time.

Lightning flashed overhead, followed by a low, ground-shaking roll of thunder. She was about to close the door, but she glanced back toward the tents and saw a dark figure running across the lawn.

Adam. What was he doing?

As she watched, he crouched beside the first rope line. Metal flashed in his hand, and she watched as the rope went slack.

He'd cut the line.

She stepped out onto the side steps, pulling the door shut behind her. Then she ran out into the rain.

She was drenched before she'd run ten feet, soaked to the skin by the time she reached the tents.

"What are you doing?" she yelled as she drew close to where Adam was crouching beside the second rope line.

He glanced up at her, his eyes narrowed against the streaming rain.

"There's a high wind warning. You're going to lose these tents if I don't drop them. Go back inside."

As if to punctuate his words, the sky flashed with lightning again. Laurie felt the force of the wind as it pushed at her, could see the strain on the ropes.

He was right. They were going to lose the tents if this kept up.

"Those pegs twist into the ground," she said. "I saw them put them in."

She knelt beside him on the sodden ground and grasped the plastic moulding on the top of the peg. She'd admired the neat mechanism when the men were installing it, and even though her fingers were cold and wet, she managed to twist it so that it popped from its socket in the ground. Immediately the rope was tugged from her hand by the wind.

"Great. I can do the rest," Adam yelled, urging her to her feet.

She pushed him away. "It's my responsibility, not yours," she yelled back. "You should be the one going inside."

"I don't suppose there's anything that I can say to make you change your mind?"

"What do you think?"

He glanced toward the sky, then back at the tent.

"Let's work fast so we can get inside out of this."

"Good plan."

He flashed a grin at her, and even though she was cold and wet and very worried, she couldn't help grinning back.

"Get moving," he said, pushing her toward the next rope line. "I'll work my way around the other side."

It took them twenty minutes to release all the rope lines. With the supporting ropes loosened, the central pillars fell and the tent dropped in on itself, collapsing over the tables and chairs her teams had set up earlier.

"Not perfect, but at least there's a chance it won't blow away now that it presents a much smaller target," Adam said.

The catering tent was faster going, and within five minutes she and Adam were working on the last two lines.

Laurie cursed under her breath as her fingers slipped for the second time on what was proving to be a particularly tricky peg. She was so cold, her fingers were turning blue and she couldn't stop shivering.

She shook them briskly to try to restore circulation, then swore under her breath as a small, wet form rushed up at her out of the darkness.

"Who let you out?" she demanded.

The puppy cowered against her, nuzzling into her body, trying to lick her face.

"Stop. Just give me a second," she told him, pushing him away.

The puppy retreated a few steps and she got a grip on the peg and twisted. It gave at last and she glanced over her shoulder and watched the tent sink to the ground.

Adam strode to her side, extending a hand to pull her to her feet.

"Come on. We've done all we can," he said over the roar of the storm.

He started herding her toward the house.

"Wait. The puppy…" she said, turning back for the dog.

Lightning forked overhead in a brilliant flash and she heard a startled yelp. A small, dark shape streaked across the lawn toward the beach.

"No! Come back here!" she called, breaking into a run.

She'd barely taken two steps before Adam caught her elbow.

"I'll go after him."

"I'm not leaving him out here."

He'd clearly learned his lesson with the tent, because he didn't try to stop her again as she broke into a jog. She was aware of him keeping pace beside her as she ran down the slope toward the beach.

"You don't have to do this," she puffed.

He didn't bother responding and she realized she hadn't expected him to, not really. Not once had he let her down in the short time she'd known him, and she knew in her heart and her gut that he wasn't about to let her down now.

They both stopped in their tracks when they reached the shore, awed by the sight of Mother Nature at her wildest. It was high tide and waves beat the shore relentlessly, throwing up wild spumes of spray, the water gray and dark. Shrubs and trees shuddered along the shoreline, whipped to a frenzy by the wind. Laurie used her hand to shield her eyes, but for the life of her she couldn't see any sign of life along the beach.

"I can't see him. But I'm sure he ran this way."

"Look!"

She followed Adam's pointing finger to where a small shape was bolting across the sand toward the line of trees that marked the beginning of the state forest that ran alongside her mother's property.

"Hey! Come back here, you silly puppy!" Laurie called, breaking into a run again.

The park was huge—at least twenty acres. If he disappeared in there the odds were good they'd never find him, storm or no storm.

Panic gripping her, Laurie lengthened her stride, her gaze pinned on the darting shape ahead of her.

"Come on, boy, come on," she called, but the storm more than drowned her out.

With a sob of helplessness she watched as the puppy disappeared into the first line of trees.

For the second time that night Adam grabbed her elbow. "Wait."

"I have to go after him. If he gets lost in there… It goes on for miles. There's no way he'll be able to find his way out. He's just a baby."

Adam's hand was warm as he reached out and pushed her hair out of her eyes.

"It's dangerous in there. With this wind, there are going to be a lot of trees coming down."

"I can't just leave him out here."

"I know. Just…stay close, okay?"

She nodded, unable to suppress the shiver that racked her body. He reached out and drew her against his side.

"Come on," he said.

They started into the forest.

CHAPTER NINE

LAURIE WAS SHIVERING, her slender frame shuddering against his side. Adam drew her closer, his arm tight around her shoulders.

The hiking trail they were on was barely discernible thanks to the thick forest canopy and the darkened sky. Debris littered the path—shredded bark and leaves, small branches.

A crack sounded and he dug his fingers into Laurie's shoulder to force her to stop. There was no way of knowing where the sound had come from, if it was one of the trees near them, if they were likely to be dodging a falling branch or tree in the next few seconds.

He wiped the rain from his eyes, wishing he'd been able to convince Laurie to go back to the house. But he knew she would never retreat from her responsibilities. She was the kind of woman who would go out into the storm every time.

He glanced down at her. She was frowning, trying to see in the gloom and driving rain. She sensed his scrutiny, glancing up at him. She looked so worried he couldn't help but drop a kiss onto her forehead.

"He'll be okay. He's small, but he's not stupid," he said.

"I yelled at him."

"Sorry?"

"I yelled at him. He ran out into the rain and I told him he was a furry pest and that he was a bad dog."

Regret and guilt were rich in her voice.

"Laurie. He didn't run away because you disciplined him."

"I was taking my temper out on him. He didn't deserve it."

"He was scared of the lightning. He wasn't running away from you."

She looked miserable and he gave her a little shake.

"Let's hold off on the recriminations until they're needed, okay?"

She nodded and they started walking again. After five minutes they reached a fork in the path.

Laurie threw her hands in the air. "This is hopeless. He could be anywhere. He sure as hell isn't following a trail. We're never going to find him. God, that poor little guy."

She started to cry. Adam pulled her into his arms. For a moment she resisted the comfort, then she rested her forehead against his chest and sobbed.

He placed his hand on the nape of her neck and placed his chin on her head, his other hand spread wide on her back. She was still shivering and he wished he had something more than his own body heat to offer her. What he really wished was that her puppy would announce his presence so they could all go home and get warm and dry.

Lightning flashed, turning the world to stark black and white. He tensed, squinting into the darkness.

Was that what he thought it was?

"I THINK THERE'S SOME kind of a building through there," he said.

Laurie lifted her head, blinking up at him. Wordlessly he led her forward. Sure enough, there was a small wooden hut set to one side of the path, its timbers painted forest-green.

"Looks like a warden's hut," he said.

Laurie stood to one side, arms wrapped around herself,

while he tried the door. As he'd hoped, it was unlocked. Which meant they were unlikely to find anything of value inside, but at least it would mean they were out of the rain.

He pushed the door open and gave the small space a quick scan. As he'd guessed, it was essentially an empty box, although the wooden floor appeared to be scrupulously clean.

He gestured for Laurie to enter, and followed her inside.

"It's going to be dark when I shut the door," he warned her.

She didn't respond and he guessed she was still giving herself a hard time about the puppy. He closed the door, then blinked for a moment in the sudden darkness.

"What am I going to tell the kids?" Laurie's voice came out of the darkness, thin with misery. "Amy already had a name picked out for him."

He wasn't surprised. Laurie was about the only person who'd ever had any doubt that she'd be keeping the puppy. He'd known from the moment he first saw her with the dog that she wouldn't be sending him back, idiot ex-husband or no.

"We don't know that he's lost. He could have run back to the house. Or he might be simply waiting out the storm like we are."

Laurie didn't say anything, but he could hear her choppy breathing. He crossed the space that separated them, one hand extended. The moment he found her, he pulled her into his arms again. She curled her hands into the wet fabric of his T-shirt and sobbed against his chest.

He'd played witness to a lot of tears in his time, but none of them had made his chest ache the way Laurie's did. He hated that she was hurting, wanted more than anything to find the magic word or deed that would make her world right again.

But this wasn't simply about finding her lost puppy—although he guessed it would go some way toward healing her pain. The misery he could feel racking her body came from a place deep inside.

"What's going on, Laurie?" he said quietly.

He felt her shake her head against his chest.

"Something's happened. What is it? Is it your ex? Something with the business?"

For a moment he didn't think she was going to answer. Then she spoke.

"My mother is…is dying."

He tensed. "What?"

"She has kidney disease. She needs dialysis three times a week to survive. But what she really needs is a new kidney. And she won't take mine, no matter how many times I explain to her that it's mine to give, that it's what I want, that I can't stand the thought of losing her. And so she's slowly going to deteriorate until finally there won't be anything more the doctors can do for her. And then she's going to die."

Her voice broke and he rubbed soothing circles on her back as she gave in to the tears again.

Peggy hadn't told him she was ill. Hardly surprising—he guessed that anyone living with a chronic illness must get pretty sick of being defined by it all the time. The information cast new light on Laurie's behavior, however. Her devotion to her mother. The intense vibe he'd sensed between them. The determination with which Laurie had thrown herself into her mother's party preparations.

It was a tough situation. On one hand, he understood Laurie's fear of losing her mother and her desire to do everything in her power to offer her a cure. But he could also understand Peggy's stand in rejecting her daughter's gift. Parents protected their children—even when it was to their own detriment.

Laurie's sobs quietened. He wasn't surprised when she pushed away from his chest, signaling she was ready for him to release her.

He let his arms drop to his side and felt rather than saw her move away.

"Sorry. It just gets to me sometimes, that's all, and then I cry and it goes away for a while again. There isn't anything you or anyone can do about it. So don't feel as though you have to say anything special. It is what it is."

"Your mother loves you very much," he said gently.

He heard her swallow. "I know."

"I've just met her, but the first thing I noticed about her was that she leads with her chin, just like Stephen. Every time that chin came up, I knew there was no compromise to be had. He was the most stubborn person I ever met."

"Mom's like that. Stubborn as the day is long. Both David and I got tested when it became clear her kidney damage was irreversible—though David wasn't a match, I was. But right from the start she refused to even discuss the possibility of one of us donating."

He was silent a moment, weighing the merit of his next question.

"Would you let your kids donate to you if the situation was reversed?"

She sighed. "No. For the same reasons that Mom cites—I could never live with the risk that something might go wrong and that they might need two kidneys themselves."

He didn't say anything. She sighed again.

"I need to accept this, don't I? Accept that she isn't going to change her mind. That this is what she wants."

"Easier said than done."

"Yeah. But I think I need to start trying harder. I brought it up with Mom again this afternoon, and I know it upsets her. I don't want this to come between us. For her to be worried I'm going to bring it up every time we see each other. For me to be so aware of it every time we're together."

"Okay," he said.

"Okay? That's all you have to say?"

"You're a smart, strong lady. You'll work it out."

A short silence fell, then he felt her hand on his arm. She wrapped her fingers around his wrist, gripping him firmly.

"How do you do that?"

"Do what?"

"How do you know exactly what to say to me, what I need to hear? How can you have so much faith in me when we've only just met?"

"I know you," he said, and he realized it was true.

From the moment he'd first met her, he'd felt the pull of attraction and recognition, and the feeling had only strengthened since then.

"How? How is that possible?" Her voice was barely a whisper.

"I don't know. But it's bloody hard to fight, let me tell you."

"I know. I keep telling myself to be smart, that you're going to be leaving soon, that there is no way that the feelings I'm feeling can be real. And then you walk into the room and I forget everything."

Her hand was very warm on his arm. He thought about last night, about their kiss and his long sleepless night. He thought about the way she'd taken shelter in his arms, crying out her grief. He thought about all the looks and the small touches and the moments of connection they'd shared over the past few days.

"Laurie—"

"No," she said.

She slid her hand from his wrist to his shoulder, then behind his neck. He felt her belly press against his, felt the firmness of her breasts against his chest as she rose up on her toes to kiss him.

It was so dark he didn't need to close his eyes but he did

anyway, all the better to drink in the taste and smell and feel of her as they kissed. She pulled him closer, then closer again, her slim arms surprisingly strong.

"You taste so good," she said against his mouth.

"So do you," he murmured.

She broke their kiss suddenly, slipping away from him. He opened his eyes.

"Take your clothes off," she said, her voice low with need.

He stilled. He heard the wet slap of what he guessed was her sweater hitting the floor.

"Take your clothes off, Adam. I want to make love. I want to be with you."

Desire heated his blood but he didn't move.

"You're upset."

"I want this. I want you. I need you."

He felt her hands on him then, tugging at the hem of his T-shirt, pushing it up his torso. He didn't help her, but he didn't hinder her, either. He couldn't decide what to do, whether he should take her at her word or hold on to the last shreds of his self-control. He wanted to be with her so badly, but her happiness was already very precious to him and he didn't want to give her cause for regret.

She successfully worked his T-shirt up his chest but she made a frustrated noise when she reached his armpits. He bit back an oath as she stepped forward and he felt the warm silken press of her skin against his. She was naked from the waist up and the contact was nothing short of electric.

She pressed a kiss to his chest, and he understood that he didn't stand a chance. She wanted this, and God help him, so did he. Tomorrow would be soon enough to deal with the consequences.

Driving his hands into her hair, he angled her head back and kissed her with everything he had in him.

LAURIE LAY IN THE DARK, her head resting on Adam's chest. The steady thump-thump of his heart sounded beneath her ear. Despite the chill of the storm she was warm, her body heated by his touch and the dying fires of their passion.

As she'd guessed, he was a wonderful lover. Attentive and earthy, at turns intense and irreverent. He'd kissed and touched and stroked her with his hands and tongue and mouth, and then he'd insisted on taking the brunt of the wooden floor, drawing her down on top of him and making love to her slowly, thoroughly, sweetly.

It had been a revelation. An awakening. Her body had never felt so heated, so hungry, nor so intensely satisfied. He was the lover she'd been waiting for all her life.

His hand smoothed down her back, tracing the line of her spine. She shivered as his palm slid over the small of her back before gently cupping her backside.

"You're beautiful, Laurie Sutcliffe."

"You're not so bad yourself, Adam Hunter."

He squeezed her bottom, sighing faintly.

"We should probably think about heading back. People will be worried about us."

She knew he was right, and yet she didn't want to move. Didn't want to lose the magic of this moment and this connection. Didn't want to step back into the real world, with all its attendant responsibilities and harsh realities.

He waited another five minutes, and she felt him take a breath, ready to speak again.

"I know," she said softly.

She rolled off him, feeling the loss of his body heat on more than just a physical level. They got dressed in silence, pulling on clammy clothes.

"It's still raining," he said.

But the wind seemed quieter. He opened the door, then held out his hand.

"Let's go."

She slid her hand into his, marveling at the way their hands fit so well together despite the difference in scale. It had been the same when they were making love: like coming home, familiar and exciting all at once.

They stepped outside. It had started to clear overhead, offering glimpses of a washed-out sky between thick banks of cloud. They set off down the trail, retracing their steps. The beach was still a grim place when they emerged from the forest, the ocean pounding the shore with violent slaps. They ducked their heads and ran hand-in-hand toward the edge of her mother's lawn. She could make out the faint outline of the downed tents as they started up the slope toward the house. A small mercy—they hadn't been blown away. No doubt there would be plenty of other damage to repair, however. The likelihood of all the fairy lights they'd installed yesterday surviving intact was slim at best.

The house was lit like a beacon as they approached. Laurie started to shiver again and Adam increased his pace.

"Five minutes till you're in a warm shower," he said.

Then they were at the side door and he was urging her inside and they were both standing on the tile, water running off of them in rivulets.

She blinked, a little startled by the brightness after the extended period in the dark. She glanced at Adam, saw he was watching her. She gave him a small, quick smile. He didn't smile back.

"You okay?" he asked.

"Yes. Of course."

"No regrets?"

"No." She shook her head. "No."

He nodded his acceptance, and she thought he looked relieved. He started toeing off his shoes and she watched him unobserved for a moment.

She didn't regret having made love with him, but the world hadn't miraculously changed while they were out in the storm. Australia was still in the southern hemisphere, and she still had two children, a business and a mother to keep her firmly anchored in her life here in America.

And never the twain should meet. The only difference was that now she knew exactly what she'd be losing when Adam left next week.

"Laurie. There you are. We've been looking for you everywhere," her mother said, Kinsey hard on her heels as she rounded the corner.

Laurie gave a gasp of relief when she saw the small, spiky-haired ball of fluff nestled in her mother's lap.

"Where did you find him?" she asked. "We were out looking for him. He ran into the state forest."

"Kinsey heard him whining outside the terrace door a few minutes ago. God, Laurie, you're soaked to the skin."

Laurie dropped to her haunches and reached out to pat the puppy's warm, slightly damp body. The puppy licked her hand and she stroked her hand down the length of his spine.

"I'm sorry for yelling at you, little guy," she said quietly.

He licked her hand again and she made a promise to herself to make it up to him as soon as she was dry and warm.

"He seems fine, Laurie. Come on, you need a shower," Adam said.

His hand landed on her shoulder, warm and heavy. She didn't need to look to know her mother noticed the gesture—she could practically *feel* the woman's interest.

"Wait. There's something I have to do first," Laurie said.

She lifted the puppy's chin with her finger, looking into his deep brown eyes.

"Your name is Atlas," she declared.

He licked her hand. She decided to take it as approval of his new moniker.

"Go get dry, for Pete's sake, Laurie," her mother urged. "The puppy can wait."

Laurie stood, a thousand other thoughts clamoring for her attention.

"I need to call the tent guys, schedule them to come back out to erect the tent again," she said. "And we need to—"

"Later," Adam growled from behind her.

Then he pushed her ahead of him toward the stairs, his hands on both her shoulders. He stopped only when they were on the threshold of her room.

"Get warm," he told her, then he dropped a quick, hard kiss onto her mouth and disappeared into his own room.

Laurie pressed her fingers to her mouth.

So many questions. So many doubts. And no answers that she could see.

Shaking her head, she went to dry off.

CHAPTER TEN

LAURIE FOUND EUGENIA laying out a pair of her mother's flannel pajamas on her bed when she exited the ensuite after a long, hot shower.

"Your mother sent them up. I've got soup coming in five."

"Thanks, but I can come down," Laurie said.

"It's up to you, but I know your mother would be reassured if you played it safe and stayed in bed."

There was a reproof in Eugenia's tone—she hated it when Peggy fretted.

Laurie gave in to guilt and let Eugenia hustle her into bed, then spent a full five minutes glorying in being warm and snug and dry. Her soup and toast arrived, and to her surprise she found herself drifting off to sleep afterward, despite the fact that it was barely four in the afternoon.

But it had been an eventful day, and clearly both her mind and body needed the downtime. When she woke again the sky was dark with night instead of storm clouds, stars twinkling in the distance. She checked the bedside clock. Nine o'clock.

She shook her head. Unbelievable. She never slept during the day for more than an hour. Ever.

She turned on the bedside light, intending to get up. Then she thought better of it and burrowed back beneath the covers.

If she got up, she might run into Adam and she wasn't sure she was ready to do that just yet. Wasn't sure she was ready to make small talk in front of whoever else might be around and pretend that her world hadn't been shifted irrevocably by what had happened between them this afternoon.

There was a light tap on her door.

"Come in," she said, sitting up and quickly running a hand over her hair.

Just in case.

It wasn't Adam, however—it was her mother, shuffling along with the aid of her walker. Laurie's disappointment must have shown on her face because her mother gave her a searching look before smiling faintly.

"Not who you were hoping for?" she said.

"No. I mean, yes." She looked away, feeling about as sophisticated and transparent as a fifteen-year-old. Which was when she registered the bulky velcro shoe on her mother's foot instead of the now-familiar psychedelic cast.

"You got your cast off!"

"Finally. You should see my poor leg—it looks like it's been on a starvation diet." Her mother sat on the side of Laurie's bed with a sigh. "Don't you dare tell Kinsey I said this, but walking around all the time is harder than I thought it would be."

Laurie managed a faint smile.

"How are you feeling? No scratchy throat or anything?" her mother asked, leaning forward to press a cool hand to Laurie's forehead, just as she had when Laurie was a little girl.

"I'm fine. It takes more than a bit of rain to stop me."

"Good, because I wanted to talk to you about something. It occurred to me this afternoon that it was something that I perhaps should have spoken to you about earlier."

"Okay."

"It's about Guy. As you know, he had an appointment with me yesterday to talk about my leaving Roland and going with him when he opens his new agency."

Laurie nodded, wondering where this was leading.

"I wanted you to know that I told him no. In fact, I told him no, under no circumstances. Not even if he threw in the keys to Fort Knox and a case of French champagne."

Laurie smiled. "Thanks, Mom, but you didn't need to tell me. I knew you'd never back him."

"Good. It wasn't until I saw you with Adam this afternoon that it occurred to me that you might have some doubt on that score."

Laurie frowned. "Why would Guy wanting to represent you have anything to do with Adam?"

Her mother gave her a dry look. "Give me a little bit of credit, sweetheart."

Try as she might, Laurie couldn't stop herself from blushing.

Unbelievable—she'd blushed more in the three days since she'd met Adam Hunter than she had in the previous ten years.

"It's not what you think."

"Isn't it? What is it, then?"

"I don't know." Laurie fiddled with the quilt. "We, um, like each other. But nothing's going to come of it."

Her mother cocked her head. "Why not?"

Surely that was obvious?

"Because he lives in Australia."

"Okay. But that's not an insurmountable obstacle, surely? If you two hit it off and can somehow find a way to keep hitting it off, it's not beyond the realm of possibility that you could make things work, is it?"

Laurie blinked. Was her mother really so romantic? So idealistic?

"Mom, my life is here. I can't traipse halfway around the world to be with a man. I've got the kids to think about, the business. People rely on me to be there for them."

"I agree. It would be hard for you to uproot your life at this stage in the kids' lives. But Adam doesn't have children."

Her mother's eyes were bright with expectation.

"Mom! Putting aside the fact that we've only just met, I couldn't ask him to give up his life. He'd have to move countries, abandon his business, the trust. That's just…that's just not going to happen."

"Why not?"

"Because I can't ask him to give up everything just so he can have me."

"Oh, Laurie. I can't tell you how sad it makes me to hear you say that. There's nothing 'just' about you. You're not a consolation prize."

"That's not what I said."

"Isn't it? Didn't you just tell me that you didn't think that being with you would be enough inducement for Adam to change countries?"

Laurie opened her mouth to deny it, but it was true. She *did* think it was too much to ask for herself. Too much to ask of him.

"What would be acceptable to ask of him, then, if you loved him and he loved you?" her mother said. "To move cities? Counties? From one side of town to the other? Across the street?"

Laurie stared at her mother, confronted.

"You're worth a great deal of risk, sweetheart. You're worthy of heroic deeds, and then some," her mother said quietly.

Laurie blinked, warding off sudden tears. Her mother reached out to take her hand, weaving their fingers together.

"I've been so proud of the way you handled yourself after Guy left, picking yourself up and dusting yourself off. But it kills me to see the doubt he's planted in you, Laurie. He left because there's something lacking in him, not because there's something lacking in you."

"I know that."

"Do you? Do you really?"

"It takes two people to make a marriage work, Mom, and two to make a marriage fail. I must have done *something* wrong." The words came bubbling up from deep inside her. A hidden truth she'd sat on for a long time.

"Because he had an affair?"

"You know what they say—men go looking for what they're not getting at home. I obviously wasn't meeting Guy's needs anymore. Or perhaps he was just bored. Or maybe it's because I'm getting older. Prue's ten years younger than me, after all. Or maybe he simply couldn't remember why he loved me anymore."

It was painful to say it out loud. But her mother was forcing the issue. And maybe it was time to get this stuff out in the open.

"Guy left because you found yourself, Laurie. Your business took off and you blossomed, and he couldn't handle it. He didn't want the competition."

"But I wasn't competing with him. I was just doing my own thing. It was nothing to do with him."

"Exactly my point." Her mother eyed her for a moment. "Did I ever tell you why I married your father?"

Laurie blinked at the sudden change of subject. "Because you fell in love with him?"

"That was part of it. But love isn't enough on its own. There has to be goodwill on both sides. And generosity. A willingness to compromise or go without to make the other person happy. Not all the time, mind—but that generosity of spirit needs to be there. I knew your father had it when he took me out for lunch one day when we'd been going out for a few months. We went to this big, fancy restaurant and he wouldn't let me look at the menu, just read the descriptions to me so I could choose what I wanted without worrying about the prices. We walked by the lake afterward, and there were these paddleboats, you know the kind you have to pedal to make them move around in the water? Anyway, your father could see I wanted to have a go on one, so he hired a boat for us for half an hour. Once we were done, he took me home and kissed me goodbye, the same as always. Then, about an hour later, his mother called. She wanted to know where he was—he'd said he'd be home by six and Lucy was always a bit of a worrier. Well, I was worried then, too, but he called me at eight to let me know he was fine and not to fret. Do you know why he was so late, Laurie?"

Laurie shook her head. She had never heard this story before. She watched in amazement as her mother's eyes filled with tears.

"Because he had to walk. That's why he was so late getting home. He'd spent everything except his train fare on lunch, and then I'd seen those paddleboats and he'd spent his train fare, too. He gave me that experience, then he walked home for two hours to pay for it."

Laurie sniffed back tears. "You've never told me that before."

"I should have. Guy has a lot of good qualities, Laurie, but he was never the kind of man who'd walk home for anybody."

Her mother squeezed her hand.

"You deserve a man who is prepared to move heaven and earth for you—and you deserve to love him so much that you'll do the same in return. Don't be afraid to ask for what you want, sweetie. You're worth it. You always have been."

She squeezed Laurie's hand one last time, then let her go.

"I'm going to stop lecturing you now. But think about what I said, okay?"

Laurie slid back beneath the covers as the door closed, leaving her alone with her thoughts once again. She knew what her mother was suggesting in her not-so-subtle way—that Laurie be open to the possibility of something developing with Adam. That she not simply rule him out of her life because the reality of pursuing a relationship with her would mean great change on his behalf.

Her mother had no idea, of course, that things had already progressed way beyond a few heated glances and a bit of flirting between the two of them. She and Adam had shared a beautiful, perfect moment this afternoon, exploring a connection that had existed from the moment they first set eyes on each other. But it had been a stolen moment, a moment out of time, a moment removed from the realities of both their lives.

Whatever she might be feeling, whatever she hoped *he* might be feeling, it seemed fanciful in the extreme to imagine that it might be the beginnings of something even more wonderful. What were the odds, after all, that four days of intensity with a wonderful man were just the prelude to a lifetime of love and happiness?

You will never know if you don't try.

No surprise that the voice in her head spoke with her mother's voice.

She squeezed her eyes tightly shut. She'd never thought of herself as a coward before, but the prospect of walking across the hallway, knocking on Adam's door and telling him how she felt and what she wanted made her stomach dip with panicky fear.

You're worth it. You always have been.

Laurie wanted to believe her mother, she really did. But the truth was that Guy's betrayal had shaken her to her very foundations. It wasn't simply that she hadn't noticed him slipping away from her, it was that he'd valued their relationship—*her*—so poorly that he hadn't even tried to save their marriage when he'd felt himself drifting. He'd known and loved her since she was twenty-one years old. No one on earth knew her better, including her mother. And he'd walked away from her without a second glance.

It was impossible not to doubt herself after he'd abandoned her and all they'd built together so easily. She'd be superhuman if she didn't.

But the question wasn't about what had happened in the past. The question she was agonizing over was about her future. About the shape the rest of her life might take. About the man who might share it with her—if she had the courage to ask him for what she wanted.

She pressed the flats of her fingers against her eyelids.

Then she took a deep breath and swung her legs over the edge of the bed and stood.

Because she'd never been a coward.

Ready or not, Adam Hunter, here I come.

ADAM ADJUSTED THE VOLUME on his laptop.

"Sorry, Syd, I couldn't quite hear you. There's an echo at this end," he said.

The young woman on his computer screen rolled her eyes.

"Don't make me say it again, Adam. You know I hate that sentimental crap," she said.

He laughed. "Seriously, the line dropped out a little."

That was the problem with Skype sometimes, but it was still an invaluable way to keep in contact with what was happening on the other side of the world. Some might even say it was a game changer. He was hoping it might be for him, anyway.

A knock sounded at his door. He glanced over his shoulder, then faced Syd again.

"Gotta go, Syd. Get back to me with your thoughts ASAP, okay?"

"Sure. But you already know my answer."

"I want you to be sure. This has to work for everyone."

"Sure, boss man."

She ended the call and Adam stood and strode to the door.

It was Laurie, of course. He'd been about to go find her, but it made sense that she'd come looking for him. The connection between them worked both ways, after all.

"Can I come in?" she asked.

She was wearing a pair of blue-and-green-striped pajamas and her hair was mussed. He wanted to haul her into his arms and kiss her, but he settled for stepping to one side and waving her into the room. There would be time for hauling and kissing later. First, there were some things they needed to discuss.

She glanced quickly around his room, then faced him, her hands finding each other at her waist. He was reminded of the other time she'd come to his room and how she'd worked herself up to ask him to reconsider staying at her mother's house.

She took a deep breath and he was man enough to notice the way the action strained the buttons of her pajama top.

He tightened his focus. This was important. He could see how important it was by how tense Laurie was—and if it was important to her, it was important to him.

To them.

"I know we've only known each other a few days. I know it's an impossible situation and that maybe I'm misinterpreting here and reading too much into what's happened and what's been said. I know there are about a million reasons why this is too hard and too crazy. But I wanted to ask you… To tell you…"

She pressed her hands flat against her belly. He could hear the quaver in her voice.

"I don't want this to be everything," she finally said. "I want more. I want…I want to see how far and deep this thing goes between us. I want to know if what I'm feeling is real."

She stopped speaking, her gaze pinned to his face. He could see the uncertainty in her eyes, the fear. It just about killed him to know that she still wasn't sure of him. After what had happened between them this afternoon, he'd been confident she knew she was important to him, that this wasn't a game or simply a way to pass time for him.

He understood her divorce had wounded her. That her ex had hurt her. He'd intended to take it slowly, to ease into things because he knew she had reason to be cautious. Her children, her recent history, their situation—there were lots of reasons why it made sense to move slowly.

But he'd never pulled his punches with her and he wasn't about to start now.

"Laurie, I love you," he said boldly. "I don't care how many days it has or hasn't been, I've been waiting my whole life to feel this way about a woman and I know it's real."

Then he closed the distance that separated them and pulled her into his arms. He kissed her, loving the way she clung to him even though he knew she had questions she still needed answering. Their bodies knew this was right, even if their minds were more wary.

He ended the kiss, feathering his lips across her cheekbone before drawing back enough to see her face.

"I've been speaking to my team back in Melbourne. My second in command, Syd, has been running the trust and the building business while I'm gone. She's happy to keep doing that for another four weeks. So I figured, if you're willing, I'll go back to wherever home is for you once the party is over, find a hotel and spend the next month proving to you that this thing between us is real."

Laurie was looking a little shell-shocked. As though she couldn't quite believe what she was hearing.

"But—" she said.

He knew what she was thinking. His business, the trust... He had a lot of stuff to sort out in order to pick up his life and move to America.

"None of it matters," he said simply. "The trust does good work, but it's established now. With good people in key positions, it will run itself. And there's no reason why the philosophy of the trust won't travel. There are needy kids everywhere."

"It's a lot to give up."

"No, it isn't."

"It is. It's a life, your life, and there's so much we don't know about each other. You don't know that I get cranky when I'm hungry and that I'm secretly addicted to bad reality TV shows. You have no idea that I steal the quilt in winter or that I always, always leave the top off the toothpaste tube. And I can be bossy and demanding and I know I have a problem with being a perfectionist—"

"I don't care."

"But you might. You might find that some of the things you don't know about me are deal breakers."

She was vibrating with anxiety and uncertainty, her body tense in his arms. He narrowed his eyes. Was he reading this wrong? Had he freaked her out with his declaration, offered her too much too soon? Was she five steps behind him, thinking only about the next date and not about the happily-ever-after stuff that had tormented him since the first moment he looked into her dusky-blue eyes?

"There's only one deal breaker for me, Laurie. What do *you* want?"

A small, worried crease appeared between her eyebrows.

"I want to believe in you, in this, so much. But I'm scared, Adam."

"Then we'll take it slow. I'm not going anywhere."

She stared at him for a long, drawn out beat, gazing up into his face with a searching intensity. He didn't waver. Not for a second. Slowly, her face relaxed and he saw the beginnings of a smile in her eyes.

"I think I'm going to hold you to that," she said. "Not the slow part, because slow doesn't seem to be our style. But the 'not going anywhere' part I like. I like it a lot."

The tension in his shoulders relaxed. He lowered his head to kiss her. She cupped his face with her hands and he could feel the depth of feeling and intensity she poured into the contact. She may not be able to say it yet, but—

"I love you, Adam," she said. "Even though it doesn't seem possible. But it feels real. *This* feels real."

"It is real." He picked up her hand and placed it over his heart. "It's as real as both of us. And it's the best thing that's ever happened to me."

She smiled, a teasing light coming into her eyes.

"I thought the best thing that ever happened to you was this afternoon?"

A slow grin spread across his face.

"That was pretty good, I've got to admit."

"Pretty good? That wasn't the impression you gave me at the time. I think you said the word *unbelievable* at one point."

"I did. But I think we can do better."

She raised her eyebrows. "Better? Better than *unbelievable?*"

"Hell, yeah. In fact, I'm going to consider it a personal challenge."

He started walking her backward, toward the bed.

There were still details to iron out, but they could wait. Right now, he wanted to lay skin to skin with her and simply hold her while he absorbed the full import of what they'd decided between them.

She loved him. They were going to do this. His life, fulfilling and challenging as it had always been, had instantly taken on a new richness and meaning.

He was no longer alone.

She fell onto her back as her knees hit the edge of the bed. He lowered himself over her, staring into her eyes. She stared back, the smile slowly fading from her lips.

"Pinch me," she said. "I need to know this is really happening, that you're not just some amazing, wonderful, generous figment of my imagination."

He brushed the hair off her forehead, traced the arc of one of her eyebrows with his thumb.

"I think we can to better than a pinch," he said.

Then he proceeded to show her.

It was very early the next morning when Laurie slipped from Adam's bed and pulled on her pajamas in the dim predawn light. It had been an incredible night, definitely one for the history books, but she wanted to wait awhile before she sprang the reality of her relationship with Adam on her mother and Nana and the rest of the household.

After a night in his arms, there were precious few doubts left in her mind, but she appreciated that her loved ones might not see the situation in exactly the same light. Once they had a chance to know Adam fully, however, they would love him the way she did. She was sure of it.

She stilled, her pajama top half-buttoned. She *did* love him. Incredible and impossible as it might seem. She had tumbled headfirst into love with him almost from the first moment, even though she'd been too scared and too gun-shy to acknowledge it.

Fortunately, Adam was a man who wasn't afraid of a challenge. She had a feeling they'd need that tenacity over the next few months.

She finished dressing, but rather than head straight for the door, she lingered beside the bed, staring down at his sleeping form. His shoulders were so broad, his body so brown and strong. And yet he was a gentle lover, infinitely patient and tender.

She reached out and rested her hand on his shoulder, just to feel the warmth of his skin beneath her hand.

This was really happening. This amazing joy bubbling up inside her was real.

She bent, pressing a kiss to his shoulder and turned for the door. She eased it open, then went to great pains to ease it quietly closed again, releasing the latch as gently as possible. Satisfied she hadn't woken Adam, she turned to cross to her room.

And nearly fell over her mother in her wheelchair.

That was the problem with wheels—they didn't make a sound on carpet.

"Mom." She could feel heat rushing into her face. Talk about busted.

"Good morning." Her mother's gaze slid over her shoulder to Adam's bedroom door. "Or should I say good night…?"

There was a definite twinkle in her mother's eye.

"Adam's going to stay on awhile. He's going to come back to Vineland with me for a month, stay somewhere nearby."

"Sounds serious." Her mother's gaze was searching.

"It is."

She said it simply, easily. She'd been worried she might sound defensive, but she didn't feel defensive. She felt…happy. Excited. Hopeful.

Loved.

Her mother smiled. "You don't have to say any more. I can see it in your eyes. I'm so pleased, Laurie."

Laurie squeezed her mother's arm. Then she gave her a cheeky smile.

"Since I've already been rumbled…" She turned back toward Adam's room. "In for a penny…"

Her mother's soft laughter followed her as she slipped back into Adam's room. Shedding her clothes quickly, she slid back into the bed beside him, wrapping her arm around his waist, shaping her body to the curve of his back.

He sighed and murmured something in his sleep. Then he rolled over and tucked her tightly against his side, pressing a kiss to her forehead.

She closed her eyes.

Strange how home could be a person, and not just a place.

A smile on her lips, she drifted into sleep.

* * * * *

Thanks to Kasey Michaels and Sarah Mayberry.
You were always there to brainstorm,
answer a question or give advice.
I'm grateful for the opportunity to
work with such generous women who also
happen to be incredibly talented writers.

ALL OUR TOMORROWS

Teresa Southwick

CHAPTER ONE

No good deed goes unpunished.

Kinsey McKeever had no idea where that saying came from, but she was living proof that it was true.

When Peggy Longwood broke her foot, Kinsey had immediately come to Cape May from her apartment in North Jersey. Her career was in physical therapy and she could help Peggy recover after the cast came off, which had taken longer than predicted because of her other health issue. And that's why Kinsey had cleared her schedule to be there from day one of the foot fiasco. Her friend and mentor was on dialysis and if a kidney didn't become available soon...

Kinsey refused to think about that possibility. She'd never looked very far into the future, always too worried about problems in the present. Now was no exception.

For the past five weeks she'd lived in the main house on the Longwood estate, pitching in for Peggy wherever she could. With the reunion about a week away and family soon to arrive, she'd been asked to move into the guesthouse where Peggy's son, David, was currently living. During summers and school vacations from the time she was sixteen until graduating from college, Kinsey had worked for his mother. And for part of that time she'd had a crush on him.

A crush was all she'd let herself feel until he'd kissed her, a full-body contact, rock-her-world kiss. It was late at night and they were alone in the kitchen. Their shoulders brushed and the next thing she knew she was in his arms, his mouth setting her on fire. She would have been his for the taking but he didn't take her.

He pulled away first, saying something about how young she was and how that would be taking advantage. She'd been in and out of too many foster homes not to get the message that he just hadn't wanted her. After that he barely acknowledged her when they were in the same room. Now they would be under the same roof.

For any other woman that would be the opposite of punishment, but not for Kinsey. Maybe he'd forgotten all about that kiss. One could hope. Or one could pretend one didn't remember.

She wheeled her bag onto the porch, took a deep breath and knocked on the door, then blew out a long breath. After several moments it opened and he was standing there.

David Longwood.

That crushing sensation in her chest had nothing to do with her heart. Not this time. Not again. She was a grown woman in complete control of her own life, her own destiny. She had a career she loved and was not dependent on anyone. Physical therapy was what she did, and it was her job to make sure his mother was strong enough for her birthday party/family reunion. She owed Peggy Longwood more than it was possible to repay in a lifetime. If this was where the woman wanted her to stay, this was where she would stay. And she would make it work.

"Hi, David."

He nodded. "Kinsey."

There was no welcoming smile, which should have detracted from his appeal, so she found it completely unfair that she only wanted him more. This would be much easier if he looked like a troll, she thought. Tall, dark and handsome, was a cliché, but he was all of that and more. Hollywood had lost leading man material when he'd become an attorney.

Brilliant and successful in mergers and acquisitions, he didn't acquire and merge quite so successfully in his personal life. Or so she'd heard. She had no independent confirmation of the rumor—and that wasn't likely to change.

She flashed her brightest smile. It was the one she'd perfected as a child going from one temporary home to another in the New Jersey foster care system. The expression was designed to charm, to show she was friendly, eager to please and easy to get along with. "Peggy said she called to let you know I was coming—"

"Right. She did. I'll get that for you," he said, as she started to wheel her bag over the threshold. Brushing her hand aside, he hefted the luggage. "Is this all you have?"

"That's it." Traveling light was hardwired into her. A kid in the system never accumulated more than would fit into a plastic trash bag. At least now she had actual luggage.

David set her suitcase down in the ceramic-tiled entry. After working for Peggy Longwood during her school years, Kinsey knew the layout of the cottage. Just around the corner from where they stood was the kitchen, including bay window, nook and center island. The great room with overstuffed sofas and a big, flat-screen TV was across from it. Down the hall were two bedrooms, each with their own bath, separated by an open study area which housed a desk and was lined with bookshelves.

"How's my mother?" he asked. "Will her foot hold up to the beating she's going to put it through during the party?"

"Peggy is a force of nature and not very good at slowing down."

"Tell me something I don't know."

Now he smiled and she was completely dazzled. It was like hitting a really big speed bump on the Garden State Parkway, except instead of losing her car's transmission, only her power of speech had gone missing.

Kinsey cleared her throat. "Peggy wanted to run a marathon as soon as the cast came off. Mobility in the foot and ankle is coming back, but not fast enough as far as she's concerned."

He was all business again but worry about his mother's condition shadowed his eyes. "This family reunion means a lot to her and Aunt Tory."

"There's every indication it will be a rousing success if escalating attendance is anything to go by."

"I know what you mean. We've got relatives coming out of the woodwork." He rested his hands on his hips, brushing back the gray suit jacket. The tailored white dress shirt fit his upper body to a T. The red power tie was, well, powerful. "How do you feel about getting bounced from the big house?"

"I'm okay with it." The bigger question was how he felt about the bounce that had landed her in his lap. "Peggy didn't want to bump me, but Cousin Corinne is frail and she wanted her in the main house so help would be close if she needs it. Plus, she has pulmonary issues and your mother wants the room thoroughly cleaned because of Atlas."

"What did Laurie's dog do?" David asked.

"Nothing. Except he sheds. Atlas feels awful about it, and has been trying alternative methods to make it stop, but so far nothing is working." And neither was her attempt to make him smile again. "There was some concern that dog hair or dander could complicate Cousin Corinne's breathing problems."

"Say that five times fast," he muttered.

"Yeah." Kinsey grinned. "Anyway, Peggy's going to have the air ducts cleaned and every square inch of it de-Atlased. She felt with all of that invasive stuff going on I'd be more comfortable here with you."

There'd been no politically correct way to tell David's mother she would rather chew her arm off than move in with him. So, here she was. And her goal was to blend in and not draw attention to herself, exactly what she'd tried to do in every new foster home, not always successfully.

"You won't even know I'm here," she promised.

"If you say so."

She studied his expression, trying to figure out what that meant, and realized the suit and red power tie meant he was going to work. "You're not off today, are you? Even though it's Saturday."

"No rest for the wicked."

He looked completely serious which was just wrong. If that wicked part were true, he'd have taken advantage of a young girl with a crush on him. He hadn't done that. It was small comfort to her bruised dignity, but he was a good man.

When he picked up her suitcase and headed around the corner, Kinsey followed. For a few moments the superior view of his broad back almost kept her from noticing that he was going the wrong way.

"Wait, David, that's not where I'm supposed to go."

He glanced over his shoulder, but didn't stop. "What?"

"I'll take the other room."

"No, you won't." He set her bag down in the guesthouse master bedroom where he'd been staying. "This is bigger and more comfortable."

"But I don't want to put you out."

"You're not. I'm condensing my use of space. The other room is storage really. I've got boxes of stuff in there from when I moved out of…the other house." It didn't seem possible for him to be more serious, but that's what happened when his eyes darkened. "Anyway, I've been meaning to go through everything, but somehow I haven't gotten around to it."

"Time flies when you're having fun." Although he didn't look as if he was having a whole lot of fun. Fun guys didn't usually wear a suit and tie on Saturday.

"So, it's settled," he said, neither confirming nor denying. "You sleep here."

"I can't."

"I insist."

"This is your home, David. I'm only staying for another week." After the reunion, she'd be out of there. "The other room is perfectly fine."

"Do you know my mother? Do you really expect me to tell her that you're sleeping in a glorified storage unit?" He shook his head. "Not happening. Besides, I was raised to be a gentleman."

"And I was raised to go with the flow. That means I'm not taking your room."

"Look, I'm hardly ever here." A muscle bunched in his jaw when he glanced at his watch. "And I'm late for a meeting so this discussion is over and I win."

"Who works on Saturday?" The question became rhetorical the moment he walked out the door.

Kinsey rolled her suitcase out of his room and into the other one. He'd been telling the truth about the stacks of boxes; one entire wall was filled from floor to ceiling with them. There was a rumor circulating through the estate staff that he'd moved back here six months ago after a bad breakup. Maybe he'd buried himself in work because of it.

She left her suitcase at the foot of the double bed and went to the linen closet where she knew the clean bedding was kept. A place to sleep was all she needed.

That was all she'd ever let herself need. The best part of being in control of one's destiny was not to clutter your life with feelings.

IT WAS AFTER MIDNIGHT when David got home and he couldn't remember the last time he'd been so exhausted. Some of it he put on the insane hours he'd been working for the past six months. The rest was Kinsey McKeever's fault.

Ever since she was a teenager and his mother had hired her for clerical and research assistance, David had seen her when he'd come home for visits and noticed that she was a very pretty girl who instantly charmed everyone around her. Then one night he'd kissed her, a kiss that came out of nowhere and surprised the hell out of him.

Their eyes met, sparks were everywhere and bam. It was completely inappropriate considering she was barely eighteen and he was seven years older. By some miracle he'd managed to pull away. With her history of being shuffled from one foster home to another he didn't want to mess with her emotions. He didn't trust himself. Not after letting down one friend already. His buddy had paid a high price for David's failings and he wouldn't chance failing Kinsey, too.

She'd been very striking as a teenager and somewhere between then and now she'd turned into a stunner with big hazel eyes.

The effort to keep his head clear of the beautiful blonde during delicate and tense acquisition discussions had taken a toll. He might have gotten home sooner but the client insisted on a long dinner break before resuming negotiations.

Now it was late and all he wanted was sleep. The house was pitch-black and turning on the lights might disturb Kinsey. Hard-hitting negotiators and bullheaded business pit bulls didn't faze him. In fact, tough talks got his adrenaline pumping. The same could be said of Kinsey, in a completely different way—a way that definitely fazed him.

For a second during their bedroom discussion, that mouth of hers had taken his breath away. Her full, sultry, defined upper lip had been created for kissing. He knew what she tasted like from that long-ago kiss and wanted to do it again.

And thoughts like that proved he wasn't ready to see her

until his batteries were recharged with sleep. Feeling his way through the dark house, he finally angled right toward the spare bedroom. He turned the knob on the door he'd previously kept closed, to shut out the sight of moving boxes and all the bad memories associated with them.

In the unrelieved darkness, he stripped down to his boxers. With a tired sigh, he slid under the covers and rolled to his side. And that's when he touched her—unquestionably a her. The softness was very much like a breast and the shriek that followed hit a decibel level some men might not hear, but could easily bring Atlas running from the main house.

"Damn it." He sat up and fumbled for the switch on the bedside lamp. Finding it was a bloody miracle, but he did and the light clicked on.

"David—" Kinsey blinked in the sudden brightness.

His gaze automatically lowered to the chest he'd just touched. "What are you doing in here?"

"Sleeping. You?" she asked.

"You're supposed to be in the other bed—room—I meant the other room. We settled this hours ago."

"I didn't think you were serious."

"I'm always serious," he said.

"Who knew you were actually being noble? You made a grand pronouncement about winning, then walked out. Nothing was settled as far as I was concerned. Then it got late and you didn't come home, so I did what I thought was best."

She shrugged and the movement did amazingly interesting things to her breasts. They were small and firm and would fit nicely in… Wait a minute.

His ears were still ringing from her scream, which apparently had affected rational thinking. It was the only explanation for the turn his thoughts had taken.

"I'm sorry if I scared you," he said. "I take full responsibility for this misunderstanding."

"There's no reason for you to do that. It takes two. Stuff happens."

"Not to me."

One dark-blond eyebrow lifted. "You never make a mistake?"

"Hardly ever."

"Don't you ever want to throw caution to the wind and let go of being perfect?"

"I can't afford to," he answered. "You?"

"At least once a day."

She shrugged and the skinny, silky strap of her camisole slid down, leaving her smooth, tanned shoulder bare. For the second time that day she took his breath away. And this time it was more than a second. Worse, he couldn't stop himself from looking at her mouth.

And less than a heartbeat later that mouth was on his. A soft moan was trapped between their lips and he couldn't swear that it hadn't come from him. The kiss was heady and hot, full of sizzle and sin.

David lifted his hand with every intention of cupping the back of her head to make the contact of their mouths more firm, but she pulled away. Her breathing was ragged, her eyes wide with surprise.

"I think this is a personal best," she said unsteadily. "It's barely tomorrow and I've already thrown caution to the wind."

That made two of them. He held himself to a much higher standard than this, especially where Kinsey was concerned.

"I'm sorry. I shouldn't have done that."

"Oh, please. I'm a big girl."

She left out the word *now,* but the memory of that long-ago kiss was thick in the air between them. Their gazes were locked and sparks were everywhere just like the last time.

Then she did that shrug thing again, proving that she wasn't a kid anymore. Although, as far as he was concerned, after that kiss there was nothing left to prove.

Behind her he could see the packing boxes that were a constant reminder of his personal failure and knew he was hovering on the edge of another one.

David slid out of bed, his own breathing still too fast. "This is fifty kinds of wrong."

"Why?"

"It just is."

He walked out before looking at that mouth of hers that could tempt him to stay. Needing a good night's sleep more than ever, he knew the odds of that now were slim to none. He didn't want to be the latest in a long line of people to let her in then let her down. So he was backing off before making another mistake. If that kiss just now was payback, it was diabolical as hell and he deserved every bit of the mental punishment that would only compound while they shared quarters.

So much for not knowing she was there.

CHAPTER TWO

IF THIS HAD BEEN A FOSTER HOME Kinsey would be packing her bags to leave. She'd thought about that kiss into the wee hours of the morning and wasn't completely convinced that she'd made the first move. Her mouth was only a whisper away from David's and he'd looked like a man who was all work and no play. The thought had crossed her mind that he could use a little play, then someone had moved. Now she had another awkward David memory and, technically, two made it a list. With any luck this wouldn't become a pattern.

In spite of her regrets and inability to rewind and delete the incident, the sun had still come up. As the first one in the guesthouse kitchen, Kinsey felt duty bound to make the morning coffee. That attitude told her David's underwhelmed reaction to kiss number two still smarted, especially since she was almost positive he'd been as turned on as she was.

"He could use some pillow talk tutoring," she mumbled to herself. "Fifty kinds of wrong my backside."

She measured grounds into the filter, then poured water in the reservoir before pressing the on button. The drip and sizzle started almost instantly and soon the smell of coffee filled the room—a kitchen she'd always thought set a high bar for hominess.

Hanging on the walls were black-and-white drawings of the main house and the ocean, all from different perspectives and signed by David's father, Peter Longwood. He'd been a renowned architect and it was her understanding that he'd designed the estate. In her opinion, he'd done a brilliant job. And the drawings weren't bad, either. Of the two houses, she was most comfortable in the smaller one. Especially this kitchen.

A round oak table and four spindle-backed chairs filled the nook with a bay window looking out on the Atlantic Ocean. Black granite with flecks of beige topped the rectangular island and countertops. The matching stainless steel appliances were top-of-the-line. Only the best for the Longwoods. Which made her wonder why Peggy had paid any attention to her all those years ago.

They'd met at a social services event at the state home, a fundraiser combined with publicity to highlight the benefits of adopting children. For some reason Peggy Longwood had been there and seemed to like Kinsey. On the spot she'd offered her a job and it lasted through college, on weekends and vacations.

Although there was friendship, too, in Kinsey's mind she worked for the Longwoods. It was easier to make it business and just be an employee. And, by God, she would be the very *best* employee.

"And don't you forget it," she said to herself.

"Is this a private conversation or can anyone join?" David's voice came from the doorway behind her.

Oh, for Pete's sake, now he'd caught her talking to herself. Add number three to the inventory of awkward David moments. And it occurred to her that over the next week there was great potential for acquiring a very impressive list.

She turned and forced a grin, a trick she'd learned growing up. Smile no matter what and pretend everything is okay. "It's private, but exceptions can be made on a case-by-case basis."

"Coffee smells good."

"I wondered if it would get your attention." Unlike her

kiss last night, she thought. Kinsey took two mugs from the cupboard and poured coffee into them. "You're not working today?"

"No."

David was wearing khaki pants with a long-sleeved powder-blue shirt tucked into them. This, apparently, was his nod to casual. As far as casual went, it looked good on him. But she felt underdressed in her shorts and a tank top, even though this was *her* work attire. Peggy Longwood refused to be a patient and didn't tolerate scrubs when she was having physical therapy.

"It's Sunday," he added, as if that explained the fact that he wasn't working.

"The day after Saturday. Imagine that. Two days of the week that most people take off to recharge their batteries and clear their heads."

Although not in her case. Kissing David had done the exact opposite of clearing her head. In fact, her head felt more full than ever. He took the mug she handed him and sipped. No cream and sugar for him, which she found insanely charming and appealing in a rugged, manly sort of way. More stuff to fill her overly crowded mind.

He met her gaze. "Yesterday's meeting was an emergency. Acquisition talks dragged on longer than expected and the company negotiators were scheduled to leave town over the weekend."

"Emergency? Really?" She poured milk in her mug, then stirred in noncalorie sweetener. "I define an urgent situation as either open heart surgery or dead by morning. But maybe that's because I work in the health care field."

"This was a business crisis, not life and death. But people's employment is at stake." He shrugged as if that explained everything.

"Don't companies that merge also merge the existing work-force and cut jobs?"

"Sometimes. But if the merger makes the company health-ier, it can grow and create more employment opportunities."

"I never thought of it that way," she said. "Which means I wouldn't be very good at crunching numbers. Listening to party-of-the-first-part will hereafter be referred to as…"

"It's actually fascinating stuff," he said.

"If you say so." David grinned and she found it made him look incredibly fascinating, as well as dashing. That kick-started her pulse which in turn triggered her curiosity. "When I was a kid, reading was one of my favorite things. Just me and the book." No one could let her down, except maybe the author. But starting a new story was exciting, unlike the mystery of a new foster home. "Your mother's books were never a disappointment. From about the third grade through the sixth, Davy Daring was my absolute favorite storybook hero."

"The character she based on me." He set his mug on the counter, then leaned back and crossed his arms over his chest.

"He solved mysteries. Took chances. Learned lessons. Davy Daring was awesome." She'd had a little crush on literary David even before meeting the real one. And escaping into the stories had gotten her through some tough times. "Your exploits awakened in me the call to adventure. A call that will take me to Greece for several months. It's the trip I postponed when your mother broke her foot."

"The exploits she wrote about weren't mine," he said, and there was a grim sort of quality to his voice.

"Maybe not word for word, but the escapades were inspired by you."

"You're wrong about that. I'm no one's inspiration." He

shook his head. "No one should make the mistake of holding me up as a role model."

She studied him, the thick dark hair and brown eyes. His broad chest tapering to a trim waist, muscular thighs. The man could be Indiana Jones, Han Solo and Captain James T. Kirk all rolled into one. His mother was a gifted storyteller, but not all of the adventures came from her imagination. Once upon a time David must have been a high-spirited and exuberant boy with a passion for life that had fueled Peggy's imagination.

Kinsey tilted her head to the side. "There's a distinct lack of daring in the grown-up David. It's disillusioning, really. What the heck happened?"

For just a second his eyes looked haunted, hinting at something deeper, darker. Then he shrugged. "Everyone has to grow up sometime."

"And some of us grow up too soon," she shot back. "God knows I'm an example of that. In my experience it's hard to have a *child*hood in the *child* care system. That doesn't mean you give up a free spirit. I sure didn't."

"Is that what made you kiss me?"

And there it was. They were finally talking about the elephant in the room instead of just feeding it peanuts.

"We were in bed. Practically naked. Seemed like a good idea at the time." That was the best explanation she could come up with for something she didn't understand.

"Do you always act on your impulses?" There was a definite smoldering look in his eyes that he probably wasn't even aware of.

"Not always." Sometimes her whims worked out spectacularly, but in this case not so much.

Although she wasn't really sorry. In the throes of her crush, she'd wondered about David Longwood, fantasized about spending time with him. Wondered what kissing him would be like. Then she found out, learned another lesson in rejection and made herself stop fantasizing so it wouldn't hurt as much.

It never occurred to her that she'd ever get the chance to do it again. So, when the opportunity had presented itself, she'd gone with the impulse. Partly because deep down she knew there wouldn't be another shot at showing him she wasn't too young anymore. And she knew that kiss was even more spectacular than the first one.

"As it happens," she said, "I have a physical therapy session with your mother this morning."

"On Sunday?" One of his dark eyebrows raised.

"Yeah, the day after Saturday. Imagine that." She smiled. "Peggy is pushing herself because of the reunion. It's my job to make sure she doesn't push too hard and do more harm than good."

"Thanks, Kinsey. For helping her."

"It's not necessary to thank me. I'm happy to do anything for her."

She passed him on her way to the front door and the fresh, masculine scent of his cologne spiraled through her. It put a vision in her head of the two of them facing each other in bed, and she knew if opportunity presented, she would probably make the same mistake.

The problem was that she liked spontaneity, prided herself on the spunk. Only this time she could have used a little less spunk and a lot more caution because now she had to spend her last week with the Longwoods resisting David. He would probably be spending the next seven days lighting candles and praying to the gods that the wacky woman down the hall didn't attack him in his sleep.

KINSEY WISHED ALL OF HER physical therapy patients were as rewarding to work with as Peggy Longwood. The pink cast was hardly dry when she'd taught Peggy to navigate the wheelchair on the estate's marble floors, which were responsible for the foot breakage in the first place. In addition, they'd worked on how to successfully transition between the wheelchair and other surfaces such as office chair and bed.

Now that she was walking with the chic and ever-so-elegant Velcro boot, Peggy's physical therapy was moving forward. They worked in her bedroom because it was a big, comfortable area and she could sit on the bed, letting her legs dangle for an important series of exercises.

"I want five more dorsi and plantar flexions," Kinsey told her.

"And I want to be thirty years younger." Peggy was nothing if not quick with a retort.

She was a tall, thin woman with summer-sky-blue eyes. Her salt-and-pepper hair was cut short and she wore it straight, a very becoming style. Today she was wearing a pink warm-up suit for their session.

"Is this a mutiny?" Kinsey made her tone firm as she would for any client. But Peggy wasn't just anyone and wouldn't be intimidated. "Because we both know what happens to people who can't take orders that are meant for their own good."

"No, what happens?" Peggy frowned, but there was a twinkle in her eyes.

"In your case they wind up stiff and walking like a woman closer to ninety than sixty."

Sitting on the bed, Peggy wagged a warning finger. "Don't let Nana hear you say that. She's ninety and thinks she walks like a supermodel and doesn't look a day over seventy."

Kinsey laughed, then quickly put her professional face in place. "Seriously, after an injury, scar tissue forms and soft tissue contracts. It's important to stretch properly to keep from getting stiff and compromising full function."

"Okay." Peggy sighed. "Talk me through it. But you really

need to change the message on your cell phone to—Hello, you've reached Helga's House of Pain."

"I'll take that under advisement," she said, her lips twitching. "Now, slowly point your foot up toward your knee, hold it for five seconds and gradually return to starting position. Good," she said, watching the movement. "Now slowly point your toe downward and away from the knee. Hold for five seconds, then return to starting position."

Peggy was all concentration as she performed the small but important movement, so her next question caught Kinsey off guard.

"How are your sleeping arrangements working out with David in the guesthouse?"

"Fine." The answer was automatic and her tone more tense than the casual, professional one she'd intended.

"Good. I felt just terrible about asking you to move."

"Not to worry. It wasn't a problem." Moving at a moment's notice was a lesson childhood had taught Kinsey well.

"Cousin Corinne is a distant relative on my biological mother's side. And she's coming from Pennsylvania, determined not to miss out on anything. Since she's older—"

"Sixty?"

Peggy's expression turned wry. "I believe she's older than me, smarty-pants."

"It's okay. I understand. The focus is getting you back on your feet for the reunion. That's my job. It's why I'm here."

"I worry about you, Kinsey. Is David making you feel comfortable?"

"Yes." She hoped that sounded just the tiniest bit truthful because in reality it was a big fat lie.

And so the whole good deed, punishment scenario became clear. Kissing him last night had released an attraction she'd thought was safely locked away. It wasn't like her. She didn't let attraction get the upper hand. By design, her frequent travel plans and short-term assignments put the brakes on personal feelings, just the way she liked it.

Peggy was giving her an odd look. "You're sure everything is all right? If David is—"

"It's fine. As a matter of fact, David is busy acquiring and merging."

"He works too hard, just like his father." The other woman pointed her toe and held it for five seconds. "And he doesn't do well with failure no matter how many times I've told him it's just a learning experience."

"He's definitely an overachiever." Kinsey was not talking about his career.

"He wasn't always so serious. As a teenager he was pretty carefree?"

"Davy Daring?"

"Yes." Peggy smiled fondly. "But he changed. I didn't notice for a while, but looking back it started after his friend Mark was hurt in an accident. Actually the boy was being reckless—as boys sometimes tend to be—and sustained a spinal cord injury. He became a paraplegic."

"Oh, that's awful." Something like that would certainly shatter a young man's bubble of invincibility. She had a bazillion questions, but didn't have the right to ask. "So he turned into a superachiever?"

"I'm afraid Peter and I may have contributed to the pressure he puts on himself. As you know my husband was a successful architect and I had my bestselling book series. Plus our marriage was a long and happy one." For just a moment, sadness mixed with the wistful expression on her face. "I think David feels he has to walk in our footsteps—professionally and personally. Which is why he perceives his broken engagement as the worst of failures. He and Danielle had bought a house together and when the engagement ended, he walked away from it and took over the guesthouse for what was supposed to be a temporary stay. He's going to get a reputation for being peculiar. I just don't know what to do if he gets a cat. On top of that, what woman wants to date a man who lives with his mother?"

Mentally Kinsey raised her hand. "He's not actually living with you."

The other woman winced as she let her leg relax. "That's just a technicality. You know what I mean. I'm worried about him."

Kinsey thought about the moving boxes stacked up in the room where she was staying. Did David leave them there as a horrible warning or a bittersweet reminder of lost love? Neither option boded well for a rebound relationship, not that she was in the market for one.

She watched Peggy do the inversion/eversion exercise where she turned the sole of her foot outward and inward, holding each for five seconds. She'd done ultrasound therapy and electric stimulation to speed healing. Now her employer's long-term well-being was dependent on consistent exercises that could be done on her own. The sooner Kinsey got on the road again, the better off she'd be.

"You know, Peggy, you're my star patient. As much as I like being in charge of Helga's House of Pain, you don't need me. I've taught you all the exercises and as the saying goes, you just have to do it."

Peggy smiled proudly. "How can I ever thank you?"

She didn't have to, Kinsey thought. She owed this woman, not just for the job years ago, but for financial assistance in college. Peggy called it "student loans," but would never accept repayment. And, because of that kindness, Kinsey had stayed longer than she normally would for a patient.

"You're the one who did the work," she pointed out. "And you can keep it up on your own. My presence here is redundant."

"Never."

Kinsey caught the corner of her lip between her teeth. "The thing is, I've got the trip to Greece coming up soon. And I could use a little extra time to get ready."

"Are you trying to get out of the reunion?" This time Peggy's frown was real.

"Of course not." She was trying to get away from David and the feelings he'd awakened in her that could turn into something she *really* didn't want to feel.

"It's only a few more days, Kinsey. I want you to be here for the party. It's not every day a girl turns sixty, and I want my family there for the big event. You're part of my family and, as such, it's your duty to stick around and make tasteless jokes about me driving an *Old-mobile* and the deafening sounds of snaps, pops and cracks when I stand up or sit down."

"Okay, then." Kinsey smiled but her heart wasn't in it. "I'll put together my best material."

"That's my girl." Peggy reached out and squeezed her hand. "I need you to motivate me."

"In that spirit, I'll leave you with this reminder. Rotate your ankle in both directions and write the alphabet with your toes. Five times a day, missy."

"I just gave up the power in this relationship, didn't I?" Peggy grumbled good-naturedly.

"If only," Kinsey said.

This was so ironic. She'd spent her childhood hoping that the next placement would be the last and she could stay in one place. Now she was looking for a way to leave earlier than scheduled.

So the lie was right out there in the open. She was *not* okay with getting bounced from the big house into the guesthouse with David.

CHAPTER THREE

DAVID BREATHED DEEPLY, drawing in the stimulating scent. Coffee. It was the third morning in a row that he'd smelled it. Something a man could get used to, especially if it was attached to a beautiful blonde in shorts and a tank top. That's something he'd enjoyed for three days in a row, too.

He slid his tie on, then turned down the heavily starched collar of his white dress shirt, letting the sides dangle before slipping on his dark suit coat. From the Longwood estate situated right on the ocean, the highway he took to the office could be congested in the summer. People trying to get to and from the beach tended to clog the roads. He'd allowed a generous amount of time, but one never knew.

He walked past the kitchen. The smell of the gods' elixir was stronger here, almost calling out "good morning" just before he opened the front door.

"Hold on, buster."

Kinsey's voice was a mixture of sugar and spice and Scotch on the rocks. As he turned, David braced for the wallop that always accompanied his first sighting of her. She turned him inside out and a guy needed to brace for that.

"Buster? What am I? The dog?"

"Maybe." She settled her hands on slender, fantasy-inducing hips. "If you walk out that door without eating the breakfast I slaved over, you're lower than a dog."

He stared at her, all big eyes and luscious lips, then cleared his throat. "I can live with that."

Before he made it out the door, she was there, looking up at him and smelling as sweet as the temptation to walk on the wild side.

"I made enough food to feed a small army and wasting food is a sin where I come from."

A reference to growing up in the state system on the taxpayers' dime. As if he needed a reminder not to start something he might mess up. "In my world punctuality trumps everything."

"Not nutrition. As a health care professional I know this for a fact. Breakfast is the most important meal of the day, David."

"Isn't it up to me to decide whether or not I want to eat? I'm a big boy now."

For some reason the words made her smile and humor sparkled in her eyes as it turned up the corners of her mouth. "That was so *Davy Daring Runs Away from Home* of you."

"He's a fictional character. It's not me." At least it hadn't been for a long time. He'd left that reckless part of himself behind when he was a teenager.

"Be that as it may, if I remember correctly, every time Davy Daring didn't listen to his mother there was hell to pay."

"You're not my mother," he said, pointing out the obvious.

If she were, and he was feeling the way he was feeling, he'd need a lot more than a morning meal to fix him up.

It was that damn kiss.

He could have gone on ignoring the way his body hummed whenever she walked into a room if only he didn't have a very recent reminder of how good she tasted, how soft and warm her lips were. And the feel of her small, firm breasts pressed against his chest was the stuff of dreams that weren't fit for fans of the *Davy Daring* series. He couldn't seem to stop looking at her through that kiss. And it was always at the edge of his consciousness that she was sleeping just down the hall.

"I'm your mother's physical therapist. Along with anatomy and physiology classes that were part of getting licensed, I took nutrition courses. They call it *breakfast* for a reason. Break fast. Because of sleeping, your body hasn't had fuel for hours. Just as a car won't go without gasoline, your system can't function efficiently without food. Including your brain. And I can't tell you how much I hate wasting food."

She could have been reciting the phone book and he'd still have been fascinated. How cute was that slight lisp she had going on? And the sincerity and intensity she expressed reminded him that in addition to food, he hadn't had sex in a long time, either. There's a fast he'd like to break.

"I have to go. I'm going to be late for a meeting."

"Okay. Suit yourself, food waster." She folded her arms over her chest.

David almost groaned at the things that ordinary movement did to her breasts. His palms itched and fingers tingled with the desire to touch her.

While he stared her down, the aroma of fresh biscuits and bacon drifted to him and his mouth started to water. "Just out of curiosity, what's on the morning menu?"

"Hash browns, scrambled eggs, biscuits and gravy. Wheat toast if you prefer."

"Smells good."

She shrugged, but her expression was nothing if not determined. "Never underestimate the unique skills of a physical therapist."

And it would be incredibly intriguing to take those skills out for a spin. If only… But stock prices had dropped and his bargaining position for this multimillion dollar merger was stronger than ever. They were in the best possible scenario to close this deal. The only thing standing in his way was

Kinsey McKeever and what she'd cooked up in the kitchen. Her powers of persuasion made him glad she wasn't opposing counsel.

"Okay," he said, closing the front door. "Maybe five minutes couldn't hurt."

"How very Davy Daring of you," she said dryly, turning away. "Coming right up."

She meant food, but watching her walk away gave the words a whole different meaning to him. And the realization made him crabby.

In the kitchen she was filling a plate with eggs, fruit, hash browns and biscuits. She handed it to him and said, "There's a place set at the table."

"I'll stand." He watched a gleam steal into her eyes and added, "Do *not* say Davy Daring cuts off his nose to spite his face. Someone like you doesn't understand and respect deadlines and punctuality."

Her expression lost its humor and that was troubling. "Someone like me?"

"Yes. A person who kisses a man just because he happens to end up in her bed." While she was mulling that over he managed to get down several bites of egg and some hash browns.

"You know, David, someone like you doesn't recognize that being in a rut can stifle your soul."

"Someone like me?" he asked, echoing her question.

She made a plate for herself and opened the door that led to the patio. "I'll take my free spirit over your stuffed shirt any day of the week. And, just my opinion, but you might want to think about having that stick surgically removed from your ass."

For several moments David frowned at the place where she'd stood. Clearly the two of them had philosophical differences as wide as the Atlantic Ocean. They couldn't be more different, and yet he was very strongly attracted. That was out of character for him. He chose serious, focused women, not a stealth kisser.

And yet his reaction was what it was. If he had to give this a title, it would be *Davy Daring Gets Physical with the Sexy Physical Therapist*.

LATE IN THE AFTERNOON Kinsey decided a walk on the beach would be just the thing. She loved it so much, felt so lucky that Peggy had offered her a job years ago. But with every positive there was always a negative. Tit for tat. Quid pro quo. Yin and yang.

David was the yang to her yin and she needed a walk on the beach to clear her head of him. Someone like *her?* What was that about? And why had she been so pleased that the smell of her cooking had changed his mind about skipping breakfast? The whole "way to a man's heart through his stomach" thing didn't wash because she didn't want his heart. Good thing since he didn't approve of her.

She tied the arms of a sweatshirt around her waist, kicked off her flip-flops and opened the front door. David was standing there with a briefcase in his hand, obviously just home from work. She hadn't heard his car.

"Hi," he said. "Going somewhere?"

"For a walk."

"You know, stretching my legs would feel good. Traffic was a nightmare. I feel like I've been in the car for a year. Want some company?"

"Suit yourself. It's a big beach." Barefoot, she went out on the porch. After setting his briefcase inside, he closed the door and fell into step beside her.

In minutes they were trudging over the pristine white sand, easier for her since she wasn't doing it in expensive, black, leather wing tips. Or a suit and tie.

The sun was low in the sky, turning the wisps of clouds pink and orange. A stiff breeze blew her hair away from her face and made David's striped, silk tie flap around.

He stood on the hard-packed sand at the ocean's edge, inches away from where each wave crept up onto the shore. Taking a deep breath he said, "I can't remember the last time I strolled on the beach at sunset."

"That's a crime," she said. "It's practically right outside your door and you have no appreciation."

"I appreciate the hell out of it. It's time I don't have."

"You should make time." Kinsey turned into the wind and started to walk, her feet in the water.

"I have responsibilities with my job."

"So do I. But there's more to life than work."

"You make it sound like an excuse," he protested.

"No. Work is necessary. Affluence is your excuse. You're so busy accumulating more affluence, you only have time to smell the roses. You don't stop to pick them. And that smacks of taking this wonderful opportunity for granted."

"Oh? And what is it about your physical therapy training that makes you an expert in psychology?"

"That was defensive, sorry," she said, sliding a glance up at him. "I wasn't being critical, just realistic. You've never known anything different—there's always been money. That's not how I grew up."

"How did you?" he asked.

"The New Jersey foster care system and children's services," she snapped. "You know all about that. It's not a secret."

If there was pity in his eyes, it didn't show because the setting sun was shining directly into them. "I meant what happened to your family? Your mother and father?"

"That's a good question and no one knows the answer, including me. I'm told that someone found me as a newborn on the steps of a building at the corner of Kinsey and McKeever Streets. As an infant I had medical issues that scared people off so I wasn't adopted. I outgrew them, but it's more difficult to find permanent homes for older children. I went to a series of foster homes with stopovers in the state facility when there was no other alternative."

"That's a lot of moving around."

"It was." She hated talking about it because usually the person listening felt the need to be sorry. She was grateful that he didn't say the words. "I like to think of it as basic training for my love of traveling. I plan to see the world."

David slid his hands into the pockets of his slacks. "How is it I didn't know this about you?"

"Need to know, and you didn't?" She shrugged. "You were in law school and not around much when I started working here for your mother. Why would she discuss the hired help with you?"

"Mom doesn't think of you that way."

"It doesn't matter." That was only a small lie. "My past doesn't define me."

"You're wrong about that." He stopped and looked down at her. "It defines you in every positive way. You could so easily have been a tragic statistic, but you're not. You have a career and a life. I admire you, Kinsey."

"Thank you, David."

This conversation was heavy and too personal, she thought. Couldn't have that. She was about to jog off and leave him behind, but remembered the flat, tired, depleted expression in his eyes when she'd opened the guesthouse door and found him there. It's why she hadn't been able to tell him not to walk with her. He needed some fun. ASAP.

She bent and cupped her hands in the water, then tossed it at him.

"Hey," he protested. "This is an expensive suit."

"One that belongs in the boardroom, not the beach." She scooped up more water and let it fly, catching him in the face before he could jump back.

His gaze narrowed just before he moved toward her. Kinsey backed away into water up to her knees. "Now what, hotshot?"

"I think I'm going to use my affluence to buy another suit." He pursued her into the surf, then reached down with the side of his hand and sent a wave of water over her.

She turned, but his counterattack got her pretty good from the waist up. "Them's fightin' words," she warned.

"Bring it."

When she laughed, his sneak attack hit her in the face and the battle was on. She splashed him as fast and furiously as possible. But his hands were bigger and sheer volume did more damage as he moved steadily closer. She stopped to push her dripping hair out of her eyes and David grabbed her upper arms, pulling her against him.

Both of them were soaked to the skin and breathing hard. The twilight wrapped lovely purple and midnight-blue arms around them and suddenly the flat, tired expression was no longer in his eyes. They were full of heat and challenge. Awareness shot through her as he slowly pulled her to her toes, closer to his mouth. He was going to kiss her.

Part of her said *bring it*. The other street smart part said *not so fast*. A third kiss was like starting a pattern to personal attachment and she couldn't do that.

"Race you back to the house. Loser cleans the bathroom." She broke free of his hands and took off up the beach, running as fast as she could. Running for her life.

It was true what they said about opposites. She and David couldn't be more different, but there was definitely an attraction. An undeniable spark. But acting on it would be worse than stupid.

She didn't stay in one place long enough to be a forever-after kind of girl. Being his rebound relationship could do what growing up without a family of her own had not. Turn her into a tragic statistic for a sad article in a women's magazine.

CHAPTER FOUR

DAVID WALKED BESIDE KINSEY on the way to his mother's for dinner. And they were late, thanks to her starting a water war. "Just for the record, you wouldn't have won that race back to the house except my soaking wet leather shoes slowed me down."

Kinsey slid him a saucy, challenging look. "Since when does Davy Daring make excuses?"

"Since he got beat by a girl."

A girl he'd almost kissed in the ocean. The same girl who'd annihilated a very expensive suit, tie and shoes. A girl he wanted to kiss even now, in spite of the fact that they were late. They stopped at the main house's front door and the glow from the porch light made her look radiant. It was all he could do not to take her in his arms right there.

Kinsey glanced up. "Does my hair look okay?"

David liked the fact that it had only taken her fifteen minutes to clean up and put on jeans and a T-shirt with a navy blue hoodie over it. She'd pulled her wet hair into a sassy, sophisticated ponytail and he liked that, too.

"No one will know that just a little while ago you were getting hammered in the battle of the Atlantic—a battle you started, by the way."

"Oh, please. I had you and we both know it."

"Hardly."

It was awareness that he'd planned to kiss her that had sent her into retreat. That's what he knew.

Before she could retort as he could feel she desperately wanted to do, David opened the front door and called out, "Mom? Company's here."

"In the dining room. You're late," his mother called back.

When they walked into the room, Eugenia Babcock was ladling split pea soup from a tureen. The housekeeper stared at them for several moments, then muttered, "Looks like you two could use something warm."

"Kinsey, sit on this side and, David, you're here." His mother was at the head of the table and they both took the seats she indicated on either side of her. Her gaze narrowed on each of them, but it was curiosity more than disapproval. "So, what have you two been up to?"

"Just a walk on the beach," Kinsey answered, then quickly changed the subject. "How was your day?"

Way to deflect, David thought appreciatively.

Peggy dipped her spoon in the soup. "I had a lovely day, dear, after you got finished abusing me."

"I'm the best part of your day," Kinsey countered. "Deny the truth if it makes you feel better, but we'd both know it's a big fib."

"I cannot tell a lie." Peggy smiled. "You do lift my spirits."

In spite of the light mood there were dark circles under his mother's eyes, a telltale sign of her fight for life. They'd found out a while ago that his sister, Laurie, was a match, but his mother had flatly refused the kidney, believing that could endanger her daughter.

David had been bitterly disappointed that he wasn't a match. Negotiating was what he did and he'd have found the words to convince her to take his kidney and save her life. But Peggy Longwood didn't easily give in to weakness and he wouldn't spoil her good mood now. Given the banter with Kinsey, he knew it was safe to talk about the recent injury.

"How's the foot, Mom?" David took a spoonful of hot soup that tasted so much better than it looked.

"Better every day. It's made all the difference having my own physical therapist here. I was so upset when I slipped on that damn marble floor in the entryway. Even though your sister has taken care of all the event details, I was afraid the accident would spoil my reunion experience. But I'm moving around pretty well, if I do say so myself."

"Where is Laurie?" he asked.

"Adam took her out to dinner. And your aunt Tory is out with Sam." Peggy smiled fondly. "The newlyweds had talked about seeing a movie, but if you ask me, I think they're parked somewhere having car sex."

"Mom!"

"What?" The innocent look didn't fool him. "David, I never get tired of setting you up. It's just too easy to get a spectacular reaction from you."

Kinsey held up her hand and the two women high-fived. "Good one, Peggy."

"Has anyone ever told you guys that two against one isn't fair?"

His mother looked at Kinsey and they both answered at the same time. "No."

What really wasn't fair, he thought, was a defenseless baby girl abandoned on a street corner. Going from home to home and being raised by strangers. Against the odds, Kinsey McKeever was a charming, bright, beautiful and successful woman. He wasn't so sure he agreed with her shoot-from-the-hip, leap-before-looking style, but he liked her.

And there was no denying that he was incredibly attracted to her. He had a do-over list, things in his life that he wished he'd handled differently, and right at the top was that kiss in her bed. He'd retreated and, even though he was protecting her, it was a regret that wouldn't go away.

After dinner, Eugenia served dessert and coffee. While they ate, Peggy looked from Kinsey to David. "So, this is the last quiet night before people start arriving for the reunion. Everyone else has abandoned me, what are you two doing?"

Kinsey was just taking a sip of coffee and nearly choked. When she was finished coughing, she said, "What makes you think there's an 'us two'?"

"I don't know." Peggy shrugged. "Maybe because you both were late for dinner and came in with wet hair."

"That's a leap, Mom." He noticed the shameless expression on Peggy's face. Worse, he knew her. "No more car sex comments, please. I'm still impressionable and it could send me into therapy for the rest of my life."

"As much as it pains me, I'll be good," Peggy promised. But her dramatic sigh said it took a toll. "As you lawyers are so fond of saying, let me rephrase. Kinsey, do you have plans for the evening?"

"As a matter of fact…I'm going to the tavern in town. It's karaoke night. Always entertaining."

"Do you get up and sing?" David asked.

"Of course. That's half the fun."

David wasn't so sure. "Don't tell me. The other half is pointing and laughing at everyone who can't carry a tune in a bucket."

"Exactly." Kinsey gave him a look as sassy as her ponytail. "You should try it sometime."

"I'm not sure making a spectacle of myself is what I'd call fun."

"David, you should go. Give it a try," his mother urged. "It might just be a good time."

He had every intention of saying no, that he had work to do. Then he looked at Kinsey and saw challenge mixing with laughter in her eyes. It was a powerful combination and astonishingly effective.

"You're right, Mom. I should give it a try." And by *it* he meant Kinsey.

THIRTY MINUTES LATER Kinsey and David walked into O'Toole's. It was a jeans, sneakers and T-shirt kind of place filled with summer tourists and vacationers. He stood out like a fly in milk wearing his long-sleeved shirt with the buttoned down collar and perfectly pressed slacks. Loafers, with tassels, completed his too-serious look.

They headed for the one empty table in the place in a back corner. A woman, Molly, was singing "The Wind Beneath My Wings." The wooden tables and chairs were close together, and as they squeezed by, everyone greeted Kinsey by name and looked curiously at David. This was the first time she'd come in with a guy.

When they sat down, a waitress stopped. "Hi, Kinsey. The usual?"

"Sounds good."

David said, "I'll have what she's having."

"Two beers. Tap. Coming right up," she shouted over the singing.

Moments later the song ended and the crowd applauded enthusiastically, though the performance was pitchy and out of tune. But Molly smiled and held out the mic to Kinsey.

Kinsey shook her head. "I don't want to take anyone's turn."

"Anyone mind if Kinsey goes?"

The crowd spontaneously started chanting her name and she looked at David and shrugged before walking up to take the microphone. Someone in the back shouted out, "What city are you singing?"

Kinsey flipped through the catalog of choices then entered the code. "'I Left My Heart in San Francisco.'"

Nerves jumped in her stomach—that didn't usually happen. The difference tonight was David. She could tolerate pointing and laughing from anyone but him and didn't like it one bit that she cared so much what he thought. So she tried to forget he was there, watching her so intently. She focused on getting the familiar words and melody in sync and as loud as possible. When she sang the last word, whistling, cheering and clapping filled the silence.

Before she could hand off the mic, someone at the next table pointed to David and hollered, "Duet."

"No," he said emphatically, but the demand only increased in volume.

Kinsey wasn't about to let him off the hook. That move in the ocean earlier, when he'd almost kissed her had turned her inside out. And she didn't like knowing that his positive opinion mattered. So now it was his turn.

She moved close and the scent of his spicy cologne filled her head when she leaned over to whisper in his ear. "They're not going to let you out of it," she warned. "Come on. Davy Daring would love being the center of attention. It's not brain surgery or rocket science. You don't have to be perfect. This is what's called having fun. Maybe you've heard of it. And laughter. They say that's the best medicine."

He shook his head and glared. "I will probably never forgive you for this."

"I can live with that."

When she'd tugged him onstage, someone called out, "What city?"

She said to him, "I always choose a song about a place. I'm the token travelin' girl."

"What about 'New York, New York'?"

"I love that one."

The beginning of the song started too low for her pathetically limited vocal range and she was no Frank Sinatra. Or Liza Minnelli. But David nailed it and only got better. Kinsey motioned to the crowd and encouraged everyone to join in. By the time they got to the last line, "It's up to you, New York, New York," everyone in the place was singing at the top of their lungs.

David grabbed her hand and together they took a bow as if they'd been doing it for years. She put the hand mic on the stool and they walked the few steps to their table to sit out the thirty-minute break.

He took a sip of his beer. "That was fun."

"Told you."

"Is there anyone in this place you don't know?"

She scanned the room. "Probably."

"You walk in and no one is a stranger." He glanced around at the dark wood walls covered with pictures, framed needle-point sayings, shamrocks and the Irish flag. "I grew up a mile from here and don't know anyone."

"It happens," she said. "So you don't feel like a spectacle?"

"Only because the crowd favorite took pity on me and had my back." He grinned that drop-dead gorgeous David Longwood grin. "I can't remember when I've had such a good time."

Six months ago he'd been in a long-term relationship. There must have been some good times. "What did you and what's-her-name do for fun?"

"Danielle?" His expression was unreadable, as if he were deliberately suppressing painful memories. "Dinner. Movies. Plays. Museums. Nothing like this. Nothing so carefree."

"Sounds to me like you dodged a bullet. It's probably a good thing you called off the engagement."

"I didn't."

She waited for him to elaborate, but that was all he said. And it was darned frustrating because she wanted to know everything. And that was darned annoying. Details of his romantic past shouldn't have mattered to her any more than his opinion of her karaoke skills. The problem was it was all beginning to matter too much.

"Tell me she didn't break up in a text message," she said.

"She'd rather text than talk." He shrugged.

"Wow. That just gave me a warm fuzzy."

"A lot of people do that," he said defensively, then looked at her as if he were bracing himself. "Go ahead. Let me have it. Point and laugh."

"What?"

"I expected something more to the effect of the real Davy Daring doesn't get dumped."

"I wasn't thinking that at all."

"No?" He drank the last of his beer.

"No." Kinsey turned her nearly full glass. "As well as being Danielle Dull and no fun at all, your ex is an idiot for letting you go."

"Really?"

"Now you're fishing for compliments."

"No. I'd rather not talk about it."

That just made her want to know more. Kinsey could oblige with more compliments if he would tell her what happened, but the sadness in his eyes told her he still had feelings for that idiot who'd ended the engagement. Maybe not talking about it was for the best. Kinsey didn't want him to see any more than she'd already revealed. She didn't want him to see how much she liked him now, how much she'd always liked him and how much she could *really* like him if she wasn't careful.

CHAPTER FIVE

THE NEXT DAY DAVID CANCELLED all his appointments for the rest of the week. His secretary couldn't have sounded more shocked if he'd said he was moving to Micronesia to start a scuba diving business. The decision to take time off had nothing to do with being out until 2:00 a.m. with Kinsey McKeever. It was about taking a couple days off to spend time with his family.

Kinsey didn't have one, at least not biologically, but she made her own, judging by the way everyone at O'Toole's had embraced her last night. Maybe that warmth was contagious because he wanted to embrace her, too.

After making his phone calls, he took a deep breath and realized there was no smell of coffee or food. Further investigation revealed the guesthouse was empty—except for him. Funny, it hadn't felt empty when he'd moved back after his engagement fell apart. It hadn't felt empty until just now, when he couldn't find Kinsey.

He walked outside and up the path to the main house. His mother was sitting on the porch with his aunt Tory. They were having coffee and as he approached, the same expression slid into identical pairs of blue eyes. He was about to get grilled like raw meat.

"Good morning, David." Peggy tried to look casual and failed miserably.

"Morning. Aunt Tory."

His aunt, a scaled down version of his mother except for the chin-length bob, looked at his jeans. "I know times are changing, but since when do successful lawyers do 'casual Friday' on Wednesday?"

He leaned back against the white railing. "I'm not working today."

"Are you sick?" His mother put her coffee mug on the table between the two Adirondack chairs.

He knew what was coming. The hand on his forehead checking for fever. There was no denying he had one, but it wasn't the kind a thermometer could measure. The heat in him was generated by one curvy little blonde who could belt out "New York, New York" with the best of them.

"I'm not sick, Mom. Stand down."

"Then why aren't you going to work?"

"I decided to take the rest of the week off and help get everything ready for the reunion."

Peggy glanced at her sister. "That's it. I'm calling Stan Freeman."

"I don't need a doctor."

"Who said it's for you? The shock of you taking time off just might give me a heart attack." His mother looked at her sister. "He never misses work unless he's deathly ill or there's a crisis."

"He's the picture of health," Tory said. "So what's the crisis?"

"He went to a bar last night with Kinsey. Maybe he's developed a crush on my free-spirited physical therapist."

"I guess that could come under either 'deathly ill' or 'crisis.' Depending on your point of view," Tory added.

"Ladies," he said. "I'm standing right here."

"About that—" His mother nodded toward the house. "If

you're looking for Kinsey, she's inside helping Eugenia get rooms ready for people coming in tomorrow and Friday."

The door beside them opened and Kinsey was there with a pot of coffee. She saw him and smiled. "Good morning."

She didn't look like a woman who'd had very little sleep and the fresh, sunny sight of her kicked up his pulse. Especially the sight of her mouth. He knew how it felt, knew the taste and texture of it. The knowing made him want more.

"Want some? Coffee," she said, holding up the pot. Probably she'd brought it to warm up his mother's and aunt's.

"Yeah."

After she poured some for the two sisters, she met his gaze. "I'll get you a mug."

"That's okay. I'll come with you." When she went back inside, he looked at his mother. "Not a word."

"I wouldn't dream of it."

Kinsey felt more than heard David come into the kitchen. Outside, leaning against the railing, he'd looked dashing in his jeans and white cotton shirt. And so handsome, really good for a guy who'd stayed up late.

She poured coffee into a mug, then turned and handed it to him. Their fingers brushed and the swift and sudden contact was like an electrical jolt through her system.

"So-o-o," she said, drawing out the word to pull herself together. "You're not working today? Stayed out too late last night? Had too much fun?"

He took a sip of coffee and his gaze never left hers. It was dark and focused and far too unsettling. "I had a great time and stayed out too late. But that's not why I didn't go to work."

"Care to share?"

"I actually took the rest of the week off. To help with preparations for the reunion."

"That's great. I'm sure Peggy appreciates it."

"She's ready to call the doctor and do a barrage of tests to make sure I'm of sound mind and body."

"You have to admit that this is out of character for a man who's spent days at the office without coming up for air," she pointed out.

"I don't have to admit anything unless I'm under oath."

"Still, I'm sure your mother is very happy you're taking some family time."

Kinsey remembered his mother's concerns about him working too hard, and wondered if he was burying himself in work to get over a broken heart. She wanted to tell him again what an idiot his ex-fiancée was, and before she accidentally let that slip out, it was time for one of them to get to work.

"Speaking of reunion preparations, I've been commandeered by Eugenia to help. She gave me a long list. So, if you'll excuse me—"

"I'll give you a hand."

Which probably meant he would watch and applaud. Before she could say no, he set his empty mug down, took her elbow and steered her out of the kitchen. "What are we doing first?"

"Cleaning and changing sheets in two of the upstairs rooms. The ones with bathrooms," she added, thinking that might change his mind.

It didn't.

Kinsey wasn't sure why she wanted to make him go away. She'd enjoyed spending time with him last night. She'd liked his sense of humor the most, but he definitely wasn't hard on the eyes. More than one woman in O'Toole's had checked him out. That shouldn't have mattered because she worked solo—career and life. It was just the way she rolled.

Now there was a snag in the fabric of her life. She'd hung

out with him last night and now today. This had all the makings of a pattern, one that could bite her in the butt.

But his persistence paid off for her because all that focus actually turned out to be helpful. Between the two of them, the first bedroom was finished in record time. In number two, they dusted every square inch, including the white shutters, then teamed up on changing the sheets.

Together they scrubbed the attached bathroom. While working on the shower and tub, she slid glances at David and felt a tug on her heart. Serious concentration crinkled the corners of his eyes and pulled his mouth tight. It was awfully cute, but he was just as appealing, possibly more so, when having fun.

The removable showerhead attached to the long hose was in her hand, the water on. Without thinking, she aimed the stream in his direction and gave him a quick shot. It caught him on the side of his face and shoulder.

"Hey—" He looked over, surprise and irritation replacing serious. It was another appealing look and convinced her he didn't have a bad one. "Do you have something against me being dry?"

She shrugged. "Devil made me do it."

"Them's fightin' words." His eyes narrowed with the light of battle and determination.

Quickly, Kinsey shut off the water before he could use that. In seconds, David was behind her, his front brushing her back as he tried to switch on the showerhead.

"No you don't." She blocked him with her body as he tried to reach past her.

"There's more than one way to get from point A to point B." His arm slid around her waist and he lifted her off her feet.

Being held and touched by David Longwood felt more

wonderful than she wanted it to. But he dropped her back to earth when there was a noise behind them.

Eugenia stood in the doorway. The fifty-ish woman was tall, slim and always had her dark hair pulled back in a tight bun. A black dress completed her uniform. "Having fun?"

Kinsey had learned over the years that the housekeeper wasn't as severe as she pretended and would do anything for Peggy Longwood. That explained the humor lurking in her eyes. She approved of the fact that her employer's son had lightened up, even if it meant a little water on the tile floor.

"I was just minding my own business and she let me have it with the water," he said. "It was an unprovoked sneak attack."

"That's too bad." The housekeeper looked a little wistful. "For just a moment you reminded me of the fun-loving boy you used to be."

Kinsey noticed the way his mouth tightened, as if his memories weren't as warm and fuzzy. She wanted the fun-loving David back, too. "Sorry, Eugenia. That darn showerhead is kind of hard to control."

"Especially when you're using it like a rocket-propelled grenade." David pushed dripping wet hair off his forehead.

Kinsey ignored him. "We're almost finished in here, Eugenia. I just have to mop up the floor."

"Indeed." The older woman arched one dark eyebrow. "David, your mother would like you to do a chart of the family tree."

"I can whip one up on the computer," he said.

"If possible, she'd like it large enough to put on display at the reunion."

"Consider it done," he said. "Kinsey can help me."

The housekeeper nodded, but her mouth twitched. "So long as there's no water involved. I'm not proficient with technology, but even I know that electronics and liquids are incompatible."

Kinsey thought about protesting this new assignment with him but knew resistance to helping him was futile. It would just create questions she was unprepared to answer. But one thing was for sure. Being joined at the hip with David was getting on her nerves. It felt too nice. She didn't trust nice. In her world nice never lasted.

CHAPTER SIX

As it turned out David had to make work-related calls all afternoon and didn't get to his mother's request until much later that evening. Kinsey was in bed and he was glad to have something to take his mind off her and his vivid memories of being with her in that same bed.

His home office and computer were set up in the study and he'd been there for several hours dealing with the family tree. Looking at it now, he was satisfied with the format. Suddenly a bright flash of lightning drew his attention outside just before he heard a rumble of thunder. This seemed as good a time as any to print out a hard copy of the work for his mother. After she proofread it, he'd enlarge the finished product for her big bash.

When there was more lightning and a louder, closer crash of thunder, he shut down the computer.

That's when he felt Kinsey behind him.

He swiveled his desk chair and saw her standing in the doorway. She was wearing a short terry cloth robe and an anxious expression.

"I couldn't sleep," she said. "Thought maybe I could help with the computer work."

"It's shut down. I think the storm is moving this way." He shook his head. "I hope it isn't as bad as the last one. Laurie and Adam had to collapse the tents to keep them from blowing away."

"Can you believe this luck?" Kinsey asked. "Two storms

in less than a week. Your mom is worried about the weather on the day of the reunion."

"I know. But if anyone can will the weather to cooperate it's Peggy Longwood." He pointed to the family tree he'd just printed. "Take a look at this and let me know what you think."

When she moved closer and he smelled the sweet, fresh scent of her skin, he realized the strain she was putting on his self-control. A friendly evening hanging out at O'Toole's was one thing, but right this second he badly wanted to take her in his arms and kiss the daylights out of her. But that would be selfish and wrong.

He had a busted engagement to his discredit and Kinsey already had a hard time believing in people after bouncing around in the foster care system. Getting involved when he couldn't do justice to a relationship would hurt her and he cared about her too much to do that.

"I don't know all these names," she said, "but the layout looks good."

"Mom and Aunt Tory only know that their real family name is Haswick and they were adopted through the state of New Jersey. Their biological brother, Stephen, is deceased," he told her. "Then I branched off with their adoptive families. Underneath that I've got children and grandchildren."

"There's Laurie and Josh and Amy."

David felt a stab of regret that unlike his sister there were no children under his name. "I put Adam Hunter in parenthesis. By all appearances he'll one day be a member of the family since my sister is in love with him. I hear they're going to work on the logistics of being together, what with him being an Aussie and all."

"Yeah. What is it about Australian men?" Her grin disappeared and was replaced by an uneasy look when there was another flash of light outside followed by rumbling thunder. "It's getting closer."

"These things usually move through fast."

"The one the other day didn't." She looked anxious before staring at the family tree. With one finger she traced the names at the top. "Peggy and Tory were lucky."

"Because after all this time they found each other?"

"That. And they were adopted."

Kinsey never had been he realized. That's probably part of the reason his mother had connected with her when Kinsey was a teenager. "Tell me about growing up."

She turned her head to look at him and their mouths were awfully close. "I already told you."

"Not about how you felt." He saw that she was about to shut him down. All he wanted was to understand. "If we were in court, I'd argue that you opened the door to this line of questioning with that comment about my mom being lucky."

She stared at him for several moments, then nodded. "I went back and forth from the state home to foster families. When I was little, every time I went to a new one, I was sure that this time they'd want me to stay permanently."

"But it didn't happen." The forlorn look on her face said more than words could and made him want to fix it, to somehow erase the painful past.

"No. But what doesn't kill you makes you stronger. Each time the social worker broke the news that the foster family was too strained, or had personal issues or whatever the problem was that time and I had to move, I'd pack my things in a big plastic bag and went to the next place."

"You didn't have a suitcase?"

"No. Most of the kids didn't." She shrugged and put her spunky face back in place. "I know your mom's life wasn't perfect, but she had a family and that's so cool. Just so you know, that's not self-pity talking. It's envy."

"You're the least pathetic person I know." He was only sorry she'd had a rough childhood, but he couldn't feel sorry for her. The experience had turned a little girl into a smart, strong, beautiful and interesting woman.

There was a dazzling flash of lightning then and almost instantly thunder boomed overhead, shaking the house. Kinsey jumped. Their arms brushed and David could feel her trembling. He saw the scared child she'd once been and everything went out of his head except the need to show her she wasn't alone.

He stood, then folded her against him and she didn't fight it. She clung to him, her arms going around his waist, holding tight.

"Sorry to be such a baby. I've hated storms for as long as I can remember."

Since she was a little girl without parents to reassure her that nothing was going to hurt her. He couldn't fix her past, but he could do something about the now.

"It's okay," he whispered, his lips brushing her hair. "I could give you all the science about why the thunderstorm can't hurt you as long as you're not outside, but it would be boring. Come to think of it, that might put you to sleep in spite of the noise."

She eased away and looked up, the sweet and sassy expression on her face shredding his resolve. "What would Davy Daring do?"

"This—"

He bent his head and touched his mouth to hers, sipping on the sigh of pleasure that escaped her lips. As sudden as lightning, the kiss changed and he wasn't looking to give her comfort or ease her fears. Something had been simmering between them and it boiled over now. He wanted her more than he'd ever wanted anything in his life.

He slid his hands down to her hips, boosting her up so she

wrapped her legs around his waist. Her arms encircled his neck and somehow their mouths stayed connected as he carried her into his room and set her down beside the bed. Both of them were having trouble drawing in air.

As they tugged at each other's clothes, quickened breaths became gasps that turned into moans of pure need. Together they tumbled onto the bed as lightning flashed outside. When the thunder crashed, she was in his arms while he pushed inside her, making her shiver but not from fear.

He moved and she quickly caught his rhythm. She was sweetness and silk and shadows, yet he held back, keeping himself on the edge to savor her potent pleasure for as long as possible. But when he heard her moan, heard the break in it, he let himself go over that ledge with her. When the trembling stopped, and their breathing returned to somewhere close to normal, he wasn't anywhere near ready to let her go.

David rolled to his back and reached out to pull her to him, but he encountered unexpected resistance.

"Thank you for that, David."

"Back at you." David raised up on his elbow and watched her slide off the bed. "Stay."

"I can't." Kinsey bent and touched her lips to his in a kiss so soft it might have been in his imagination. Her voice was full of a yearning she probably didn't know was there. "I have to go."

He watched her walk out of the room. Without the lightning, without Kinsey, darkness closed in around him along with the smell of failure. He'd broken his promise not to start something with her.

Now the storm was gone, and he only had himself to blame that she was, too.

"THAT WAS QUITE A SHOW last night."

Kinsey wanted to look at Peggy, but hadn't been able to

manage it since the therapy session had started. Did the other woman know Kinsey had slept with her son? Mind-blowing, tangled sheets, naked sex?

It was the end of the physical therapy session and she was watching Peggy to make sure the ankle rotation was done properly—and trying desperately to act as if David hadn't completely rotated her world last night.

Suddenly Peggy's ankle stopped moving. "Kinsey?"

"Hmm?"

"Are you all right?" Peggy was sitting on her bed, while Kinsey knelt on the carpet in front of her.

"Yes." She didn't look up, but studied the injured foot. "No swelling."

"It's feeling better every day." She began rotating in the other direction. "Laurie and I were very concerned about that storm."

"Oh?"

Kinsey was concerned, too, but her storm had nothing to do with lightning and thunder, and everything to do with the earth moving. She should have put a stop to it. She should have gone back to her bed and hidden under the covers with the pillow over her head, just like she'd done as a child.

But David had been there, sympathetic, strong and completely irresistible. And don't forget sexy. She'd thought being in his arms was the best until he kissed her. Then that was the best until he'd carried her to his room and made love to her. She didn't think anything would ever top that. Unless she repeated the experience with David.

But that wasn't going to happen.

"Kinsey, seriously, is something wrong?"

"Sorry. No. I'm just a little tired. The thunder kept me awake."

"Tell me about it. I thought Laurie was going to have a stroke. That's twice she was afraid the outdoor preparations for the reunion would be ruined. Fortunately Adam talked her off the edge and calmed her down, convinced her that whatever happened they could fix it together. Even more fortunately, that storm was all flash and bang. Unlike the last one there was no bluster to wreak havoc."

Havoc was in the eye of the beholder, Kinsey thought. And she was feeling it big-time. Along with conflict. She had learned not to ever count on staying in one place too long and embraced that spirit through her travels. But, for the first time since she was a child, she wanted to stick around. And that was exactly the reason she should go. Right now.

But she had promised Peggy she'd stay through the reunion. She simply couldn't break her word to the woman who had done so much for her. Realistically, she was almost home free. After the reunion she could leave with a clear conscience.

And really, what more could possibly happen?

She watched Peggy finish up the last of her repetitions and nodded with satisfaction. "Good job. Since your schedule is going to be grueling—"

"But fun."

"Right. I think you should cut yourself some slack on exercises for the rest of the day."

"Twist my arm." The older woman grinned like a kid on the last day of school before summer vacation.

"Okay. Good. I'll see you later." Kinsey started toward the door.

"We're finished?"

"Yes." She moved closer to escape.

"Just a darn minute, young lady."

Kinsey winced. "Is something wrong?"

"You tell me." Peggy put on her stern look that fooled no one. "You didn't bully, badger, pep talk or make smart-aleck jokes about old people during the session. That's not at all like you. Something's up and you're not setting a foot outside this room until you talk."

"Nothing. Really. I'm just tired."

A shrewd expression crept into her face. "It's David, isn't it?"

"Of course not. Why would you think that?"

"Because he took time off work and claimed it was to help with the reunion, but that was baloney. He followed you around like a smitten puppy and cleaned bathrooms."

"He just wanted to help," Kinsey protested.

Peggy wasn't buying it. "He couldn't pull the wool over my eyes when he was a boy and he can't now. Neither can you, missy. I've known you since you were sixteen. Maybe you can speed charm and fool the rest of the world, but I know better. You like David."

Like seemed such a bland word for what she felt. But Peggy was right. Might as well come clean, but not quite all the way. There was no need to reveal they'd slept together.

"Yes, I like David."

"I knew it," Peggy said triumphantly.

"It's not like that. The two of us couldn't be more different. But…"

"Ah, but." The other woman nodded knowingly. "Did it ever occur to you that chemistry is the most important component in a relationship? My husband and I were quite opposite. He was an architect who worked with exact measurements—lines, angles, arches were his stock in trade. I, on the other hand, make stuff up. Nothing is precise in imagination. Yet we were happily together for many years and burned up the sheets, if you get my drift."

"Did I need to know that?"

"Yes, indeed. Because I have a point. Isn't it possible that you're too restless? Maybe David could give you roots?" She held up a hand when Kinsey started to answer. "And maybe

he's too serious. You can give him laughter. Embracing differences *is* common ground," Peggy insisted.

"I never thought about it that way."

"Well, you should."

"Do you ever get tired of being right?" Kinsey asked.

"The crown is heavy, but someone has to wear it." Peggy
raised her chin, a regal pose.

Kinsey laughed, then moved close and impulsively leaned
down to embrace the other woman. "You're not old, just wise
beyond your years."

"And you're a joy," she answered, hugging back. "Thank
you for being here, sweetheart."

Kinsey left the room, her heart both light and heavy at the
same time. She should never have doubted Peggy's understanding, but she couldn't afford to let hope get the upper hand.
She'd learned the lessons of a nomadic childhood and trained
her heart too well to not believe in anything permanent.

But Peggy's health was precarious. When Kinsey left this
time, as much as she hated to even think about it, she didn't
know if it would be the last time she saw David's mother. And
she didn't want to think about how it would feel to not see
him again.

CHAPTER SEVEN

DAVID HEARD THE GUESTHOUSE front door close and glanced at the clock on his desk. Eight-thirty in the morning—and Kinsey was on day two of her campaign to avoid him. This was about sex—the mind-blowing kind they'd shared. The kind he wanted with her again and was almost positive she wanted, too.

He grabbed his BlackBerry and followed her. Footwear wouldn't be necessary since she'd be walking on the beach as usual, and there was no point in ruining another perfectly good pair of shoes. With Kinsey, one should always expect the unexpected. It was quickly becoming one of his favorite things about her.

Yesterday he'd given her space. After all, sex had complicated things for her. He, on the other hand, was seeing more clearly than he had for a long time. Being with her made him feel as carefree as a boy—all his tension and stress disappeared. On paper it should work the opposite, what with her unpredictability. It sounded like the worst cliché in a beginner writing class, but hanging out with Kinsey McKeever was like the sun breaking through thick fog.

This was the day of the big reunion and it was going to be perfect weather. There wasn't a cloud in the sky and no heat wave predicted. He hurried down to the beach and looked left, then right, spotting the lone, small figure strolling barefoot at the water's edge. She stopped and stooped to pick something up, probably a seashell. Then she threw it into the surf.

His heart stuttered and sighed as he watched her. From what she'd revealed to him, he realized she'd always been alone. There was no way to change the past, but it wasn't happening today, not on his watch.

David jogged over the dry sand, to the dark, hard-packed part where the waves lazily lapped on the shore, then went after her. He wasn't sure if she'd heard him behind her when he got close or felt the vibration of running, but she stopped and turned. Surprise and pleasure turned up the corners of her mouth.

"David."

"You were expecting the friendly, neighborhood serial killer?"

"I wasn't expecting anyone."

He stuck his hands in his pockets and started walking past her, then called without looking back, "You coming?"

She caught up with him and fell into step. "Since when do you walk on the beach?"

Since he couldn't stop thinking about her. When he wasn't with her he wished he was. When he was with her, it was a toss-up between never wanting to leave and wanting badly to kiss her senseless.

"I'm told it clears the head," he said.

"Something on your mind?"

"Like what?"

She glanced up and shrugged. "I remember a Davy Daring book where our intrepid hero had some girl trouble. He liked someone who didn't like him back."

David could interpret the law and a judge's ruling without a hitch, but women were another story. She wanted to know something, and had brought up women, so it must be about that. The only woman before Kinsey had been his fiancée.

"It's over between Danielle and I."

"So you said. Do you want to talk about it?"

"Waste of time. There's nothing to say."

"Have you talked to anyone about it?" she asked.

"What part of 'there's nothing to say' did you not understand?"

"Pretty much all of it."

"This thing females have about dissecting details of a relationship is beyond me."

"Cope. It's what we do." She grinned.

He watched the way the golden fingers of the sun caressed the curve of her cheek and highlighted her beautifully defined upper lip and the full lower one. She wasn't wearing a bit of makeup. Her blond hair was tousled as if a man had run his fingers through it last night. He wished he'd been that man.

"I'd much rather dissect you," he said.

"How?"

"What is your favorite thing to do?"

"You really have to ask?" A wave rolled gently over their feet, the water warm compared to the still cool air. "Even after my choice of karaoke songs the other night?"

He thought about that and remembered her musical selections had been cities. "Travel?"

"Give the guy a prize."

"So where have you gone?"

"Italy. France. The British Isles. South America." She thought for a moment. "I'm going to Greece right after the reunion. The only thing that limits my wanderlust is money."

"So working is inconvenient but necessary in the pursuit of seeing the world?"

"Well, sort of—but I do really love what I do." She turned to look up at him and the breeze blew a strand of hair across her face. After tucking it behind her ear again, she said, "You don't have financial limitations. I bet you've been everywhere."

"Not really. Italy and France with my folks. Dad was heavy into the architecture. I've traveled on business to London."

He shrugged. "Oh, Danielle and I went to Hawaii. That's about it."

"What a shame."

He wasn't sure if she meant the trip with Danielle or the fact that he hadn't traveled extensively.

"If I could, I'd go to China. Japan. Australia. If I had your resources…"

When she hesitated, he asked, "What?"

"I'd go all over the world."

"Why? What makes you want to do that?" he asked.

"When I realized I didn't belong anywhere, I decided to go everywhere. I remember exactly when the seed was planted. I'd just moved again after only a few months in one foster home. I was in school studying history and geography. The teacher said that thanks to modern modes of travel, the world is a lot smaller than when Christopher Columbus took his voyage. I realized then that I really could go everywhere."

"I see."

So when life gives you lemons, make lemonade. She was a classic example. The odds had not been in her favor, but she'd made a life for herself on her own terms. Hell of a woman. She wasn't sad about her past, so he wouldn't feel that way for her.

"And," she added, "my favorite book at the time was *Davy Daring Goes on an Unexpected Trip.*"

David had put the Davy Daring away a long time ago. It was a struggle not to give in to that reckless part of his nature—the part that wanted to act without thinking, without considering the consequences to himself. Or others. Come to think of it, Kinsey had brought out his daring and he'd taken her to bed. More to feel guilty about.

"I don't remember that one," he said.

"I can't believe you don't know every book your mother ever wrote."

"A few come to mind, but not that one."

"It was one of my favorites." The happy memory danced in her eyes. "Davy plays hooky from school and hops on a train. The conductor catches him and since he can't go home until the next station, the guy teaches him about the rails and traveling from town to town. Oh, the people he meets."

"Probably perverts," David joked.

"The conductor was taking care of him."

"Why? What did he want? There must have been something in it for him." He stopped, knee-deep in the water. "He had a job to do and shouldn't have had time to babysit a boy who was ditching school and breaking the law by stealing a ride."

"There were consequences later, but Davy was having an adventure. Can't you suspend your disbelief?" She pointed a warning finger at him. "You could take lessons from Daring, you know."

"Lessons? From a juvenile delinquent in training?"

Her eyes narrowed on him. "Do you always suck the joy out of everything?"

"It's a gift. I'm practical."

"I'll show you practical." She bent and scooped water into her hands, splashed him with it, then did a little victory dance in the thigh-high surf.

"You have no shame."

"It's a gift." She twirled and the movement was so unselfconscious and carefree and irresistible that it was impossible to be annoyed even if he wanted to. Revenge, on the other hand, was a different story.

"Prepare for payback," he growled, scooping her up in his arms. Then he walked farther into the water until it hit him midthigh and got his shorts wet. "Take a deep breath. You're going in."

Kinsey grabbed him around the neck, an unexpected revenge perk. "You wouldn't."

"Oh?" He bent as if he were going to drop her and she shrieked, holding tighter. "Thanks to you I ruined an expensive pair of leather loafers. And you got me in trouble with Eugenia for getting water all over the bathroom."

"She wasn't mad," Kinsey protested.

"Well, I am." He faked dropping her again and she squealed.

Then she reached down and plucked the cell phone from his pocket. "How expensive is this BlackBerry?"

"You wouldn't."

"Oh?" She arched a dark blond eyebrow. "How much damage can salt water do to this baby? As Eugenia would say, water and technology are incompatible. Is your whole life on a chip the size of an eyelash? What about all the work stuff? Take a deep breath. It's going in."

He wasn't sure whether or not she would follow through on the threat, but the uncertainty had adrenaline pumping through him. The problem was he had his hands full and couldn't do anything. "This isn't funny."

"I think it's hilarious." She held his phone over the water by two fingers. "Unless you put me down on dry land, this baby is toast—or whatever salt water does to delicate electronics."

He could do just that and overpower her with size and strength, but he was reluctant to let her go.

Before he could decide, she looked more closely at the phone. "It's vibrating. I think you have a text. Work just doesn't have the decency to leave you alone."

Obviously she knew her way around a BlackBerry because she pressed some buttons and read the caller ID. Then all the fun was sucked out of her face. "It's Danielle."

After moving back a couple steps to where the water was more shallow, he set her down. She gave him the phone and he read the message from his ex.

"What does it say?"

Kinsey tried to sound casual which was a challenge because of how betrayed she felt. But she knew that was seven different kinds of stupid since she was nothing to David. Maybe a friend? With benefits, but surely not more. Although on her part it *was* more. In spite of her best efforts and all the warnings in the world, hope had been implanted in her soul—and one text message had crushed it.

"She's coming to the reunion."

"Why? She dumped you before Peggy and Tory even found each other and started planning this get-together."

"Out of respect for my mother, she says." David dragged his fingers through his hair. "When the reunion idea came up I invited her."

What had possessed him to do that? she wondered. Then she remembered what his mother had said, about him detesting failure. He was hoping to get back with his ex and cancel out the failure.

"So, it's really not over." Kinsey wasn't asking. She just wanted to say it out loud and get the message from her brain to her heart. She turned and started back toward the house.

"Yes, it really is over," he said, falling into step beside her.

She waited for more information, details of how he could be so sure. When it didn't come, the thought of screaming held a lot of appeal. Frustration stirred the pot of multiple emotions rushing through her and squeezed out everything else.

She stopped suddenly and slapped her hands on her hips. "Is it a guy thing?"

"What?"

"The tendency to not share personal stuff? Or do you care so much about Danielle that it's too painful to talk about?"

His already dark eyes darkened more. "I don't talk about her because it's irrelevant and a waste of time. But if the details are that important to you, I'd be happy to share. Ask me anything."

Questions were difficult to choose since she wanted to know everything. "How did you meet?"

"Work."

For a lawyer, he was certainly stingy with his words. But that wasn't really what she wanted to know anyway. She needed much deeper information. "What is she like?"

"Blond. Blue eyes. Tall. Slender."

"Those are physical characteristics. What's she *like?*"

He thought for a moment. "She's beautiful and cultured. Comes from old money. She's a lawyer like her father."

A high achiever who followed in the family footsteps. Kinsey wasn't sure what she'd wanted to hear, but that wasn't it. The details she was looking for were more along the lines of she snorted when she laughed or that she ate crackers in bed and got crumbs all over the sheets.

"She sounds perfect for you." Damn it.

"I thought so."

Kinsey knew she should just keep walking back to the guesthouse. This was none of her business, but she just couldn't keep her mouth shut.

"You know, David, failure isn't a black mark on your soul. It's not a measure of character and no one expects you to be perfect. Did it ever occur to you that failure is nothing more than an opportunity?"

"How do you figure?"

"It could be the gateway to another path, a different life."

"Or not." His expression was grim, his mouth tight. The muscle in his jaw jumped as intensity gathered in his eyes. He looked at the text message on his phone and frowned. "She says she's having second thoughts."

Then there was nothing left for Kinsey to say. And what

was the point? Her time with the Longwoods had only ever been temporary. Leaving had always been the plan.

The realization hit her, as real as if David had actually dropped her into the cold ocean. And her stomach clenched.

The feeling reminded her of the rejection she'd felt every time she'd found out her stay in a foster home was over when she so desperately wanted to stay. So, the takeaway from this was to be careful what you ask for.

This time her stay had gone on just long enough for her to fall in love with a man who was still in love with someone else.

CHAPTER EIGHT

KINSEY HAD SAID ALMOST NOTHING to David on the walk back to the guesthouse. One minute she'd been easygoing, teasing and laughing. The next she was marching up the beach like a woman whose digital video recorder had malfunctioned for the final episode of *The Bachelor*. Danielle had loved that show and any glitch in the recording resulted in lawsuit threats. It would take an idiot not to know Kinsey's shift in mood had something to do with the message from his ex.

But that was over.

Except the expression on Kinsey's face, in her eyes, wasn't about anything as superficial as a botched recording for a TV show. He'd seen hurt bubbling up and knew he could have handled things better and was ready to do that now.

But he couldn't do anything with her barricaded in her room. He'd heard water running for a shower. Later the hum of the blow-dryer leaked out. In the past thirty minutes there'd been no sound and he was bracing himself to face her. Lining up his defense strategy like any attorney worth his five hundred dollars an hour. Granted, he didn't practice criminal law. His specialty was mergers and acquisitions, but one still went step-by-step in any legal undertaking.

His mother thought jurisprudence was incomprehensible. David disagreed. He wished the working of the female mind were as easy for him to understand as the legal system.

He looked at the clock on the microwave as he paced by the kitchen. Did it always take Kinsey this long to put herself together? Not in the short time he'd spent with her—and for some reason it was important to him to spend *more* time with her. Maybe she was taking extra care because of the family reunion today.

David was prepared to wait her out. But if she didn't show soon, he was going in after her.

Ten minutes later he was readying himself to do just that when her door opened. He stopped pacing and stood in the living room. Instead of relief when she appeared, there was more confusion than ever. She had her rolling weekend bag, purse and car keys. He couldn't say it was all her worldly possessions, but was undoubtedly everything she'd arrived here with.

"So you've been in there packing all this time."

"Yes." Her stubborn little chin lifted slightly.

"Why?"

"When one is leaving, it's customary and efficient to place one's belongings in some kind of container to facilitate their removal and relocation."

"That's not what I meant and you know it. You're not staying for the reunion." It wasn't a question and the resulting anger surprised him.

"I have a trip of a lifetime to Greece coming up," she defended.

"You promised to stay."

"And I'd planned to. But…" She set her purse and keys on top of the standing suitcase. "Have you contacted Danielle?"

"No."

"You should. Ignoring her is rude."

"So is cutting someone loose in a text message," he pointed out.

"You should call her. Maybe she'd had a bad day and shot off that text without thinking."

"And how do you explain the lack of contact for the last six months?"

"There's no time limit on changing her mind." Kinsey shrugged. "Just because she ended things that way doesn't mean it's the best method of couples' communication. Start this phase of your relationship off on a better note and actually speak. Wouldn't it be nice to hear her voice?"

Why was she pushing him at Danielle? He'd been so sure she was jealous. Smart money was on that emotion, not this charming attempt at matchmaking.

"I'll contact her," he said. "And politely tell her that I'm rescinding her invitation to the reunion."

"Good strategy. Play hard to get." Kinsey nodded approvingly.

"I'm not playing anything." He stared at her. "But you can't say the same."

"What does that mean?"

"I don't…" He took a deep breath. "We—Mom, Laurie and I—do not want you to leave. Before the reunion," he added.

"I'm sorry but you don't get a vote on my schedule." Hints of that hurt little girl clouded her eyes. "This isn't a Davy Daring book where you get everything your way."

That did it. Frustration, anger and guilt intertwined and snapped through him, lowering his breaking point threshold.

"You keep bringing up Davy Daring as if he's a real person. He might have been once, but he's gone and has been for a long time. I lost him when I lost my best friend."

"Oh, David—" Her eyes grew wide. "I'm so sorry. Losing someone at a young age must have been devastating."

"He's not dead. But he told me once that he wished he was."

"I don't understand. What happened?"

"I was sixteen. Just got my driver's license. A bunch of us

took two cars to Ocean City, about thirty miles from here. It has a better boardwalk. And a bridge. The Ninth Street Bridge," he said, as if that was really important information. "We were hanging around there—"

"And?" she prompted softly.

"I got the bright idea to walk on the railing."

"Oh, my God. Did you fall?"

"No." He laughed and heard the bitter irony in the harsh sound. "I didn't even get the chance to try. There was a girl with me and I had to get her home for a curfew. But Mark thought it was an awesome suggestion and tried it."

"You weren't there?"

"I'd just left. But it was my idea. He would never have thought of it if I hadn't been shooting off my mouth. He tried it and fell. Hit the water wrong. Now he's a paraplegic in a wheelchair for the rest of his life and it's my fault. Way to go, Davy Daring."

Kinsey moved closer and put her hand on his arm. Her gaze was filled with all the sympathy he didn't deserve. "You didn't make him do it, David. He was a kid and kids sometimes do stupid things."

"And sometimes they just come up with stupid schemes and stand back while others do something that otherwise might never have occurred to them."

"What did your parents say?"

"They just knew Mark had an accident. They were sorry for him and his folks and glad it wasn't me."

"And you never told them the whole story?"

"I didn't want to disappoint them," he said.

"But ever since, you've been punishing yourself more than they ever could or would have. Not to mention the guilt that has been cutting off the blood supply to your personality." When he didn't say anything she asked, "Do you see Mark?"

"Yes. Now and then. But it will never be like it was." That state-of-the-art motorized scooter would always be a technological reminder of what happened.

"What's he doing now?" she asked.

"He's a structural engineer. Married with two kids."

"So you're still friends." She wasn't asking a question. "He's living his life."

"Half a life."

"How do you figure? He's got a family and a career. Is he happy?"

David raked his fingers through his hair. "I guess."

"Isn't it up to him to decide whether or not his life is full? He's handled his limitations and moved on. Don't you think it's time you moved on, too, David? You're not responsible for what Mark did. He didn't think it through and had to pay a price. A horrible price, but that's what we call suffering the consequences of our actions."

Maybe finally telling someone was responsible for a shift, but what Kinsey was saying made sense to the adult David in a way it hadn't to the immature Davy Daring. After all these years it was like he could breathe again.

He smiled. "I didn't mean to dump all that on you."

"I don't mind. It's about time you got it off your chest."

His chest actually felt lighter, which is probably how that expression had started in the first place. "Thanks for listening."

"No problem. Way past time for you to let it go."

Oddly enough, he could probably do that now. But her words reminded him that she was going. "So, now you know my dark secret. I think there's some kind of rule. After someone bares their soul, it's obligatory to stick around for a family reunion."

Whether she knew it or not the look in her eyes said she wanted to stay. He was about to close the deal when there was a knock on the door. Kinsey was closest and opened it. After his description a little while ago there was no way she didn't know the tall, blue-eyed blonde.

"You must be Danielle."

"Yes. I'm here to see David."

She stepped aside. "He's right here. My name is Kinsey and I was just on my way out."

"Not so fast," David said.

"There's nothing you can say to talk me out of it."

"So you're leaving without talking to my mother?" Apparently he'd been living with guilt so long he now felt the need to spread the joy—plus he thought it might stop her.

"I'd never do that," Kinsey protested. "I was just on my way to see her. After that I'll come back for my things and be on my way."

"To Greece."

"That's right." For someone anticipating the trip of a lifetime, she didn't look all that happy. "Goodbye, David."

This wasn't goodbye. Not if he could help it.

David started to follow after her until Danielle put a hand on his arm.

"Can we talk?"

He looked at Kinsey's stiff, straight back as she hurried across the lawn to the main house. Making things right with her was the most important thing. Then he realized, first things first.

"I think we need to clear the air," he said.

"I'm in complete agreement. This separation has opened my eyes, made me reevaluate our relationship." She tucked a strand of golden-blond hair behind her ear.

Once upon a time he'd thought her hair stunning. Now he found his taste ran more to honey. "You dumped me, Danielle. We don't have a relationship."

She slid her hands into the pockets of her navy slacks. A red sweater was tied around her neck, over the white silk blouse. "I've missed us as a couple, David."

"You want me back because you don't like being alone?"

He'd once thought this woman one of the most independent he'd ever met until Kinsey taught him the true meaning of the word.

"I miss you, David." She looked sincere. "We were in a rut and I shook things up."

"No kidding. Breaking it off in a text message will do that. You couldn't have given me a heads-up and said we needed to talk?"

"I'm doing that now." She reached into her pocket and pulled out her phone and read a message. After responding, she slid it back out of sight. "Let's fix this."

There was nothing to fix. Whatever he'd once felt for this woman was gone.

Kinsey was right. He'd definitely dodged a bullet.

"If that's why you came today, I'm sorry but it was a wasted trip. It's over between us. There's no way to get back what we had."

Her blue eyes went wide and surprised, but there was no hint of tears. "Are you sure?"

"Absolutely."

"Because of Kinsey?"

His gaze jumped to hers. "What?"

"I saw the way you looked at her. If you'd ever looked at me that way…"

He never had because there were no deep feelings to back it up. For the first time he realized that their relationship was a successful failure. They hadn't taken the final step to make it permanent because it wasn't love.

"You and I weren't working and hadn't been for a long time," he told her gently.

She met his gaze for a moment, then nodded. "I think I knew that deep down."

"Maybe you came today for closure. To move on. Because texting isn't the most satisfying form of communication."

"Maybe."

"So this time we're doing it in person. A mutual calling off the relationship."

"If it's that important to you, okay."

"It is," he said. "Because you can't build a future without closure on the past. Besides, Davy Daring doesn't get dumped."

IT WASN'T EASY, BUT KINSEY held herself together after walking out the door. David's description hadn't done the woman justice, which convinced her that hope was the cruelest of all emotions.

As a little girl she'd hoped to be adopted, but no one chose her to be in their family. Why would she believe David could want someone like her when flawless Danielle was his for the taking? It was a double win for him. He'd get the girl and cancel out the failure. Life would be perfect.

After leaving the guesthouse she stood on the beach for a while, looking at the ocean. When she couldn't put it off any longer, she walked up to the main house and saw that some people had already arrived. It wasn't even noon yet and her world had turned upside down. But the Longwoods were ready to party hearty.

On the back lawn facing the Atlantic ocean there was a white tent with tables and chairs set up beneath. Laurie had arranged this in the event of rain or sun. Fortunately, today had an abundance of the latter along with a breeze off the water that made the day practically perfect.

She saw Laurie overseeing the caterers who were in red T-shirts and blue aprons. They were arranging food—potato salad, sandwiches, vegetable and fruit trays to be circulated throughout the afternoon. A barbecue was planned for the evening festivities. It was all low-key and laid-back, just like the woman who'd inspired the event.

Peggy Longwood was standing on the lawn, talking on her cell phone. In a completely different way, this goodbye was going to be just as heart wrenching as the one with David. She'd said the words countless times and thought the formula to feel nothing was still working for her. However, the hitch in her chest and the nerves doing a samba in her stomach told her different.

"Peggy," she called out, moving up the slight, grassy rise.

"Kinsey's here, I have to go," the other woman said. She held up a finger and listened for a moment. "Understood."

When she disconnected and slid her cell into the pocket of her pink knit slacks, Kinsey painted a smile on her face. Lyrics from an old song flashed through her mind— "Smile, though your heart is aching. Smile even though it's breaking. You'll get by."

But only if she made a run for it as quickly as she possibly could.

"Peggy, I have something to tell you—"

"Kinsey, sweetheart, just the person I wanted to see. I'd like you to meet Cousin Corinne." Her tongue got stuck and she stumbled over the words, then laughed. "Say that five times fast."

That's what David had said. Her heart gave a sad little lurch. "I wish I could, but—"

Peggy's arm slid over her shoulders and drew her toward the house. The older woman went on as if Kinsey hadn't spoken.

"Cousin Corinne is the 'mature' lady you gave up your room for. She just arrived yesterday and wants to meet you."

They went in the front door and Peggy took her arm as she stepped onto the marble entryway floor. "Damn slippery stuff. While I love being the center of attention, I'd rather it wasn't for a pratfall at my own party."

"I've got you," Kinsey said.

"I know, sweetheart. I'm counting on you."

Surely not now. David and Laurie were there for her and they were family....

In the living room a plush area rug interrupted the slippery tiles of death as she and Peggy liked to refer to them—and held a cushy, plush corner sofa with big fat throw pillows. There were several people in the room, but conversation stopped when Peggy walked in.

"Everyone, I'd like you to meet Kinsey McKeever. She's the miracle worker I told you about. Without her bullying me into physical therapy that would have bent and broken a lesser woman, I literally might not be standing here now. Well, I'd be standing probably, but not for as long, and it would hurt." She put her arm around Kinsey and pointed out a gray-haired, fifty-ish man. "This is Rod Connelly, a distant cousin on Nana's side. And the beautiful blonde beside him is his wife, Marcella."

Kinsey had so wanted this to be like pulling off an adhesive bandage—quick so it would hurt less. There was no way to do that without making this situation awkward for Peggy and she wouldn't do that.

"It's nice to meet you," she said, smiling at the couple.

"And this is Cousin Corinne, from my biological mother's side."

Peggy stopped beside an overstuffed chair that made the white-haired woman sitting there look like a character from Honey I Shrank the Grandparents. She had a nasal cannula and portable oxygen tank, visible reminders of her pulmonary problems.

Cousin Corinne took her hand and squeezed her fingers with surprising strength. "Thank you, dear. Your room is so lovely."

"It's not really mine, but I'm glad you're comfortable there."

"Very. And I wouldn't have missed this reunion for anything."

Kinsey was tired of rationalizing. There were so many people here, and with more coming, surely one less would make things easier. She just needed to get away. She was prepared for the aftermath of leaving and could deal with it. But this long goodbye was breaking her heart.

"It's a dream come true, everyone coming together like this. The family of yesterday, today and—" Peggy slid her arm around Kinsey "—tomorrow."

"Well put," Corinne said.

Peggy looked around the room. "Now if you'll excuse me, I need to check on everyone outside and introduce this young lady."

Arm in arm they left the living room and Kinsey heard the conversation resume. She and Peggy walked onto the back porch, shaded by what was the master bedroom balcony upstairs, and here below it doubled as a patio cover.

"I want you to meet Aunt Hilda and Uncle Jim. They're from my adoptive father's side. They're the ones talking to Tory over where the family tree is set up. Did you see what a beautiful job David did?"

On the computerized printout? Or me, Kinsey wondered. She'd seen what he accomplished on the computer just before he proved that the earth really did move when David Longwood made love to a girl. The memory stabbed her heart and all she wanted was for the piercing pain to stop.

"Wait, Peggy. I really have to tell you something."

"What is it?"

"I have to go."

"Did Laurie assign you a chore today?" The older woman nodded knowingly. "She planned and worked and delegated so everything would go off without a hitch, but I know she has a select and trusted few on call if needed."

"No. I meant that I'm saying goodbye. I have to go. There's a lot to do before my trip. Passport. Paperwork. Shots."

Peggy's eyes went soft with understanding. "Since when do you need shots to go to the Mediterranean?"

"I was kidding about the shots, but I really do have a lot to take care of."

"And it can't wait a day?"

Not if she was going to get out of here with her heart in one piece. "I'm afraid not."

"Where is that brave girl who told me she had a lot to offer if she only got the chance?"

"What?"

"You were barely sixteen years old. That's what you said to me when we met. I saw a girl with a spine, a straightforward young woman who was fearless, strong, charming and needed a hand up not a handout. That woman showed up when I broke my foot, but that's not who I'm seeing now. What happened to her, Kinsey?"

"I'm still the same."

Peggy shook her head. "You're running away and I'd really like you to explain why. What is so important that you're compelled to break your promise?"

CHAPTER NINE

IF SHE DIDN'T BREAK HER promise David would break her heart. More accurately, the damage to her heart was already done and seeing him would simply prolong the pain. The sooner she got out of here, the faster she'd get over him.

Maybe.

"Talk to me, Kinsey."

"The fact is I don't really understand why you want me to stay." Sidestep the question, that was the ticket. "I'm not that important."

"That's where you're wrong, sweetheart." Peggy smiled. "Everyone in this family is very important to me."

"But I'm not part of the family," she pointed out.

"Just because your last name isn't Longwood?"

"Kind of. Yeah."

"For a well-educated young woman you're not very bright about certain things."

Kinsey was taken aback. "Did you just call me a dimwit?"

"No. I prefer to think of it as selective stupidity."

"Good, because that's so much better."

"It's understandable," Peggy went on. "It's brought on by an emotional vacuum during childhood."

"That's your official diagnosis, Dr. Freud?"

"No. The official one is that you're afraid to let yourself care because it could all be yanked out from under you."

Peggy folded her arms over her chest. "When will you see that we're not going anywhere?"

"Of course not. I'm not as dim as you think. You've lived in this house for a long time. Your husband designed it."

The older woman rolled her eyes. "Yes, and I have no plans of ever living anywhere else, but that's not what I meant. And for all we know it could burn to the ground one day, or we could lose it because of financial setbacks. But I'm not talking about a structure when I said we'll be here. I'm talking emotionally. Don't you understand?"

"What?"

"Family isn't limited to people who share DNA. If that were the case, Nana would just be a ninety-year-old woman who lives in my house when she's not on a bus to Atlantic City for a gambling junket."

"That's different," Kinsey said. "Nana adopted you."

"She embraced me into the family."

"But it was a legal adoption," she added.

"I see." Peggy nodded. "So in your definition of *family* one needs DNA and/or legal documentation."

"It doesn't hurt." Even Kinsey could hear the lack of conviction in her voice.

It was very clear to her now from which parent David had inherited his negotiating skills. This woman knew how to argue a case. The problem was that whether or not Kinsey stayed for the reunion wasn't at the heart of the matter.

"Oh, sweetheart, don't you know that we make our family as we find it? As we go along. Yes, it was important to find my sister and that's the best birthday present I could have. But Nana is my family, too, and everyone on my adoptive father's side. I only add the adjectives *biological* and *adoptive* for clarification because we've doubled in size. But, the heart doesn't know biological from adoptive. They're all family." Peggy nudged her chin up with a knuckle. "But you've been family since about five minutes after we met. Do you know why I offered you a job?"

"No." In fact Kinsey had always wondered why the woman would take a chance on a teenager without experience.

"I fell in love with you and wanted to take that sad expression out of your eyes."

Kinsey wasn't aware that it showed and wasn't sure she could let herself believe the words. "I just worked here."

"And I gave you responsibilities that taught you self-confidence. Just as I did Laurie and David." Peggy's blue eyes took on an "aha" look. "That's it."

"What's it?"

"David. You're in love with him."

"No." Kinsey heard zero conviction in the lie. "As you said, you taught us both independence. He's like my brother. And, for the record, let me say, 'Eww.'"

"You're throwing up roadblocks where none exist." Peggy tapped her lip. "So, reading between the lines, you're running away from your feelings for my son."

Nailed. Busted. Outed. There was no point in wasting more energy on a denial. Peggy Longwood read her perfectly and always had.

"It doesn't really matter how I feel. He's getting back together with Danielle. Why wouldn't he? They were together for a long time."

"Getting? They're a couple again?"

"They were working on it when I left."

"She's here?"

"He invited her." Kinsey shifted her feet and looked at the grass. "Isn't that ironic? Reunion is in the air."

"Don't be so sure."

Kinsey looked up. "Why?"

"You're right. David was with her for a few years and she's

a nice girl. But that doesn't make her the perfect match for him. They didn't get married and I think there's a reason."

"Timing. Work schedules incompatible with having a ceremony."

Peggy shook her head. "It can take five years to find out someone is wrong for you but only five minutes to know the love of your life. Which makes it frustrating when we overthink a relationship."

"I'm not doing that."

"You're wrong," she said directly, but not unkindly. "But I wasn't talking about you."

"Then who?"

"My sister. Tory and Sam were always in love. They wasted a lot of time being apart and unhappy because of decisions they now admit were stupid. And she ran away, too."

"I'm not running," Kinsey protested. "It's a trip to Greece."

"You say potato, I say po-tah-to." Peggy nervously tapped her foot and scanned the expanse of grass as if she were waiting for someone. "If you keep running, you'll never get what you want most."

"Which is?"

"A family." Peggy shaded her eyes with her hand and heaved a sigh. "Finally."

"I'm sorry?"

"Here comes David."

Kinsey's heart sank. So much for a quick and easy departure. Peggy waved him over and he walked toward them. Six-plus-feet of hunkalicious maleness and she felt her heart squeeze painfully. He was everything a woman could want, but one-sided wanting was the basic ingredient for your worse than average romantic disaster.

"Hi, Mom." He smiled, then kissed her cheek and whispered something.

"Good." She looked up at him. "Kinsey just told me Danielle is here."

"She wanted to wish you a happy birthday."

"That's nice. Did you know Kinsey isn't staying for the reunion?"

"Yes." He didn't look upset or disappointed. In fact there was an almost smug expression on his face. "I was told there was nothing I could say to change her mind. So I'm finished trying."

Since when did he listen to her? Kinsey wondered.

"Then I suppose I've been wasting my time and goodbye is inevitable. You were good enough to postpone your travel to help me recuperate." Peggy bent to hug her. "Have a wonderful trip, sweetheart. I want to see all the pictures and hear every detail when you get back."

"I'll call you—" Kinsey stopped as unexpected emotion choked off her words.

"I can never thank you enough for getting me back on my feet."

"Any time." She shook her head. "Strike that. You're not allowed to slip on the tiles of death ever again."

"She means the marble floor," Peggy explained.

"I connected the dots," David assured her. "A week with Kinsey has been educational, to say the least."

Educational? That's all it had been to him? Kinsey felt the earth move and he'd rotated her world. She was changed, changes that would last a lifetime—and the loss would last even longer.

She lifted her hand in farewell, then turned to go down the hill. David fell into step beside her.

"Where are you going?" she asked.

"To help you with your luggage."

"I can handle it by myself." She always had and it appeared there was no reason to believe that would change any time soon. He'd certainly backed off on trying to convince her not to leave. It was surprising how much that hurt.

"A gentleman would never let a lady carry her own bags." He looked determined, and recently it had become clear that the Longwoods could be stubborn.

"Okay. Thanks."

Maybe at least this part of her farewell would be quick and easy.

"So, lots of people are showing up today." It was lame to state the obvious, but Kinsey felt compelled to fill the awkward silence as they walked to the guesthouse. "Peggy must be pleased about the turnout."

"Yeah." He glanced at the driveway with its three-car garage. "Laurie hired someone to direct traffic and parking and a van to shuttle people back and forth so they don't have to walk too far from where they parked down the road. And there's the occasional taxi bringing someone in from the airport."

"Your sister has thought of everything. She did a great job of organizing this event."

She glanced at her small, fuel-efficient compact car parked off to the side. Because his sister had thought of everything, her car wouldn't be blocked in by another vehicle.

David slid his fingertips into his shorts pockets. He'd showered and shaved after she walked out earlier and the fragrance of his cologne slipped inside her, warming everywhere it touched. In his red, white and blue tab front shirt and dark sunglasses, he looked every inch the handsome, prosperous playboy at play.

Not fair, she thought. He wasn't a playboy. He was a one-woman man and unfortunately she didn't happen to be that woman.

"You're going to miss a great party," he said.

"I know. But with this big crowd no one will miss me."

"You're wrong. Everyone will miss you."

"Not possible. I don't even know most of those people." She stepped onto the guesthouse porch.

"But the ones you do know will miss you very much." David's voice was different from earlier.

It was lighthearted, almost teasing. Probably because he'd worked things out with Danielle. Dark glasses hid the expression in his eyes, but she figured it matched his tone and that made her sad. Although skeptical, she would allow that there was a miniscule possibility that she would be missed, but not by the one man she most wanted to miss her. They stared at each other for several heartbeats and he didn't say the words.

"That's very sweet of you to say, David." She put on the happy, no-one-can-hurt-me face that had carried her through so many leavings in her life. "But I need to go. I'll just get my things."

"Okay." He opened the door and walked inside. "I'll grab them for you. Did you leave everything in the bedroom?"

She walked in behind him, but he was tall and his broad shoulders blocked her view. How could he not see the rolling bag she'd left right there inside the door?

Moving around him she saw the space was empty, except for her purse. "Where's my stuff?"

He slid the sunglasses to the top of his head. "Where did you put it?"

She spread her arms and indicated the vacant area. "Right here. It's gone."

"Are you sure this is where it was?"

"Positive." But he was a lawyer and could argue about the meaning of *where* until hell wouldn't have it. "And there's one way to find out."

She walked into her bedroom and a quick glance told her what she already knew. It wasn't in here. Without his permission she went down the hall and glanced through his room. Nothing.

She marched back to the entryway. "Someone stole my stuff."

"Why would anyone do that?"

"How should I know." She met his gaze, her own eyes narrowed. "What do *you* know?"

He shrugged. "I was in the shower. Didn't see anything."

All she wanted was for this long goodbye to be over, but fate wasn't merciful. It was just stuff. All replaceable. Unlike David who was one of a kind. "I can live without it."

Kinsey walked back outside to the driveway where her car was parked. A breeze from the ocean cooled her hot cheeks and blew the hair away from her face. The sun, in a cloudless blue sky, turned the swell of the water into sparkling diamonds. Fate had been kind to the Longwoods and given them a perfect day for this party. For Peggy's sake she was really glad.

She unlocked her car door and David reached around to open it for her. "Drive carefully."

"I will, thanks." She fit her key into the ignition and turned it.

That was when she realized how attuned she was to sound cues. There's always a moment when your mind fills in what you expect to hear just before it registers total silence, if you didn't count the clicking noise of the key turning. She tried again and nothing happened. No engine coughed to life.

"Damn it. What the hell is going on?" She looked up at David.

"This is really weird," he said.

"Oh, please. Don't even try to tell me it's a coincidence."

He held up his hands and backed away. "Perish the thought. I'd never try to tell you anything."

"Do something," she said.

"I'd be happy to do some investigating, make inquiries." He gestured to the people gathering, chatting, eating and sitting in chairs under the white tent. "But I'm expected to mingle with the guests. Care to join me?"

"No." Kinsey felt something that was a lot like panic growing inside her. She was close to losing it and when that happened, she wanted to be by herself. "I'll walk into town."

That startled him. "And do what?"

"Call a garage. Have my car towed. Whatever."

"Stay," he urged. "Do it tomorrow."

Just then a cab pulled into the driveway and an older couple got out. They paid the driver, then walked to the front door where a sign was posted with directions to the main event on the lawn.

Kinsey was only surprised that her mind, in a state of being so upset, had worked fast enough to see the taxi as a solution to her problem. This was actually the first and only lucky break she'd gotten all day.

"I'll take a cab." She lifted her hand to hail the driver and he nodded.

David took her arm to stop her. "You should count to ten and think about this."

"What can I say? I'm spontaneous."

"There's a fine line between spontaneity and spinelessness."

"Did you just call me a coward?" She glared at him, grateful for something tangible to be ticked off about.

"It's an observation." He put his hands on his hips and there was a thread of irritation in his voice. "You know what your problem is?"

"I don't have any problems unless you count missing luggage and a car that won't start."

"Your problem," he said, ignoring her sarcasm, "is that as a child you learned to charm everyone for your emotional survival. You still do it. But anyone who really knows you, someone like me for instance, is aware that it's largely a coping skill and a load of crap."

"What does that mean?"

"I've seen you crabby and it doesn't put me off in the least. In fact, I like it. So you can be yourself with me. And one more thing." There was intensity sparking in his eyes. "You're an adult. You can make your own choices. No more being at the mercy of the system. This time if you lose a good thing, there's no one to blame but yourself."

Kinsey couldn't think of a comeback and that almost never happened to her. Could be that the emotion choking her was also blocking blood to her brain. She tugged her arm from his grasp and turned away before he could see the tears fall. "I can't keep the cab waiting."

She moved away, part of her hoping he'd stop her again or say the one thing that would.

He didn't.

CHAPTER TEN

—

THE SUN HAD JUST GONE DOWN and David figured that was good because he was ready to put away the phony happy-reunion face that was making his jaw hurt. There were other places that hurt, too, deep inside, but he wasn't ready to do a battle damage assessment yet. It would result in the opposite of happy-reunion face and someone would notice. He didn't want to spoil his mother's party. In the shadows now he could at least stand down.

The part of him not pouting acknowledged it had been a good day. He'd met his cousin Allie Gibbons, Aunt Tory's daughter, who'd set this whole reunion in motion by finding her father, Sam McCormack. Allie and her husband, Mark, lived in South Carolina with their three children—Quinn and twins Molly and Megan. Along with the other children of cousins from both his father's and mother's sides of the family, the Gibbons kids were running through the grass, squealing and having a great time while the adults chatted and promised to stay in touch.

David was sitting on the patio by the main house with his back to the guesthouse he'd shared with Kinsey. The positioning was deliberate, all the better to not be reminded of the best week of his life. Unfortunately, when his mother walked outside he was facing her and the inside light must have revealed his unhappy-reunion face because her big smile turned into a frown.

"Don't pout, David. Your face might freeze that way."

"I'm not. That would be childish."

"And manly men never act like children." There was a note of sarcasm in her voice. She patted his arm before taking the chair across from him. "When little boys grow up, pouty faces are called brooding."

"That works for me."

"Just keep in mind that the look you're wearing has been known to contribute to the advancement of wrinkles." She tapped her lip thoughtfully. "Do young women these days like wrinkles and hair graying at the temples on men? Or not? I can never keep up."

"I don't know and it really doesn't matter," he said.

She sighed. "I'm sorry I couldn't talk Kinsey out of leaving."

"Me, too." It didn't even occur to him to wonder how his mother knew the reason for his mood. If he asked she'd just say it was a mom thing.

"Don't give up, sweetheart. She'll get the wanderlust out of her system. You heard her say she'll call me. She always comes by after a trip to share pictures and experiences. When that happens, you can be here, just a coincidence—"

"That doesn't work for me, Mom."

"Why not? Do you have a better plan?"

"That's just it. There shouldn't have to be a plan. If she wanted to be here she would be here. What is that saying? About letting a bird go and if it comes back of its own free will it was really yours in the first place?"

"That might be true if Kinsey were as uncomplicated as a cockatiel, but she has a past and issues to work through."

"Nice try, Mom. I know all that. And it doesn't make me feel much better. Just when I thought I'd found a woman as interesting as Dad found you, she goes to Greece."

"How very sweet of you to say that." Peggy leaned over and patted his knee.

"And you know what? I don't want to talk about it."

"Then I don't know what to tell you, son."

"Since when?" Tory sat down beside her sister across from him.

David studied his aunt and tried to remember if she'd looked this beautiful when he first met her, after she and his mother had reunited. Or was it reuniting with Sam, the love of her life, that gave her big blue eyes that happy glow? He was glad for her, but such visible happiness was damn hard to be around when he was having such an excellent pout.

"Seriously, what's got you two looking like there was E. coli in the salad?" Tory glanced from him to her sister. "And, Peggy, you always know what to say. It's one of the things I like best. Talk to me, you two."

"He's brooding over Kinsey," his mother said straight-out.

"For Pete's sake, Mom."

"What's wrong?"

"Isn't this my disclosure?" David wasn't comfortable with his private pain put out there for public consumption. Like Kinsey said, it was a guy thing. "You couldn't have just made something up? It's what you do."

"And so do I, including illustrations. I'm very good with capes," Tory said. "But how can we help without knowing the truth of what's going on?"

"That's what I'm saying," David clarified. "There's nothing anyone can do. And I really don't want to talk about it."

"About what?" Laurie came up from behind him and took the last remaining chair, beside his.

"David's brooding over Kinsey," Tory said.

His sister eagerly leaned forward. "So there is some-thing between you two. I was getting a vibe, but with all the last-minute details for the reunion, I didn't have time to get into it."

"And you did a magnificent job on this gathering, sweetheart," Peggy said to her daughter. "Thank you for all the hard work. It's perfect."

"I'm glad you like it, Mom." Laurie's chic, short dark hair made her eyes look huge and they shone with pleasure. "Now, little brother, spill your guts. Tell me what's going on with you and Kinsey."

"Nothing." That was absolutely true because she'd run out on him. And what was it about the women in this family getting better-looking lately? Laurie had fallen for her Australian guy and the happiness just radiated from her. But not even that could burn off the big, bad brood he had going on. "And I don't want to talk about it."

"Which one of you wants to tell him that we don't really care whether he wants to talk or not?" Laurie asked, glancing from her mother to her aunt.

David thought about his father often, but he couldn't remember missing him more than he did right now, surrounded by women who wanted to talk about his feelings. A shudder went through him. The least his parents could have done was given him a brother.

Then he had another, more painful thought. Kinsey would have been a good fit with the bright, beautiful, exceptional women in his family.

"Come on, David. My professional reputation is on the line," Laurie said.

He glanced at her. "I'm not exactly sure what talking about my mood has to do with your reputation."

"Then I'll explain it to you." His sister held up her hand and started to tick things off. "You don't look happy. If anyone notices you don't look happy they might conclude that there was a problem with this event. I organized this event, therefore the conclusion could be reached that there was a problem with the service I provide."

"So it's all about you?" he said dryly.

"Exactly." Light spilling through the house windows revealed her grin.

"When you put it like that…" David decided to talk because it was three against one and the sooner he knuckled the better his chances of being left alone. "The truth is I'm not having a good time, but it's got nothing to do with the reunion." He thought a moment and said, "Actually that's not true. I'm having a lousy time because Kinsey isn't here with me."

"Don't you feel better getting that off your chest?" Peggy asked.

"No." He shifted in his wooden chair. "The thing is, I wasn't this down and depressed when Danielle dumped me. It was almost a relief, but I didn't get that at the time because my pride and sense of failure were dinged."

"I never liked her," Laurie said.

"Yes, you did, sweetheart," her mother interjected. "And you talked to her for a while today. But your loyalty to your brother is admirable."

"What are you feeling now, David?" Tory asked.

He said the first thing that came to mind. "It's as if I've lost the one person in the whole world who can make me happy."

The three women sighed, then groaned in unison.

"That's so sweet," Tory said.

"Romantic and sad in equal parts," his sister added. Then she looked at her watch and stood. "I wish I could stay, but I'm needed for the grand finale."

"I have to go find Sam and give him a big kiss and tell him how much I love and appreciate him." Tory slid out of her chair and started to walk away, then stopped. "Oh, I almost forgot, what with David's brood, but Stan is looking for you, Peggy. He's afraid you're overdoing it today."

"That's because he's my doctor."

Tory leaned over and hugged her sister. "It's not about being your friend or a doctor. Anyone with eyes can see that he cares deeply for you. I don't want to say *love,* but..."

"You can't help yourself. When you're in love, you want everyone else to be in love, too." Peggy laughed. "Tell him I'll be there in a few minutes."

When it was just he and his mother, David asked, "Do I know how to clear a room, or what?"

"Our fault not yours. This probably wasn't the best time to try and crack your code of silence." Peggy stood, too. "It was leaked to me that there's a big surprise to close the festivities. And I need to find Stan before it starts."

"Don't mess with Laurie's schedule. After all, her professional reputation is at stake and we wouldn't want to jeopardize it. Go get your surprise and your doctor." David felt more than heard someone come up behind him and then he saw his mother smile.

"And *your* surprise just arrived," Peggy said, just before she walked away.

David turned. The only woman in the whole world who could make him happy was standing there. Suddenly, he had sincere happy-reunion face that had nothing to do with his family coming together and everything to do with Kinsey.

"You came back."

"Only because I didn't get a chance to meet Aunt Hilda and Uncle Jim."

"Is that the only reason?" David stood up slowly.

Kinsey could come up with a million, but there was only one that really mattered. And she would get to it.

She walked closer and could feel the warmth of his body, smell the wonderful spicy scent of his skin. Feelings poured through her and she knew then that she never would have been able to outrun what she'd found with him.

"I wanted to show your mom that stupid doesn't run in the family."

He looked puzzled. "You might want to explain that."

"Peggy told me that her sister and Sam wasted a lot of years because of decisions in the past that they now admit were stupid. And she ran away."

"Ah." His body was all lanky and loose, but his eyes simmered with dark intensity. "How far did you get?"

"O'Toole's."

"You spent the afternoon singing karaoke?"

"Not exactly."

She'd spent the afternoon missing him and the rest of the family. And in between missing him, she'd kicked herself for being an idiot. For voluntarily walking away from the man she loved and the family she loved.

"Why did you run, Kinsey?"

"Funny you should ask. I spent most of the day trying to figure that out."

He folded his arms over his chest. "And?"

She met his gaze. "I thought it put me in control of the situation. That's important to me because as a child I never was in charge of my destiny. At least it never felt that way."

"So why did you come back?" His voice was deeper, a little hoarse, with expectation around the edges.

"I found out my destiny is here. With you. At least I hope it is."

The corners of his mouth curved up. "Just so you know, Danielle and I cleared the air."

That name started a slow leak in her bliss balloon. "What did she say?"

"After she guessed that I have deep feelings for you?"

Her heart did a happy dance. "Yeah. After that."

"We agreed that the relationship was over and had been for a long time."

"You could have told me that before I left," Kinsey said.

"I would have but you took off unexpectedly. I would have told you I love you, too."

"You do?"

"Yeah."

"Me, too. Love you," she said.

He grinned. "Come here."

"Not so fast." She backed up a step. "You stole my luggage and broke my car to show you care? Some men just send flowers."

He shrugged, which wasn't a yes or no—such a lawyer thing to do. "I'm not some men."

"Tell me something I don't know." Like how he managed that stunt. She'd wondered all afternoon. "I wasn't gone from the guesthouse all that long. How did you pull it off?"

"I called mom and she stalled you while Eugenia hid your stuff and handyman George disabled your car. Not permanently, by the way. So the answer is that I had backup in the form of my loyal family." He rocked back on his heels looking very full of himself.

"I don't know what to say." That was a lot of trouble for them to go through for her. If cynicism hadn't been carved into her, she would have let herself believe that all of them did what they did because they cared about her. But the lifetime of doubts were like a comfortable pair of jeans that were hard to part with. "What if love isn't enough? You know I have issues."

"I noticed. So do I. Who doesn't?" His gaze never left hers. "I'm a little too stuffy and you're a free spirit. But I believe that's called balance—yin and yang."

"Are you yin or am I?"

He laughed. "I think you all but admitted to being part of the family, and we'll always be there for you—all of us. If you stick around long enough you might just end up with the name Longwood."

"I'd like that a lot." More than she could say.

Peggy was right. Belonging somewhere *was* what she wanted most in the world. Kinsey knew with instincts honed by self-preservation that the Longwoods would accept and keep her whether or not she was with David. But, he was irresistible and she loved him with every bit of her being.

"So, if I agree to stick around, what else is in it for me?" Even a heart overflowing with happiness couldn't suppress her sassy side.

He grinned his I've-got-her-now grin. "For starters, you'll get to hang out with Mr. Excitement. Did I mention the conspiracy idea was mine?"

She returned his smile and took a step closer. "How very Davy Daring of you."

"It's Captain Daring now. I think my mother is planning to put me in a story illustrated by Aunt Tory. There's a rumor that she's very good with capes."

"Sexy."

"I know. A man has to do what a man has to do to win his woman." Settling his hands at her waist, he said, "Thanks to you, I found my inner Davy Daring again. I'd love to travel the world with you. Share your adventures. Love you with everything I've got."

"Nothing would make me happier. As long as we always come back here. To our home base. Our family."

"You're a tough negotiator, Kinsey McKeever." He smiled down at her. "But since it gets me everything I want…done and done."

David took her in his arms and touched his mouth to hers, then bent her back in a dashing kiss. As sizzles and sparks erupted inside her, there was a loud explosion and bright lights in the sky.

Fireworks.

Peggy's surprise.

The family spectators gathered on the lawn applauded the first salvo in the reunion's grand finale, and Kinsey wasn't quite sure whether it was because of the fireworks display or David's romantic one.

She just knew it was the perfect backdrop for the perfect beginning of the best part of the rest of her life.

* * * * *

EPILOGUE
The Future Is Now

PEGGY HAD ALWAYS LOVED fireworks. She didn't know why, except that she had a vague memory of colors in the sky, bright exploding lights, the booms and bangs that came without warning…and someone's loving arms around her as she buried her head against a soft breast and occasionally peeked up at the glorious displays that to her, were simply magical.

They were magical tonight.

Stan slipped his hand around hers, and she decided there was magic enough to allow her to rest her head on his shoulder as they stood at the edge of the grass and listened to the *oohs* and *ahhs* of her family and guests.

To her left, Allie Gibbons was sitting on a blanket spread on the lawn, cradling little redheaded Megan to her, while Molly ran in circles as her father warned her to be careful, clapping at each new burst of color to light up a starry night over the water. Quinn stood between Tory and Sam, the three of them holding hands, their faces tipped up to the sky.

Family. The past gone, the bonds of love as strong as if they'd been there forever.

Laurie stood to Peggy's right, Adam Hunter's strong arms encircling her waist, his chin resting on top of her head as he stood behind her. Laurie positively glowed, the years of unhappiness, of worry, that had once squeezed at her mother's heart all gone now. Her life with Adam and the children wouldn't be perfect, nothing ever is. But the love was there, quick and fierce and true, and really, what else did anyone need?

Peggy lifted her head and asked Stan, "Did you see David? Don't tell me he and Kinsey are arguing again. Do you know, I actually think they enjoy it."

Stan craned his head, his gaze traveling the wide lawn and the mass of partygoers enjoying the show. He looked back at the house, and then smiled. "There they are," he said, pointing up at the house. "No, not on the terrace. Look up. Higher."

"Where? I don't—oh, for pity's sake." Peggy smiled as she raised her hand and waved at her son and Kinsey, the two of them perched on the slate roof just outside one of the attic windows, giving them the best possible view of the fireworks. "I've got my Davy Daring back, don't I, Stan? Their children are going to be living terrors, and it serves them right. Lord knows at least half these gray hairs I've got came compliments of my son."

"I love your hair. I love you, Peggy," Stan told her, and then had to repeat what he'd said because of the boom of the finale of the fireworks. "I said, *I want you to marry me, Peggy. I love—*"

"Well, it's about time you got around to that. All you needed were some fireworks lit under you, I guess," Eugenia interrupted as she approached, looking fairly flushed and breathless. "I've been looking all over for you," she continued, addressing Peggy. "Phone call. Oh, and congratulations. I'll book the church for next month. You're too old to drag this out, you two. Now, answer the phone."

"There's really a phone call for me?" Peggy asked, looking at the cordless phone her housekeeper was now holding out to her, but much more interested in what Stan had just said, and in answering him with a resounding *yes*. After all, if everyone else had a tomorrow, why shouldn't she? It was time; there would never be a better time. "*Now?* Why didn't you just take a message, Eugenia?"

Eugenia was blinking rapidly, her spine stiff and straight, her tight bun nearly quivering with some Herculean effort to contain her composure that clearly wasn't going to work much longer. "It's the transplant coordinator at the hospital. I thought you'd want to take the call."

"It's…it's the…*who?* But it's after ten. I mean, why would she call me after…?" Peggy looked at Stan, who put his arm around her waist, lending her his strength. "Stan, do you think it's…?"

He took the phone from Eugenia and handed it to Peggy. "There's only one way to find out."

She nodded, taking the phone in both hands, as she was suddenly trembling, and lifted it to her ear. "Hello? Margaret Longwood here. I'm…I'm sorry to have kept you waiting."

As the woman spoke to her, and Peggy managed mostly one-word answers, Eugenia was bustling about, whispering to Tory and Laurie and the others. Mark Gibbons kissed his wife and began running across the lawn to the stairs leading to the terrace, wildly waving his arms to get David's attention.

"Yes," Peggy was saying to the question as to her general health, "the cast is off and I'm not ill, I have no fever or cold. Yes, in fact, my family physician is with me now, if you'd like to speak to—oh, all right, if it isn't necessary. Um…when do I need to be—yes, I can do that. Immediately. Um…thank you. Thank you…"

"Mom?"

Peggy allowed Laurie to take the phone from her and push the end button. "That…that was Dr. Vincente, from the hospital. She…she says they have a kidney for me. We have time, but she'd really rather I drive to Philadelphia now."

"Oh, Mom…" Laurie threw her arms around Peggy and kissed her, held her tight.

"We have a kidney!" Eugenia, calm, dignified, never flustered Eugenia Babcock was running from group to group on the lawn, hugging people, even strangers, crying and laughing, and shouting out again and again, "We have a kidney!"

The crowd was all gathering around Peggy now, cheering and clapping, a few of them pushed aside as David, holding Kinsey's hand as he half ran, half stumbled, at last made it to his mother's side. He swept her up in his arms and swung her in a full circle before putting her down. "We have a kidney," he said quietly. "We have a life."

Peggy wiped at her wet cheeks with the handkerchief Stan had produced from his back pocket. She'd first been stunned by the call, and then she'd been swept up in the euphoria all around her. All these people who loved her, who cared about her. All the life she had to look forward to now. It was all so much, almost too much to take in.

But there was more.

"Ask everyone to be quiet a moment, David," she said, sniffing, trying to collect herself, bring her tumbling emotions under control. "Tell them I have something to say."

A few moments later, with all eyes on her, with everyone straining to hear her every word, Peggy said what had to be said.

"Thank you. Everybody. Thank you so much. Thank you for being so very dear to me, all of you. This…this has been quite a night." She looked at the faces of her family, old, new, reclaimed. "But there is someone missing, and there is a family somewhere that isn't celebrating tonight. That family is grieving the loss of someone they love very much, someone so good, so generous, that he or she has given me the gift of life. It isn't easy, knowing that someone had to die so that you can have a chance to live. I can only say that I will honor this anonymous hero every day for the rest of the life that he or she has given me. And I'd ask you all now to join me as we bow our heads to silently thank this generous hero, and to offer a prayer of solace for the family that now mourns."

Everyone bowed their heads, and the silence that followed was broken only by murmured prayers and sounds of soft weeping. Even the children were quiet, knowing something important was happening. A family was being thanked, a hero was being remembered.

"Amen," Stan said at last, squeezing Peggy's hand. "Come on, sweetheart, we need to pack you a bag. We'll stop at my place on the way and I'll grab a few things. We need to get on the road."

"Wait," Tory said quickly, "Sam and I will go with you. Won't we, Sam?"

"I'll drive," Sam agreed. "Stan, we'll get Peggy settled in at the hospital, and then you can stay with Tory and me at my condo. The surgery won't be until tomorrow anyway."

"We'll come, too," David said, and Kinsey nodded fiercely, clearly not to be left behind.

"And us," Laurie told them, a now sleeping Molly hanging over her shoulder. "All of us. We're all coming. Aren't we?"

Sam smiled. "My condo isn't all that big."

"We'll get hotel rooms for everyone," Tory said as they all made their way back up the sloping lawn and onto the terrace. "And don't you shake your head at me, Margaret Mary. We're family. Family sticks together."

"I couldn't agree more," Eugenia said. "I'll ride with David and Kinsey. You can decide where to put your mother."

Peggy looked at Eugenia, who somehow was already in possession of her purse and the black sweater she was slipping into in preparation of leaving for Philadelphia. Nana was standing beside her, holding an umbrella, of all things. Holding an umbrella, and wearing a "don't even think about leaving me behind" expression.

"But, Eugenia, we have a house full of people here. If we

all leave, then who will—and, Mom, it's going to be a long night. Why don't you stay here and someone can bring you to the hospital tomorrow and—" She stopped, shook her head as she took in all of the suddenly mulish expressions around her. "They can take care of themselves, can't they? Hilda, Cousin Corinne, all of them. They'll figure it out."

In the end, it was a bit of a staggered parade that headed for Philadelphia over the next twelve hours—Sam driving Stan, Peggy and Tory, and with David, Kinsey, Eugenia and Nana following directly behind them. Adam convinced Laurie to take over hostess duties for her mother, and they'd leave only after the last guest was gone—which wouldn't be long if Laurie had anything to say about it!

Two weeks later, looking fit and healthy, Peggy returned to Cape May, Stan fussing and insisting she immediately go up to her room to rest while he and Eugenia fought over who would make her some iced tea. Peggy loved no longer having any restrictions on her fluid intake, and she warned him to make it a large glass.

Once he had kissed her and reluctantly left her alone, Peggy folded back the sheet and walked out onto the terrace that overlooked the beach. The expanse of sand wasn't her private beach, but it was usually empty, as the house was fairly isolated from its neighbors and the tourists tended to stay on the city-run beaches, near the lifeguards.

But the beach wasn't empty now.

Sam and Tory were jogging along at the water line, Sam slightly ahead, calling back over his shoulder at Tory, who seemed to be running and holding a hand to her side at the same time. She called out something to him and he stopped, waited for her, and then they held hands and continued on, this time walking. But Tory was determined to learn to love running, even if she'd flatly refused to eat broccoli. There were sacrifices you made for love, she'd confided in Peggy, but she saw no reason why broccoli had to be one of them.

Peggy could make out the faces of her grandchildren and Tory's grandchildren, all of them hard at work building a sandcastle, with Adam clearly in charge of its construction, while Laurie and Allie and Kinsey and David tossed a plastic saucer back and forth.

Family.

Stephen wasn't with them, but Adam was. Her brother was in her heart just as their parents were, joining with her Peter, and alongside the nameless donor who had given her a second chance at life; safely tucked away, always to be cherished.

All the yesterdays. All the todays. All the tomorrows.

Life. It was a beautiful thing....

* * * * *

Harlequin® A *Romance* FOR EVERY MOOD™

HEART & HOME

Heartwarming romances where love can
happen right when you least expect it.

Harlequin® American Romance®
Lively stories about homes, families
and communities like the ones you know.
This is romance the all-American way!

Harlequin® Special Edition
A woman in her world—living and loving.
Celebrating the magic of creating a family
and developing romantic relationships.

Harlequin® Superromance®
Unexpected, exciting and emotional
stories about life and falling in love.

SPECIAL EDITION

Life, Love, Family and Top Authors!

IN AUGUST, HARLEQUIN SPECIAL EDITION FEATURES
USA TODAY BESTSELLING AUTHORS
MARIE FERRARELLA AND *ALLISON LEIGH.*

THE BABY WORE A BADGE
BY *MARIE FERRARELLA*

The second title in the **Montana Mavericks:
The Texans Are Coming!** miniseries....

Suddenly single father Jake Castro has his hands full with
the baby he never expected—and with a beautiful young
woman too wise for her years.

COURTNEY'S BABY PLAN
BY *ALLISON LEIGH*

The third title in the **Return to the Double C** miniseries....

Tired of waiting for Mr. Right, nurse Courtney Clay takes
matters into her own hands to create the family she's
always wanted— but her surly patient may just be
the Mr. Right she's been searching for all along.

REQUEST YOUR FREE BOOKS!

2 FREE NOVELS
FROM THE ROMANCE COLLECTION
PLUS 2 FREE GIFTS!

YES! Please send me 2 FREE novels from the Romance Collection and my 2 FREE gifts (gifts are worth about $10). After receiving them, if I don't wish to receive any more books, I can return the shipping statement marked "cancel." If I don't cancel, I will receive 4 brand-new novels every month and be billed just $5.99 per book in the U.S. or $6.49 per book in Canada. That's a saving of at least 25% off the cover price. It's quite a bargain! Shipping and handling is just 50¢ per book in the U.S. and 75¢ per book in Canada.* I understand that accepting the 2 free books and gifts places me under no obligation to buy anything. I can always return a shipment and cancel at any time. Even if I never buy another book, the two free books and gifts are mine to keep forever.

194/394 MDN FELQ

Name	(PLEASE PRINT)	
Address		Apt. #
City	State/Prov.	Zip/Postal Code

Signature (if under 18, a parent or guardian must sign)

Mail to the **Reader Service:**
IN U.S.A.: P.O. Box 1867, Buffalo, NY 14240-1867
IN CANADA: P.O. Box 609, Fort Erie, Ontario L2A 5X3

Not valid for current subscribers to the Romance Collection
or the Romance/Suspense Collection.

Want to try two free books from another line?
Call 1-800-873-8635 or visit www.ReaderService.com.

* Terms and prices subject to change without notice. Prices do not include applicable taxes. Sales tax applicable in N.Y. Canadian residents will be charged applicable taxes. Offer not valid in Quebec. This offer is limited to one order per household. All orders subject to credit approval. Credit or debit balances in a customer's account(s) may be offset by any other outstanding balance owed by or to the customer. Please allow 4 to 6 weeks for delivery. Offer available while quantities last.

Your Privacy—The Reader Service is committed to protecting your privacy. Our Privacy Policy is available online at www.ReaderService.com or upon request from the Reader Service.

We make a portion of our mailing list available to reputable third parties that offer products we believe may interest you. If you prefer that we not exchange your name with third parties, or if you wish to clarify or modify your communication preferences, please visit us at www.ReaderService.com/consumerchoice or write to us at Reader Service Preference Service, P.O. Box 9062, Buffalo, NY 14269. Include your complete name and address.

Celebrating

Blaze™ **10** *years of*
red-hot reads

Featuring a special August author lineup of
six fan-favorite authors who have written
for Blaze™ from the beginning!

The Original Sexy Six:

Vicki Lewis Thompson
Tori Carrington
Kimberly Raye
Debbi Rawlins
Julie Leto
Jo Leigh

Pick up all six Blaze™
Special Collectors' Edition titles!

August 2011